'Goodnight, Miss Cartwright. And thank you for an evening far more enjoyable than I ever expected it to be.'

He took her hand and lifted it to his lips, lingering a little over the kiss, wishing he dare kiss her properly but knowing he would be forever damned if he did.

It was several seconds before she could repossess herself of her hand and by that time she was tingling with a sensation she could not describe. It was a feeling of being on the verge of something so exciting, she was shivering. Her stomach was churning, her heart beating so fast she could hardly breathe, and her toes and fingers curled involuntarily. She climbed into the curricle without ever knowing how she got there. This man was dangerous! He threatened everything she stood for. She must be on her guard, always on her guard, lest he undermine her confidence and the tenets by which she lived crumbled to nothing.

She flicked the reins and, as the pony started forward, trotted round the circle before the door and out of the gate, she found herself murmuring, 'Remember whose daughter you are, Charlie Cartwright. And remember whose son he is.'

Born in Singapore, **Mary Nichols** came to England when she was three, and has spent most of her life in different parts of East Anglia. She has been a radiographer, school secretary, information officer and industrial editor, as well as a writer. She has three grown-up children, and four grandchildren.

Recent novels by the same author:

TALK OF THE TON
WORKING MAN, SOCIETY BRIDE
A DESIRABLE HUSBAND
RUNAWAY MISS
RAGS-TO-RICHES BRIDE

THE EARL AND
THE HOYDEN

Mary Nichols

MILLS & BOON®
Pure reading pleasure™

First published in Great Britain 2008
Large Print edition 2009
Harlequin Mills & Boon Limited,
Eton House, 18-24 Paradise Road, Richmond, Surrey TW9 1SR

© Mary Nichols 2008

ISBN: 978 0 263 20663 0

Set in Times Roman 16 on 17¾ pt.
42-0509-80705

Printed and bound in Great Britain
by CPI Antony Rowe, Chippenham, Wiltshire

THE EARL AND
THE HOYDEN

Chapter One

1814

Seven o'clock on a fine spring morning was the best time in all the world to be out riding, Charlotte decided, as Bonny Boy took her over the park surrounding Mandeville and into the woods above it, where the soft ground deadened the sound of his galloping hooves. It was good to be home again after the uncomfortable heat of Jamaica and the unpleasantly rough voyage, though, thank goodness, she had not succumbed to seasickness. She had missed the worst of the long hard winter, although the Atlantic had given her a taste of it as they buffeted their way homewards in the *Fair Charlie*.

On one side of her, the wooded slopes, a mixture of dark green conifers and deciduous trees just beginning to show their pale green hid Mandeville from view. On the other, the heather-covered hills separated Mandeville from Amerleigh. The heather was not yet in bloom, but the gorse brightened the terrain with its butter-coloured blooms. Mandeville was hers, and had been ever since her father's death two years before, along with the cotton mill at Scofield, five miles distant; the Jamaican plantation; the *Fair Charlie*—a slaver that, since the abolition of the abominable trade, had become an ordinary trading schooner— together with the lead mine under the ground over which she was riding, though that had become so deep and so frequently flooded it was hardly profitable. Did having all that make the sacrifices worthwhile?

What had she sacrificed? Her girlhood, perhaps. Her chance of marriage and children because she was well aware that her mode of living would put all but the most desperate and greedy off courting her. And the desperate and greedy she was easily able to rebuff. She did not want to marry; marriage meant handing everything she owned over to her husband and becoming his property, just as the plantation slaves had been her property, to do with as she pleased. She had been aware of the injustice of that long before her father died, but he always said he could not afford to give them their freedom; he needed their labour to produce the sugar on which a large proportion of his wealth was founded. 'Besides,' he had said, 'free men can be dismissed if they do not work hard enough and that means they also lose their homes. They know they are better off as they are.' Being a child at the time, a child brought up to believe her papa was never wrong, she had accepted his argument. A year after his funeral she had taken the long voyage to the West Indies to see things for herself.

The conditions in which the slaves lived and their treatment by the overseers had appalled her. She had offered them freedom, but as they had nowhere else to go, she had given them a weekly wage to remain in her employ. Daniel Mortlock, her plantation manager, had told her that acting arbitrarily would make the slaves on neighbouring plantations discontented and ready to cause trouble, but she had simply said what her neighbours did was no concern of hers, but if they had an ounce of humanity they would follow her example. She was adamant no human being ought to own another and he had been obliged to back down.

If she had a husband, everything would be in his hands and she was not prepared to forgo her independence. Not for anyone. Her biggest regret was that she would have no children. She told herself she would have to make do with other people's children and that included the villagers and those who worked in her mill, but it could never be the same as having a child of her own, someone she could love, as only a mother can love a child.

If her mama had not died giving birth to her, things might have been different. She might have had brothers and sisters and her mama would have guided her, taught her how to behave, brought her up to be a lady, seen her safely married, and her brothers would have taken over from her father. Instead, her father had treated her as the son he never had, making no allowances for her femininity. He had called her Charlie, which she had accepted as his playfulness, but she knew now it was more than that. It was a refusal to see her as a daughter, when all he wanted was a boy in his own image.

She supposed he had loved her in his way, but he had never told her so, never by so much as a kiss on the cheek let it show. Sometimes, when she was small, she had lavished her affection on her governesses, but they had been chosen by her father for their strictness and practicality and she had been rebuffed. She had soon learned not to show her feelings. But the gentler side of her nature could not quite be stifled and she could, and did, show compassion to those less fortunate and could never be cruel to any living thing, human or beast.

She had become a fearless rider, fished the swirling rivers and hunted over the hills and dales. She was a good shot with both pistol and shotgun, and was not above acting as midwife to horses, sheep and dogs. Encouraged by her father, she had developed a good business head and was perfectly conversant with bookkeeping and accounts, a fact that sometimes flummoxed Jacob Edwards, her legal adviser, and William Brock, the mill manager, and had certainly shocked the manager of her plantation when she visited Jamaica. Oh, it was good to be home again!

She was so deep in thought she did not hear other thundering hooves until a rider suddenly appeared out of the trees to the side of the path she was using and caused Bonny Boy to rear. It took all her strength and skill to keep her seat and bring him under control, while the other rider had his work cut out to pull his own mount to a halt.

'You confounded idiot!' he exclaimed, still wrestling with the reins and not looking at her. 'What, in heaven's name, were you thinking of, racing about like a madman? You could have killed me.'

'And you me.'

The sound of a female voice made him turn and look at her. What he saw caused him to stare in amazement. The figure riding astride the big horse was a woman, there was no doubt of it, but what a woman! Dressed in a man's riding coat, her only concession to womanhood an open riding skirt, which revealed tan leather breeches and brown riding boots. In spite of his annoyance he could not help admiring her long shapely leg. Neither did she seem to subscribe to the feminine insistence of shielding her face from the sun because she was hatless and her skin was tanned and glowing. Her abundance of chestnut-coloured hair, streaked with the red of sunrise, had escaped from its pins and drifted across her face in wild curls. Her eyes were neither brown nor green, but a mixture of both, and they were regarding him angrily.

'One does not expect to come across a lady jockey on one's own land,' he said, affecting annoyance, though he felt bound to acknowledge her skill in controlling her mount. 'Especially one set on winning a race…'

'I was galloping, not racing,' she snapped. 'If you had been looking where you were going instead of jumping out on me like some highwayman—' She stopped suddenly to look more closely at him. He was a large man on a very big horse and towered over her. He was wearing a dark green uniform, its jacket decorated with black leather frogging and fastened with silver buttons. His breeches were also dark green and tucked into black riding boots. A dusty riding cloak was carelessly flung over one shoulder. On his head he wore a black shako beneath which his handsomely rugged features were set in a fierce line of disapproval, but even so she thought she detected a hint of humour in his dark eyes. 'Did you say *your* land?'

'Yes,' he said. 'You are trespassing on the estate of the Earl of Amerleigh.'

'Oh.' Her heart gave a sudden lurch as her defiant gaze met his. She could not look away, it was as if some alchemy, some chemistry in their make-up, had fused and produced a new element, something akin to fire, which threatened to consume them both in its heat. For a moment she simply stared at him. This was the man who had humiliated her so profoundly she had never quite forgotten it, had not been allowed to forget because her father had conducted a determined vendetta on the old Earl ever since. But the Earl had died six weeks before and here was his successor, larger than life.

'So you are the Earl's cub,' she said, using the name her father had given him. 'Then you ought to know the extent of the Amerleigh domain, and this stretch of land does not belong to it.'

He did not like being called a cub, but let it pass. 'Of course it does. I used to roam here as a boy. I know every inch of it.'

'But you are no longer a boy, are you, my lord?' It was said with a false sweetness that disguised the bitter memories which the sight of him had invoked. And to rub salt into the wound, he did not remember her. 'Things have changed since you went away. I advise you to speak to your lawyer before you accuse anyone of trespassing in future.' She paused suddenly. 'You do know…'

'That my father died. Yes, Miss Cartwright, I do know.'

'My condolences. You mother will be glad to have you home again.'

'No doubt,' he said, wondering how well she knew his mother or whether she was simply making small talk. She did not strike him as someone who went in for that sort of thing.

'Now, you must excuse me, my lord, for I have work to do, even if you do not.' She turned her horse to leave him, but he leaned forward and seized her reins.

'Not so fast, madam…' He did not know why he wanted to detain her, nor what he meant to say to her, but he was given no opportunity to find out because she slapped the back of his gloved hand with her crop, making him release the reins. He looked startled for a moment, then threw his head back and gave a hoot of laughter, which infuriated her.

'If you think manhandling a lady is a subject for humour, then you are more uncouth than even I expected,' she said, digging in her heels and galloping away, leaving him staring after her.

What had been going on in his absence? Six years he had been away, serving with the army in Portugal and Spain, six long years, during which the fortunes of war had ebbed and flowed, and the army had marched the length of the Portugal and back more than once. Now Viscount Wellington was on the offensive and preparing to rid the world of the upstart Napoleon for good. He was on French soil and marching towards Bayonne. If it had not been for the illness and death of his father, Roland would have stayed to the end, would have exalted with the rest of the troops in the hard-won victory.

He had written to his father once or twice in the early days of his service, but receiving no answer, had given up. If his father wished to forget him, then he would forget his father. Even his letters to his mother had been ignored, though he was sure that was because she had been forbidden to communicate with him. But three months before, she had written to tell him the Earl was gravely ill. 'Come home, if you can,' she had written. 'We have removed to the dower house. It is more convenient.' He wondered what could be more convenient about it. Compared to the rambling old hall where he had grown up, it was a doll's house. He could not imagine his autocratic father living there.

The letter had been addressed to his headquarters, but at the time it arrived he had been behind the enemy lines, surveying the land and producing maps. It was weeks before the letter was put into his hands and by then a second one had followed it, informing him his father had died and he was now the Earl of Amerleigh.

He had obtained leave of absence and, with his personal servant, Corporal Travers, had returned to Lisbon and embarked on a transport ship. They had landed at Portsmouth and travelled by stage to Shrewsbury, where they had purchased mounts to take them the rest of the way to Amerleigh, taking a bridle path over the hills and ignoring the road. He had not expected to find a wild woman in men's clothes galloping across the estate.

He turned as Travers caught up with him. 'You have just missed the most extraordinary creature,' he said.

'I saw her.' Ben grinned. 'I could see you were enjoying your conversation with her, so I held back. Who is she?'

'I have no idea.' He stopped suddenly and laughed. 'Oh, it couldn't be, could it? Oh, my, I do believe it was. What a homecoming!'

'You know who she is?'

'I think so. No, I am sure of it. Her name is, or was, Charlotte Cartwright and I have a feeling I shall be crossing swords with her again.'

The new Earl had matured into a handsome man, Charlotte admitted to herself as she rode away, remembering the slight figure he had been at twenty-one, good-looking, yes, with his curly brown hair and classical features, but proud and disdainful, disdainful enough to humiliate her beyond endurance. But she had been proud too and that meant not showing her hurt. Nor would she remind him of it now. If he had forgotten her, so much the better. But they were sworn enemies and would remain so.

She slowed to a walk, ruminating on what had happened six years before and all her anger bubbled up again. It had been her father's wish to be accepted by society, and to that end he had entertained and had brought in teachers to show Charlotte the accomplishments a lady should have, including sewing, drawing and dancing, none of which she had particularly enjoyed. Besides, it was too late by then, her unconventional character had already been formed and she found it impossible to change, but to a certain extent he had achieved his aim simply because he was the richest man for miles around and could make or break any man he chose, and that included the Earl of Amerleigh. But not his cub.

To be rejected by a stiff-necked, conceited sprig, in a voice loud enough to be heard by anyone standing within ten feet of him, had been the outside of enough. It was the first time her father's money had not been able to buy whatever and whomever he liked. Hoyden, the sprig had called her. Well, she supposed that was not so far from the truth. And plain. Was she plain? Her father had assured her she was not, that she was every bit as beautiful as her lovely mother had been, and the silly young fop needed his eyes seeing to. But looking in the mirror on her return home from the ball which both fathers had confidently expected to end in the announcement of the engagement of their respective offspring, she had admitted that perhaps Roland Temple had the right of it. And coming to that conclusion had in no way lessened her sense of grievance; if anything, it had heightened it. Oh, how she wished her father had never made that bargain with the late Earl. But wishing did not mean she would undo what he had done. Never, never, never.

She entered by the wrought-iron gates of Mandeville and was filled with the pride of possession. The red sandstone mansion ahead of her had been built by her father to tell the world how a mere nobody could, by dint of hard work and clever management, make a mint of money. It stood out from the surrounding countryside because the great trees that had been planted to make the park were still in their infancy, though there were several decorative trees and shrubs in the gardens near the house. Given a few more years, Mandeville would rival the best country seat in the area, if not the whole county. It already outshone Amerleigh Hall, which was crumbling into ruin.

She rode round the house and dismounted at the stables, an extensive range of buildings which housed several riding horses, four carriage horses and a couple of ponies. In the adjacent coach house there was a well-sprung travelling coach, a phaeton and a curricle. Having given Bonny Boy to a groom to be looked after, she ordered one of the ponies to be harnessed to the curricle and went into the house by a side door which took her through the kitchens.

She exchanged news with Mrs Cater, her cook, asked May, the scullion, about her chilblains for which she had provided an ointment, stroked the kitchen cat, which purred in delight, then went up to her room to change for the business of the day. She took not the slightest notice of the pictures that lined the walls nor the costly ornaments and furniture, all purchased by her father to impress. Her booted feet sank into the deep pile of the carpet, oblivious of the footprints she left behind. She was thinking of her encounter with the Earl and trying not to let it bother her.

Once in her bedroom, she flung off her riding coat and skirt, peeled off the breeches and washed quickly in cold water from the jug on her toilet table. Then she dressed in a plain grey skirt, a white shirt and a black bombazine jacket tailored like a man's and fastened with braided frogging. This was the outfit she had devised to go to business, not quite mannish because it fitted her neat figure perfectly, but near enough to tell everyone she meant business and would stand no nonsense. She pinned up her wayward hair and, disdaining a bonnet, topped it with a tall beaver hat with a sweeping feather. Her riding boots she changed for half-boots in fine black leather, and thus apparelled, returned downstairs where the curricle was waiting for her to drive herself down to the valley where the cotton mill stood beside a fast-flowing tributary of the Severn.

She had been away a year and in that time the measures she had put in hand to improve the conditions of the mill hands had been allowed to go by default. She had come back to find the schoolroom unused and the children had returned to the long hours and unhealthy conditions that had been prevalent when her father first took over the business from his father-in-law many years before. 'Mr Brock, there is a law about schooling the children we employ, which we have to obey, as you very well know,' she had reminded him, though she had gone far beyond the minimal lessons she was required to provide. 'We are no less bound by it than anyone else.'

'We had large orders to fill,' he told her. 'We needed every hand to the looms or the ship would have sailed half-loaded. Your father would never have allowed that.' Reminding her what her father would or would not have done seemed to be his way of objecting to her orders.

She needed Brock for the day-to-day running of the mill and so they had compromised on the hours of work and the amount of schooling the children had. She intended, little by little, to wear him down and have her own way. In the meantime she trod carefully and diplomatically, only too aware that as a woman she was despised; as the richest mill owner in the district she was treated with deference larded with a certain amount of contempt. She straightened her back, put her chin up and pretended not to mind.

Today, she inspected everything, watched the shuttles flying across the looms for several minutes, spoke to the mill manager about production schedules, dealt with her correspondence and gave a few orders, something she did almost every day of her life. Though she appeared to be her usual self, there was, beneath the cool exterior, a fluttering in the pit of her stomach, a feeling of unease, as if something was hanging over her, not quite a threat, but something that could upset her well-ordered routine. It did not take much puzzling on her part to put it down to the arrival of the new Earl of Amerleigh.

* * *

Roland rode on, noting, as he neared his home, that everything was looking decidedly neglected. Hedges were growing wild, ditches were uncleared, the workers' cottages in disrepair. He stopped and dismounted at the church and went inside to look at the family vault. His father's name, newly carved, was the last of a long line. He supposed his own name would be added in due time. Pushing such morbid thoughts from him, he returned to the road where Travers waited patiently with the horses, and they rode on towards the big house whose great chimneys and crenellated walls could be seen through a gap in the trees.

It had stood in its surrounding deer park since Elizabeth was queen and Harold Temple had become rich plundering the seas for his monarch and been made an earl on the strength of it. Succeeding members of the family had added to the house, furnished it lavishly and held sway over the village, from which it took its name, or perhaps the village grew up after the house— Roland had never been sure. Now it had a forlorn and dismal air. The lawns were uncut, the flower beds and gravel drive full of weeds. He noticed a broken window and peeling paintwork.

Roland rode on past it, down a long path beside what had once been a thriving garden and out on to a lane that led to the dower house. It was a square, red-brick building, having only a sitting room, a dining room, a parlour and four bedrooms as well as the usual offices. When he had left home six years before, it had been occupied by his grandmother, but she had died while he had been away. He had been very fond of the old lady who had defied her son and left Roland an annuity, not grand, but enough to provide him with a measure of independence, for which he was very grateful. He dismounted and handed his reins to Travers, then strode up to the door.

It was opened before he reached it and his mother flew out and into his arms. 'Roland, oh, Roland, you are home at last. I have been praying for you to come and now you are here. Let me look at you.' She stood back to appraise him. She saw not the slim, half-grown youth who had left home, but a mature, battle-hardened man, tall, broad shouldered, weatherbeaten. 'You have changed.'

'It has been six years,' he said with a smile. It was not only physically he had changed; his character had matured too. The young man who had been haughty and proud, who felt himself, as the son of an earl, to be a superior being to the man who ploughed the fields, was gone. He had learned a little humility, to judge people on merit, not on their position in society. Rank in society was not the same as rank in the army and he much preferred to be known as Major, a position he had earned, than to be made much of on account of his title.

'Oh, you don't know how I have longed for you to come home,' she said, leading him into the house.

He paused to speak to Travers. 'Find the stables and see to the horses, I'll join you when I can.'

'Did you receive my letters?' she asked, as they stepped into the hall and she relieved him of his riding cloak and hat. She was, he noticed, very thin, her face lined with worry, and he was sorry if he had been responsible for putting any of the lines there. And though she was dressed in deepest mourning, her blue eyes shone and her mouth smiled with joy at having him home again. 'I wondered why you did not come at once.'

'I was away from headquarters and could not be contacted,' he said, following her into the drawing room and refraining from reminding her that his letters home had gone unanswered. 'It was nearly two months before I returned and your first letter was put into my hand, only the day before the second arrived. I came as soon as I could. I am only sorry I did not arrive in time.'

'Never mind, you are here now. Sit down and let me look at you.'

Roland pulled up a chair and sat on it, his head full of what he had seen: the poor state of the big house, the neglected air about the village, the arrogant Miss Cartwright and her assertion Browhill did not belong to the Amerleigh estate. When and why had it changed hands?

'You are grown so big and strong,' his mother went on.

'That is down to the army, Mama. It made a man of the boy.'

'You will always be my boy.'

He smiled and reached for her hand. 'I know.' He paused. 'I passed the house. It looked thoroughly neglected. What happened?'

'It is a long story. Your papa lost heart after you left. He did not seem able to do the work he always used to do and things went from bad to worse. Two years ago he had a seizure and Dr Sumner said he was not to be worried. I wanted to write and tell you what was happening, but your father forbade it. We moved here so that he might be peaceful and hoped to let the house, but there were no takers. After his last attack he suddenly changed his mind and said he must see you.'

'I am deeply sorry I was too late. I would have been glad to be reconciled with him. Did he ever forgive me?'

'I think so, though I always thought there was nothing to forgive, except perhaps your hasty departure, when he might have come round to listening to you, and you to him.'

Roland did not think so, but forbore to say so. 'What would you have me do?'

'It was his wish that you restore the Hall. It is, after all, your home. It has been the home of the Amerleighs for hundreds of years. One day you will marry and pass it on to your sons.'

'I know, Mama.' He gave a sigh. From what he had seen, it would be a monumental task and one that would take every penny he owned and more. 'I had better see Mountford and talk it over with him.'

'Yes. He will tell you about the lawsuit.'

His heart sank. 'The lawsuit?'

'Yes, your father was in dispute with Mr Cartwright over a strip of land that he said the man had cheated him out of.'

'Browhill?'

'Yes, how did you know?'

'I came that way and met Miss Cartwright.' He smiled wryly at the memory. 'We had a few words about it.'

'Oh, no, not you too. Will there be no end to it?'

'I do not know. Tell me what happened.'

'Later. Now, I must go and have a room made ready for you, then you can change and we will have dinner.' She bustled away.

He sat on for a few minutes, gazing at a portrait of his father that hung over the mantel. It showed a big, proud man, master of all he surveyed, supremely confident. How had he come to be so far in debt he had had to leave his ancestral home? His mother seemed reluctant to tell him.

He stood up and left the room to go in search of her and found her in one of the bedrooms supervising the making up of a bed for him. His portmanteau and haversack had been brought up and put on a chest under the window. A jug of hot water had been placed on the wash stand. 'There, will that do?' she asked.

'Very well, Mama. I am used to far less than this.'

'Come down when you are ready. I do not know what Mrs Burrows is making for dinner, but I am sure she will do her best.'

He washed quickly, changed his shirt, put on his best uniform and returned downstairs where they were served a simple meal in the dining room by Mr Burrows. He had been the butler even longer than his wife had been the cook. He had always been one to stand on his dignity in the hierarchy of the servants' quarters and held sway over at least twenty indoor servants. Now, according to his mother, Mr and Mrs Burrows and one girl were all the indoor staff they had.

'And outside?' he asked, after Burrows had left them to serve themselves. 'Gardeners, coach-men, grooms?'

'We go out so little I cannot remember the last time the coach came out. I drive the gig when I want to go calling or shopping. We only have one horse and Bennett looks after it. He still does the garden and keeps an eye on the big house.'

Roland speared a piece of mutton on his fork. 'Is that all that's left?'

'Yes, but we do not need them here and would have no room for them in any case. Some of them went to Mandeville. Jacob Edwards has done very well there. You remember him; he is a year or two older than you. He used to share your lessons before you went away to school and you used to go fishing together in the holidays.'

'I remember.' Jacob had been with him the first time either of them had set eyes on Charlotte Cartwright. It was at a horse fair that had come to Amerleigh. The boys had been enjoying them-

selves going round all the stalls and listening to
the banter of the stallholders and had stopped at a
shooting range where a row of wooden ducks
were set up for the contestants to shoot down.
Jacob tried first and had hit seven of the ten.
Roland had his turn and hit the first nine, but failed
at the last.

'Missed!' said a triumphant voice. He had swivelled round to find a girl of about twelve standing
close by. She was well clad and well shod and her
reddish hair was crammed under a blue chip
bonnet, so she was not one of the villagers. There
seemed to be no one with her.

'You think you can do better?' he had demanded,
while the stallholder looked on, grinning from ear
to ear.

'Yes.'

'You are more likely to shoot yourself than the
ducks.'

She held out a brown freckled hand. 'Give me
the gun and I'll show you.'

He laughed and gave it to her and was thoroughly chagrined when he found she could load
and prime it and was astounded when, hardly
seeming to take aim, she shot down all ten ducks
in quick succession. 'I told you so, boy,' she said,
returning the gun and taking a tiny squealing

piglet from the stallholder as her prize. Any other girl of his acquaintance would have been more careful of her clothes than to hold the animal in her arms, but she did not seem to mind. Her father had come and fetched her then and given her a jobation for giving him the slip, but she just laughed at him.

It was Jacob who found out who she was: daughter of Mr Cartwright the owner of Mandeville, an estate on the other side of the hill from Amerleigh. Roland had returned to school without seeing her again that year, but on subsequent holidays he and Jacob had come across her out riding or fishing and they had shouted a greeting and sometimes stood over her on the bank to watch her fish. It was only on reflection now that he realised she had always been alone and he wondered if she had ever had any siblings or playmates. Jacob had admired her, for all the neighbourhood considered her wild and unmanageable. Roland had gone away to university and did not see her again until a few days before that fateful ball, galloping over Browhill, just as he had seen her today. She had not changed.

'Father paid for Jacob's schooling later, didn't he?' he queried, coming back to his conversation with his mother.

'Yes. He has climbed his way up to be a lawyer and is Miss Cartwright's man of business.'

'Rubbing salt in the wound.'

'Yes. It was all too much for your poor papa and he seemed to give up. The estate became neglected and he thought of nothing but revenge. It soured him, Roland.'

'And he blamed me.'

'In a way I suppose he did.'

'And you? Do you blame me?'

'No, you were young with your life before you and you did not know the whole story. I begged your father to explain the position to you, but he said he would expect you to comply simply because he said it was necessary.'

Roland closed his mouth on the comment that it was most unlikely that even an explanation would have made him change his mind. In the middle of the most lavish ball he could ever remember his parents holding, he had been told by his father that he was expected to propose to Miss Cartwright that very evening. He remembered his angry reaction as if it were yesterday. 'Not for anything,' he had said. 'The chit is barely out of the schoolroom, if she was ever in one. She is a hoyden and ought to have been a boy. She is certainly plain enough.' They had had a bitter quarrel and he had stormed up to his room where he had remained despite the entreaties of his mother to come down and his father's threats that he would cut him off without a penny if he defied him. 'If you do not obey me in this,' he had shouted through the thick oak door, 'you are no son of mine.'

Next morning Roland had left the house with no luggage except a small carpet bag and taken a stage to London, where he bought into the 95th, which later became part of the Rifle Brigade. His rise to his present rank had been made on merit as more senior officers had been killed and wounded, which he supposed was something the war had done for him.

'Why was it so important to Papa?'

'Your father and Mr Cartwright were once friends in a way, though the man had no breeding to speak of. They were both magistrates and used to meet at the courthouse and at the sheep market and talk about business. Mr Cartwright suggested our name coupled with his wealth would together make one of the most influential families in the kingdom. Miss Cartwright's dowry would be pro-digious; not only that, he was prepared to stand buff for your papa's debts, which at that time were considerable. And there was cash in hand too. All to give his daughter a title. The offer was too tempting to resist and your father accepted a payment in advance, which of course the man demanded back when you left. Unfortunately, most of it had already been spent, some on that disastrous ball, on paying debts, and on new furnishings to impress Cartwright. I also had new gowns; your father said it was a matter of pride that his wife should be dressed in the latest mode…'

'He did all that without consulting my wishes,' he said, wondering if the proposed engagement had been as much a surprise to Miss Cartwright as it had been to him.

'I am sorry for that, but he supposed you would agree for the sake of the dowry. You must not condemn him too harshly, Roland. In his day parents often arranged marriages for their children and the children rarely complained. Marriage was more of a business matter then, a joining of great houses, the making of a dynasty. If a man needed more than his wife could provide, he could easily find it elsewhere, and as long as he was discreet she would turn a blind eye…'

'Times have changed, Mama. I prefer to find my own bride and I most certainly would not expect her to turn a blind eye, as you put it.'

'Have you? Is there a lady…?'

'No. I have been too busy fighting a war to worry about courting.'

'Then it is not too late.'

'Good Lord! Surely I am not expected to pay court to the chit, just as if the last six years had never been.'

'No, I can understand you would not want to do that and it would not do. Two such strong characters as you both are would make for endless conflict. She is not one to bow to any man, husband or no.'

'How far has this litigation gone?'

'I have no idea, no one confided in me. Mountford will tell you.'

'So the new Earl has come home at last,' Mrs Elliott said, helping herself from a tureen of vegetables offered by one of Charlotte's footmen. An invitation to Mandeville for supper was worth accepting if only because the food was sumptuous, much better than anything she was able to provide at the vicarage. Tonight Charlotte was entertaining the Reverend Mr Elliott, Mrs Elliott and their son, Martin, who had just been ordained as curate and was waiting for his first post, together with Sir Gordon and Lady Brandon and their twenty-year-old daughter, Martha. 'The Reverend saw him arrive on horseback, with no luggage or servants, except one dowdy-looking fellow in army overalls, is that not so, husband?'

'Yes,' the parson agreed. 'I hardly recognised him, he was so dusty and travel-stained. He had on a dark green jacket, which had certainly seen better days, and a black shako, just as if he were a common soldier. He dismounted to go into the church and stood before the Amerleigh vault. He was there some time in quiet contemplation and it was then I guessed who he was.'

'Did you discover if he means to stay?' Sir Gordon asked. Both Sir Gordon and his wife had succumbed to good living and were almost as round as they were tall. Sir Gordon owned a cotton mill in Scofield, not far from Charlotte's, but as far as she knew, he rarely went near the place and knew very little of what went on there, but she invited him and his wife to dine occasionally because he was a great gossip and enabled her to keep abreast of what her competitors were doing.

'And why would he not? It is his home and his inheritance, after all.' This from Martin Elliott. He was a pale young man, and very thin, but not ill-looking.

'Inheritance!' Sir Gordon exclaimed. 'Millstone

would be a better description. How he will bring it about, I do not know.'

'He probably has a private income,' Lady Brandon put in, while Charlotte remained silent. She did not want to say anything that might inadvertently reveal that she had already met the gentleman in question. 'Or he has become rich by the war. It sometimes happens, I believe. The victors plunder the vanquished.'

'He will need every groat he can lay his hands on,' Sir Gordon said. 'His father has left the place in a sad state.'

'Why did they quarrel?' Martha asked, while Charlotte held her breath, hoping fervently none of her guests knew the real truth.

'No one knows for sure,' Mrs Elliott said. 'But it was very sudden. I have heard it said it was over a woman. The Viscount, as he was then, was banished in disgrace.'

'Now, now,' her husband gently chided her. 'It is no business of ours.'

She lapsed into silence, much to Charlotte's relief, but the pause was soon filled by Lady Brandon. 'Do you think we should call on him and welcome him home?' she asked. 'Though whether that be the great house or the dower house, it is difficult to say.'

'I would not go so far as to suggest that, my love,' her husband said. 'He might find it a trifle embarrassing. Hold your horses and wait to see what he does. He might not stay.'

'And whom do you suppose will take over the estate if he does not?'

'I feel sorry for him, coming back to that,' Mrs Elliott said, earning a sharp glance from Charlotte.

'Why?' Sir Gordon demanded. 'If rumour be true, it was his quarrel with his father that sent the poor old man out of his mind.'

'Was he out of his mind?' Lady Brandon asked.

'Of course he was. No man in his right mind would allow his estate to be run down like that. Do you not agree, Miss Cartwright?'

Charlotte, directly addressed, found herself saying, 'I do not see how anyone but his doctors can know the state of his lordship's mind, but it is very true the estate is in a parlous state.'

'I am surprised you have not offered to buy it yourself,' Sir Gordon said. 'No doubt you could get it for a song.'

Charlotte smiled, thinking of the Earl and his fierce claim that the land on which they had almost collided had been Amerleigh land. If she was any judge of character, he would not part with his birthright to her. But, oh, taking the Amerleigh estate from him would be sweet revenge for the humiliation she had suffered at his hands. 'What use would I have for such a place?' she asked. 'And we are talking as if the Earl is going to sell up.'

'If he has any sense he will,' Sir Gordon said.

'I would not,' Charlotte said suddenly. 'There are too many people's livelihoods depending on a healthy estate. I would look on it as a challenge.'

'Is he one to rise to a challenge, do you think?' Lady Brandon asked.

Charlotte shrugged. 'I have no idea, but we shall soon see.'

The return of the Earl of Amerleigh caused no end of gossip in the village. The main gist of their curiosity was centred on whether he had returned with a fortune and whether he had married and would be bringing his wife to the Hall just as soon as it had been refurbished. And if he was not married, why, then he might be looking for a wife! Single young ladies in the parish and for several miles around were suddenly alert to the possibilities. Hence the bigger than usual congregation at church the following day.

Wondering what to wear, Roland had surveyed his wardrobe, which did not take long. Apart from his ordinary uniform and a dress uniform that he wore on formal occasions, he had a pair of overalls, a riding coat of Bath cloth which he had been wearing when he enlisted, a pair of calfskin breeches, half a dozen shirts, a change of underclothes, and a spare pair of boots. He had never needed more. He found some of his old clothes in a trunk, which his mother had brought to the dower house. There was among them a black frock coat and breeches, but when he tried them on, he found they were several sizes too small. The Roland who had gone away had been a stripling of twenty-one, slim as a reed; the Roland who had returned was broad of shoulder, deep-chested, with muscular legs and arms. He had perforce to ask Travers to spruce up his best uniform and tie a black mourning ribbon about his sleeve. Bennett had brought out the carriage, for which Roland had hired horses, and took immense pride in cleaning it so it gleamed as it once had, and he and his mother travelled in that.

After the service, the Countess placed herself between Roland and the parson on the church path to greet everyone and introduce them to her son. Among them were Lord and Lady Gilford, who had a substantial mansion on the road between

Amerleigh and Scofield, Mr and Mrs Edward Trent of Shrewsbury; Sir Gordon and Lady Brandon, who had a country house on the slopes above Scofield, and several others whom Roland did not know. They were all accompanied by offspring.

That might have been the end of it, but the parson, conscious of his role as conciliator, addressed Lady Brandon. 'My lady, I am sure the Earl needs no introduction, but I am persuaded you would wish to welcome him back in our midst.' And to Roland. 'My lord, you remember Sir Gordon and Lady Brandon, do you not?'

Roland bowed. 'Your servant, my lady. Sir Gordon.'

Her ladyship acknowledged him with a slight inclination of the head. 'My lord.'

Sir Gordon shook his hand and then drew Martha forward. 'May I present my daughter, Martha?'

He bowed, remembering the schoolgirl he had seen about the village with her governess when he had been home in his youth. She had become an attractive young lady. 'Miss Brandon.'

She bobbed a curtsy and kept her eyes downcast. 'My lord.'

The parson had not done. 'My lord, I believe you are acquainted with Miss Cartwright.'

It was only then he realised that Charlotte stood

behind them. Gone was the strange riding gear and in its place was a watered silk gown in a soft dove-grey, topped with a matching short pelisse. Her amber hair, which had been so windswept when he had come upon her riding, was now pinned up beneath a simple straw bonnet, but he could see that it was already straining to escape.

He realised quite suddenly that plain was an inaccurate way to describe her. Not that she was a beauty; her features were too strong for that, but handsome might do. Her eyes were her most striking feature and they were looking at him in a way that made him feel uncomfortable. Disdainful, amused, irate, wary—he wasn't sure how to describe that look. As far as he knew, she had not heard the hateful description of her he had flung at his father all those years ago, but remembering them now made him feel ashamed of words that never should have been uttered by anyone calling himself a gentleman, however irate he had felt. 'Your servant, Miss Cartwright,' he said, touching his hand to the peak of his shako.

She had thought he was tall when mounted, but now she realised he must be over six foot in height, a giant of a man and not one to be easily intimidated. But neither was she. 'My lord,' she responded coolly. She had not been brought up to attend church regularly, but she had realised that not to go might make for gossip. As she did not want anyone to connect her with his disappearance six years before, she had come, telling herself that she would take herself off immediately after the service. She had not bargained for the parson's interference. She turned from him to the Countess. 'My lady, how do you do?'

'I am well, thank you. And you?' The Countess was, as ever, graciousness itself, and whatever Charlotte felt about the late Earl and his son, she liked her and felt sorry for her.

'I am in fine fettle,' she said, risking a glance at the Earl. He was looking at her intently, as if trying to read what was going on in her head. She hoped not, because her thoughts were confused. She had to admit she found his rugged good looks attractive, more so than the immature looks of the boy who had disdained her, and had to tell herself sternly that he could never be forgiven that.

'Did you have a good voyage home?' the Countess asked.

She laughed. 'The sea was somewhat rough, but I survived it.'

'Miss Cartwright has recently returned from a visit to Jamaica,' his mother explained to Roland. 'She has a sugar plantation out there.'

'Indeed?' he said. So that accounted for the name of her house; Mandeville he knew to be a Jamaican town. 'And slaves, too, no doubt?'

'The trade slave has been outlawed, Lord Temple,' she said, noticing the Countess's look of shock that he should mention such a thing.

'The trade, yes, but not the ownership.'

'True, but there would be hue and cry if the law decreed they had to be freed,' she said. 'We should have no sugar, tobacco or cotton. It would be disastrous for the British economy.' She wondered why she did not tell him that her slaves had been given their freedom instead of repeating parrot fashion the arguments her father had used when she had questioned him on the subject. Obstinacy, she supposed, and a mischievous wish to score a point over him.

His mother touched his arm, warning him not to continue. 'Point taken, Miss Cartwright,' he said, smiling as if he knew perfectly well what she was about. It disconcerted her to think he could read her mind like that.

'Have you ever visited the Indies, my lord?'

'No, never.'

'Perhaps you should.'

'One day, perhaps. Did you not find the climate uncomfortably hot?'

'I do not suppose it was any worse than the heat in Spain.'

'Probably not,' he agreed. 'One becomes used to it. But it is good to be back in England's softer climate, do you not agree?'

'Oh, most decidedly, and especially in spring-time.'

The conversation ground to a halt. His mother plucked at his sleeve. 'Good day, Miss Cartwright.' He touched his hat again and, taking his mother's arm, guided her to their carriage to return to the dower house.

'Roland, how could you?' his mother scolded him. 'It is not like you to be discourteous.'

'Perhaps I let my feelings on the subject carry me away,' he replied unrepentantly.

Charlotte walked to the churchyard gate with Lady Brandon. 'Charlotte, why did you not tell him you had freed your slaves?' her ladyship queried, watching his departing back.

'Because I did not choose to. He has no right to criticise me.'

'Do you think he is married?'

'I am sure I do not know.'

'I should not be at all surprised if he did not have a Spanish wife tucked away somewhere, and we shall be expected to receive her. And just look at him! Was that meant to be a uniform he was wearing?'

'It is the uniform of the 95th Rifles,' Charlotte murmured. 'I believe they are considered some of our finest fighters and always in the vanguard of any attack.'

'Is that so?'

'So I have read. And it seems to me that a green uniform is much more practical than a red one. It is less easily seen by the enemy.'

'That is as may be,' her ladyship said. 'But I still say it made the Earl look devilish sombre.'

'Good heavens, Catherine, he surely has reason to be sombre,' Charlotte said, surprised to find herself defending him. 'His father died while he was away and now he finds himself owner of a crumbling mansion and a run-down estate. It will be interesting to see how he comes about.'

'No doubt he will marry an heiress.'

'What happened to the Spanish wife?' Charlotte asked mischievously.

'Charlotte, is it in your nature to be perverse? Or is it simply that you enjoy provoking me?'

'Oh, I am definitely perverse,' Charlotte said, laughing.

They had reached her curricle, with its patient

horse standing in the lane, and she bade her ladyship goodbye and drove herself home. In spite of telling herself what Roland Temple did was no concern of hers, that she despised him, she had frequently found herself thinking about him since his return and wondering how they would go on when they met again, because in a village as small as Amerleigh, they could not fail to meet. And now she knew. It was war.

Chapter Two

Later that day Roland fetched Travers, and they went on foot to inspect the big house. 'I might as well go and see what needs to be done,' he told him.

Taking the great key his mother had given him, he unlocked the stout oak door and stepped inside. Even the dilapidated state of the exterior did not prepare him for the interior. The downstairs rooms had been cleared of anything of value, leaving only the heavy old Jacobean furniture, which had long gone out of fashion; there was hardly a stick of decent furniture left and most of the carpets had gone. The walls were bare of pictures, though it was easy to see on the faded wallpaper where they had once hung.

Travers followed him from room to room. 'If you don't mind my saying so, Major,' he said. 'It could be a villa in Spain after the Frenchies have done with it.'

'Yes.' It was far worse than he had expected. How had it got like this? What had his father been thinking of to let it happen? Surely his mother was mistaken and it had nothing to do with Cartwright and a worthless strip of land? An unwise investment made by his father, perhaps. But if that were so, why had Mountford not advised him against it? His mother was right, a visit to the lawyer was called for, and the sooner the better.

They went up the wide, curving staircase and wandered about the first floor, containing the main bedrooms, the gallery and the ballroom, followed by the caretaker who had arrived from nowhere and seemed to think it his duty to be in attendance. The bedchambers were dank and those hangings that remained smelled of damp. A mouse scurried along the wainscot and disappeared down a hole. 'What on earth happened?' he murmured.

'Happened, my lord?' Old Bennett was clearly agitated.

'Oh, I do not expect you to know,' Roland told him.

'No, my lord, but it grieves me to see the old place like this. We are all glad to see you home. Amerleigh needs you.'

The man's words brought home to him that he

could not please himself, that there were others involved, servants and tenants and those in the village whose livelihood depended on the work they did, directly or indirectly, for the estate. How had they been managing? The thought that some of them had gone to Mandeville incensed him, especially if this desolation was any of Cartwright's doing. No wonder his father had wanted revenge.

'Seems to me, Major, you're going to need some blunt,' Travers said as they locked up and left to go back to the dower house.

He should have reprimanded the man for his impertinence, but he was only stating a fact and they were more than master and servant: they were friends, comrades in arms who had shared bad times as well as good. 'Yes, Corporal, I think I will.'

'There's the French gold…'

The day before the battle at Vittoria, millions of dollars, francs and doubloons had arrived in the French camp and Lord Wellington, who knew of it and was always having trouble paying his troops and buying supplies, had been anxious to lay his hands on it, but unfortunately the troops had found it first and in the aftermath of the battle had stuffed their pockets and knapsacks with it. The 95th was no exception; though Wellington had threatened to punish anyone who looted, there was no stopping them. Travers had returned to their billet with his pockets jingling. He had used some of it to buy himself out of the army in order to accompany his officer home.

'I can't take that,' Roland said. 'It's yours.'

'No, it ain't, not rightly. And it seems to me you need it more than I do. There's been many a time you've helped me out of a scrape.'

'Thank you, Travers, but I doubt if it is enough to do more than scratch the surface of the problem.'

'Then scratch the surface, sir.'

He laughed suddenly. It was good to have a friend, but talking of French gold reminded him that he had a little nest egg of his own, given to him by a grateful Spanish Count the first time he had been sent behind the enemy lines. His work done, and wanting somewhere to hide up before trying to make his way back to his own lines, he had taken refuge in the stable of a large villa and hidden himself in the straw. A dog had found him early the next morning, yapping its head off until its owner appeared. She was young and frightened, but he had soothed her and assured her he meant her no harm. He had only wanted somewhere to sleep. She took him into the kitchen and while the cook gave him a good breakfast, she went to fetch her grandfather.

Count Caparosso was an elderly man, wearing old-fashioned satin breeches, an embroidered coat and a bag wig. He was also very nervous. The French were near at hand and he was frightened for his granddaughter. After giving Roland a meal and asking him all about himself, he had asked him to take Juanita to safety. 'She has an uncle in Coimbra,' he had said. 'Take her there. I shall pay you handsomely.'

'Do you not wish to go yourself?'

'No, I am too old to travel and I must stay and look after the house as best I can until this dreadful conflict is over.'

Roland had hesitated. The journey would not be an easy one, bad enough on his own, but with a gently nurtured girl it would be doubly difficult. The Count had seen his reluctance. 'She is my only joy,' he had said. 'The jewel of my bosom, but I dread what would happen to her if the French find her here. I am an old man and I would not be able to defend her.'

'How do you know you can trust me?' Roland had asked him with a wry smile. 'I might be as bad as the French.'

'No. You are an honourable man, I can see it in your eyes and the way you are so courteous to Juanita.'

'She is a lovely young lady and deserves every courtesy.'

'So you will take her?'

It was necessary for him to make a start and so he had allowed himself to be persuaded. Juanita and her maid were given into his care, and though he had protested he wanted no recompense, his host persuaded him to accept a small bag of jewels and an ancient carriage pulled by two very scrawny horses. But it had been a good disguise after all, and though they had had one or two scary moments, he had brought his charge safely to the house of her uncle. He had become very fond of her by then and they had parted with a promise from him that if he were ever in Coimbra again he would call. He had done so once, over a year later, only to find she had married her cousin and died in childbirth. Poor little thing, she had been no more than a child herself.

Apart from a diamond ring that he'd kept, thinking that one day he might marry, he had turned the jewels into ready money in Lisbon, surprised and delighted to discover they were worth a small fortune. He had banked the money, intending to save it against the day when the army no longer needed him and he had to settle down in civilian life. Believing he would not be welcome at home, he had planned to buy a farm, work the land and breed horses. Together with his annuity and half-pay, it was enough for him to make a good start. Must he give up that dream for this rotting mansion? But the rotting mansion was his birthright and his responsibility; he could not please himself, not anymore.

'I think I shall move in at once,' he told Travers as they wandered about the almost empty rooms, followed by Bennett, hanging on their every word for a morsel of information that might indicate what his lordship intended. 'It behoves the Earl of Amerleigh to live at his country seat, not at the dower house with his mama. Besides, there is very little room there.'

They went up to the attics where they found a couple of old beds with damp mattresses, one or two cupboards, a sofa and some uncomfortable chairs, which even the creditors had disdained. 'Fetch it all down and make up two bedrooms,' he told the two men. 'You will need to take the mattresses down to the kitchen and dry them off by the fire. And light fires in all the rooms to air them. I will be back later.'

He set off back to the dower house to acquaint his mother of his decision. She was dismayed and tried to dissuade him, but he was adamant. 'If I am to restore the Hall to what it was, I must live there,' he told her.

'How can you do that without servants?' she said.

'I have Travers and Bennett.'

'You will make yourself a laughing stock.'

'I will be a bigger one if I stay here, attached to your apron strings.'

She sighed. 'Shall you take Mr and Mrs Burrows back?'

'No, you need them. I will take on a woman from the village. Do you know of such a one?'

She thought for a moment. 'There is a Mrs Fields. She used to work at the King's Head, but lost her position over some dispute with the landlord. I never had a meal prepared by her, but I have heard she is a good plain cook. As long as you are not contemplating entertaining…'

He laughed. 'That I am not. Will you do the necessary for me?'

Having agreed, she insisted on making up a parcel of clean bedding for him and gave him a basket containing a cold cooked chicken, a meat pie and a boiled ham. 'You will starve if left to yourself,' she said, forgetting, or not realising, that he was perfectly capable of subsisting on his own, and had been doing so for the past six years with the help of Travers. 'I will have Mrs Burrows make something up for you every day until you take on a new cook.'

He thanked her with a kiss and left.

It was not the discomfort of the lumpy bed that had kept him awake that night, but the knowledge that he was in the devil of a fix. There was no money in the estate coffers and the only income was rent from the tenants and he had no doubt their holdings had been neglected too and would need repairs. The money from the sale of the jewels would only stretch so far and then what was he to do?

However, he had always maintained there must be mutual affection in a marriage, which was why, he supposed, he was still single. He had met no one to whom he could give his heart and now he wondered if he ever would. And if his heart was not engaged, could he bring himself to look for a wealthy bride? Would the women around here all be like Miss Cartwright—mannish, spoiled, arrogant? There was only one way to find out and that was to mix socially and assess the situation. But putting the estate to rights must come first.

He was used to rising early and it was no hardship to get up at dawn, eat a Spartan breakfast and set off on horseback for Shrewsbury. He planned to see Mountford, have a look for furniture and carpets to make the principal downstairs rooms of the Hall presentable, and buy himself some clothes.

It was a mild spring day and he stopped on the way to admire the pink-and-gold sunrise over the hills. He breathed deeply and continued on down into the valley to Scofield. As he approached the Cartwright mill, he could hear the bell, warning employees that time was running out. They came hurrying along, men, women and children, streaming in through the open gates.

He reined in to wait for them to pass before proceeding. Some of them noticed him, pointing him out to their fellows, others bobbed a knee or touched a forelock. Two of the girls he remembered seeing in Amerleigh. They were probably daughters of estate workers. He smiled at them. 'Good morning, young ladies.'

They stopped and giggled, then, remembering themselves, dipped a curtsy.

'You come from Amerleigh?' he queried.

'Yes, sir, I mean, my lord.' It was the older of the two who answered him.

'Tell me your names.' He asked because he thought he should know all his people, and they were still his people, even if circumstances meant they had to work in the mill.

'I am Elizabeth Biggs,' the elder said. 'This is Matilda.' Her sister, too shy to speak, looked at her feet.

'And do you enjoy your work?'

'It's work, ain't it?' Beth said. 'Better than the workhouse anyday.'

Everyone had gone into the mills and the clanging of the bells had suddenly stopped. 'Oh, my, we're late.' Beth grabbed Matty by the hand and ran towards the gates just as they were being closed. Roland watched, expecting the gatekeeper to hold them open for the girls, but they were shut in their faces. They stood for a moment, then turned sorrowfully away, their shoulders drooping.

'Why doesn't he let you in?' he asked them.

'No one goes in after the bell stops,' Beth told him. 'We lose a day's pay. It's to teach us not to be late.'

'But you were not late. You were here, ready to go in. If I had not detained you...' He stopped speaking and reached in his pocket for his purse. 'Here,' he said, offering them half a crown. 'I made you late, so I must recompense you.' It was more than the day's wage they would lose and they hesitated. 'Go on, take it,' he urged, holding it out.

Beth accepted the coin, murmuring her thanks, and they scampered away just as Miss Cartwright bowled up in her curricle.

She drew up beside him. He doffed his hat. 'Good morning, ma'am.'

'What was the matter with Beth and Matty?' she asked. 'Was one of them not well?'

'No, they were shut out for stopping to speak to me.'

'Nonsense!'

'I beg your pardon, ma'am?' It was a question, not an apology, uttered stiffly.

'I mean you must have misunderstood.'

'No, I do not think I did. I spoke to them and they stopped to answer. It was a brief exchange only and the gatekeeper could see them quite clearly. He shut the gates in their faces. If that is how you treat your employees, Miss Cartwright, then I pity them.'

'Save your pity for your own employees, my lord,' she retorted and drove up to the gates, which were immediately opened for her. She disappeared through them and they were shut behind her, leaving him staring at the words *Cartwright Mill* painted in large letters on them.

* * *

Charlotte left the curricle in the yard where a small boy came to walk the pony away and look after it until she was ready to leave again, and went in search of William Brock. She was seething. To be criticised by the Earl of Amerleigh over her treatment of her employees was the outside of enough. At least she was employing them, which was more than could be said for him. 'What is your policy over latecomers?' she demanded.

He looked puzzled. 'You mean the hands who are late for work?'

'Yes, the hands.'

'They are locked out, ma'am. It's to teach them punctuality, Miss Cartwright. They are rarely late more than once.'

'I assume from that you mean they lose a day's pay.'

'Yes, of course. It has always been so. All the others mills do it.'

'Not this one, Mr Brock. The two I saw turned away today are good workers and now we have lost their labour for a day. That is not good business sense.'

'Their looms are not idle, I can find good weavers who can manage two at a time.'

'Not good enough. In future, you will instruct the gatekeeper to take the names of those who arrive late and you will see that they are deducted half an hour's wages for every five minutes they are late. Is that clear?'

'Yes, ma'am,' he said resentfully.

'Good, now let us get on with the business of the day.'

They went on to discuss other matters, then she inspected the looms, peeped into the schoolroom where the young man she employed to give the children an hour's tuition during the midday break was preparing his lessons. She could not afford to take all the children off their work at once, so they came to him in two shifts. They were given a good dinner and then settled down to lessons. Any that showed promise she intended to send to school. She hated employing children, but knowing that not to do so would harm their families, she tried to make their working conditions as pleasant as possible.

By the middle of the afternoon, she had done as much as was needed and, sending for the curricle, drove herself to the Shrewsbury office of Robert Bailey, her mining engineer, to talk to him about opening a new level. The encounter with the Earl that morning had added to her annoyance with him and made her all the more determined to thwart him. He was a thorn in her side. For the first time in her life she was being illogical and unbusinesslike, but she could not help it. She did not care what it cost, she wanted that new adit.

'If you do not mind my saying so, Miss Cartwright,' the engineer said. 'You are thinking like a woman.'

'I *am* a woman, Mr Bailey.'

'So you are, but you have always figured things out like a man, pros and cons, objectively.'

'And who is to say that I am not being objective now? The deep level is causing problems with flooding, so we need to abandon that and sink another. There is lead down there, you know it as well as I, and lead commands a very high price, so we weigh that up against the cost of bringing it to the surface and we arrive at the conclusion that it will take less than three years to make a handsome profit. And it will give work to many.' Even while she was arguing with him, she was picturing Roland Temple, Earl of Amerleigh, standing where the engineer was standing now, telling her he would have his land back. When she had extracted all she could from the mine, she might offer to sell it back to him at a highly inflated price. She wondered if he would try to raise the money or give up. Why did she sense the Earl was as stubborn as she was? And why, oh, why did it matter?

Charles Mountford, who had been the family lawyer ever since the late Earl had inherited the title twelve years before, was in his forties, dark haired, dark eyed and dressed in black. He had been expecting his lordship, he said, after the usual greetings had been exchanged. 'Please take a seat.' He indicated a chair placed on the other side of his desk, then he sat down and began shuffling papers. 'May I offer condolences on the demise of your father,' he said. 'And congratulations on your coming into your inheritance.'

'And what exactly is my inheritance?' Roland asked him. 'Apart from the title, that is.'

'Amerleigh Hall and its domain—very little else, I am afraid.'

'I thought as much. Tell me what happened. My mother said something about a lawsuit.'

'Yes, that has been unfortunate.'

Unfortunate for whom? Roland wondered; not for the lawyers, he was sure, but he did not speak aloud. 'Tell me how it came about.'

The man coughed as if reluctant to begin, then, seeing Roland's look of impatience, made a start.

'The estate had not paid its way for many years, harvests had been poor and taxes heavy on account of the war, and in order to recoup the late Earl invested in stocks that he hoped would make a quick profit, but they failed, leaving him with heavy losses.'

'Did you advise him to buy them?'

'No, I did not.' The man was outraged by the suggestion. He was very small and wiry and his bony hands were continually on the move as he spoke. 'I do not know who advised him. It might have been Cartwright, but if he did, he did not take his own advice, or he was high enough in the instep to absorb the loss. As soon as I heard what had happened, I begged his lordship to retrench, but he would not. He continued going on as he always had, entertaining lavishly, buying the latest fashions for her ladyship, maintaining horses and hounds—for he was Master of the Hunt—and gaming. The more his pocket pinched, the more he gambled and the more he lost.'

'And all this happened in the last six years?'

'No, my lord, it started while you were at university, but he would not have told you of it even if you had been at home.'

Roland acknowledged the truth of that. 'So when Cartwright came along with a lifeline, he seized it?'

'Yes. Unfortunately he did not envisage you would not agree to the arrangement. Naturally, Cartwright demanded the money back. The Earl did his best, sold off a few paintings and ornaments and managed to find the initial capital, but Cartwright refused it. He wanted a vast amount of interest as well. He was a businessman, he said, and money was a commodity like anything else and should make a profit. Your father had deprived him of the profit he expected, namely a title for his daughter, so he was entitled to make it another way. He offered to expunge the whole debt in exchange for Browhill. The strip of land was nothing but heather and scrub, so I advised his lordship to agree. Soon after that Cartwright began successfully mining for lead...'

'Poor Papa. That must have galled him. According to my mother he thought he had been tricked into parting with the land and Cartwright knew there was lead there even before he suggested taking it. Is that true?'

'I have no way of knowing. It was enough that your father believed it. He thought if he could recover the land and take over the mine, the profits would be enough to set all to rights. After all, there was a war on and lead was needed for ammunition, not to mention for roofing, piping and paint.'

'Are you still pursuing the suit?'

'I have had no instructions to the contrary. Of course, if you should instruct me otherwise…' He stopped to look enquiringly at Roland.

Roland had been prepared to drop it, but the notion that his father had been bullied into agreeing to the transaction when he was far from well made him hesitate. 'Tell me, when the bargain was made, was it wrapped up tight? No loopholes?'

'That is what we have been endeavouring to discover, but Cartwright was far from co-operative and I have no reason to think his daughter will be any more so. My dealings with her have led me to believe she can be stubborn. And as money means nothing to her…'

'On the contrary, I think it means everything to her.'

Mountford gave a twisted smile of acknowledgement. 'She has that from her father. He made a fortune trading cotton, sugar and slaves.'

'So she would not mind losing a few pounds fighting me.'

Mountford shrugged. 'Who is to say? Do you want me to continue with it?'

'I will think about it and let you know. Now, what about the house and its contents? Could they not have been saved?'

'As soon as the Earl's problems became common knowledge, the dunners were on the doorstep. Tailors, vintners, jewellers, saddlers, butchers, those he has lost to at the tables, not to mention estate workers and servants, all turned up, wanting to be first in line for whatever was going. I was obliged to advise his lordship that simple retrenchment was not enough.' It was said apologetically. 'He stubbornly refused to sell, but in the end he did allow himself to be persuaded into moving into the dower house, letting it be known it was on medical grounds and as soon as his health recovered he would return to the main house. The Hall was put up for rent, but no one came forward and he was obliged to realise whatever assets he still had, except the house itself and the rest of the estate, to pay everyone off.'

'And have they all been paid?'

'I believe so, yes.'

'That, at least, is a relief.'

'If I were you, my lord, I would endeavour to sell,' Mountford went on. 'There must be someone who has the blunt to restore the place.'

Roland was reminded of Charlotte Cartwright. How she would crow! She might even put in a bid herself. He would not give her the opportunity. 'No,' he said. 'I am surprised at you suggesting such a thing. I will bring it about myself.'

The man gave him a tired smile. 'It will cost a great deal.'

'I am aware of that,' he said, standing up to leave. 'I will find the wherewithal.'

His next call was at a tailor's shop where he bought two new coats, two waistcoats, pantaloons in superfine and riding breeches in soft leather, several shirts, a dozen muslin neckcloths, and a pair of Hessians, arranged for them to be delivered, then he returned to Amerleigh, and, with Travers, set off to inspect his domain.

The estate was large and included dairy farms on the lower ground and sheep grazing higher up and some woodland in between. It had never occurred to him that it would not continue to dominate the surrounding country and its people for centuries more, not even when Cartwright had turned up and bought up the neighbouring estate, pulled down the old house and built an edifice that had the locals wide-eyed with astonishment. He was a mushroom, the detractors said, and like a mushroom would flourish for a day and then be gone. How wrong they had been. It was Amerleigh that would crumble before Mandeville unless he did something about it.

They rode round the village, noting that there were few people about. 'All working at the

Cartwright mill,' the smithy told him when he asked. ''Twas the only work they could get when his lordship let them go.' He spoke to one or two of the older women who remembered him as a boy and welcomed him home, convinced that now he was back, the jobs would return and the repairs to their cottages be put in hand. From the village, he made his way to the Home Farm where Ben Frost gave him a catalogue of grievances, which did nothing to improve his despondency: his barn leaked, the window casements on the farmhouse were rotting, and, what was worse, a wall separating his sheep from the road had collapsed and the animals were straying onto the highway. Roland promised he would do what he could and then set off up to Browhill to take a look at the disputed land.

The mine was set in the side of the hill. There was a great wheel-house in the centre of the site and several brick buildings were scattered about, one of which had a very tall chimney from which a column of smoke drifted. The sound of their horses must have alerted its occupant, for he came out to meet them.

'My lord Temple,' he said, recognising Roland. 'What can I do for you?'

'You can show me round,' Roland said.

The man was middle aged, with a stooped shoulder and a distinct limp. His name was Job Bunty and he had once been an Amerleigh game-keeper, shot, if memory served Roland correctly, by a poacher he had tried to arrest. The man picked up a lantern from a niche in the rock and lit the candle inside it with a flint. 'This way, my lord.'

'Is it worked out?'

'No, my lord, but it's got mighty deep, two hundred foot and more. After all the rain we've had, there's a deal of water down there and the pumping engine don' seem able to shift it all. Mind your head, my lord, the roof's low.'

Roland did not need telling; the lantern cast an eerie glow over a narrow tunnel running steeply downwards. They had to proceed in single file, almost bent double. And then it suddenly opened out to a huge vault. Roland stepped cautiously forwards and, taking the lantern from Bunty, swung it over a great void, noticing the ladder attached to the side, disappearing into the murk below his feet. He picked up a stone and dropped it down the hole. After several seconds he heard the splash. 'Come, let us go back and you can show me the rest.'

Back on the surface, they passed several men

who had just come up from a different level and were extinguishing the candles stuck on their hats. Two young lads, stripped to the waist, were pushing a loaded truck on rails. Their guide led them to the washing floor where the ore was separated from the dirt and other minerals in running water. 'In Mr Cartwright's day it was done by small boys,' Bunty told Roland as they walked on. 'But Miss Cartwright won't have them standing in water in bare feet and now it's the bigger lads who do it and they are provided with boots.'

They arrived at another building where the ore was crushed to prepare it for smelting, work which was done by women, usually the wives of the miners. Next was a blacksmith's shop, where the smithy sharpened the miners' picks and drills, and the changing house, where the single men lodged, which was ill lit and gloomy. Everything was covered in fine, grey dust. They were just going to walk up the hill to look at the smelting mill when Charlotte arrived on horseback. Seeing the two men, she dismounted and strode over to them. 'What are you doing here?' she demanded without preamble.

'Assessing the situation,' Roland answered lightly.

'Oh, I see, you still think this is Amerleigh land.'

'Naturally I do.'

'Then you are mistaken. I would have expected your lawyer to have told you that.'

'He told me that it was wrested from the late Earl under extreme duress.'

'I know nothing of duress.'

'No, I can understand you would not even know the meaning of the word,' Roland said. 'But I can tell you no *gentleman* would have dunned another in so vindictive a fashion.' His emphasis on the word gentleman was not lost on her.

'And no *honest* man would renege on a debt,' she retorted.

He wondered if she knew exactly how the debt had occurred. 'My father offered the capital sum back, but your father insisted on exorbitant interest.'

'There is nothing illegal about that.'

'No, but my father would have found it given time. He was not given time simply because your father was set on making himself more money from the deposits in this mine.'

She laughed, wondering if there were any truth in what he said. 'I suppose I am to take it that you are going on with that ridiculous claim.'

He had been wondering if it was worth the time and money, not to say stress, the lawsuit would involve. Thinking about what Mountford had told him, it seemed to him his father was as much to blame as Mr Cartwright. The old Earl should not have spent the money he had been given before making sure his son would do as he wanted, and when he had not, should have offered it back immediately without being asked, then Cartwright could not have dunned him. It was six of one and half a dozen of the other, a silly squabble that should never have occurred. Roland regretted that he had been involved, albeit unwittingly. On the other hand, if the mine really did belong to the Amerleigh estate, the profits could certainly be put to good use. 'You could revert the land to the Amerleigh estate and then there would be no need for the lawsuit to continue.'

'Certainly not,' she said, determined not to give an inch. 'I am about to open up a new adit. Now, please leave. I am too busy to argue with you.'

Roland bowed and returned to his mount, followed by Travers, doing his best to keep a straight face.

'You may laugh,' Roland told him as they rode back to the village. 'She is a veritable shrew, but I shall get the better of her, you shall see.'

'Oh, I am sure you will, Major.' Travers found it difficult to give his master his proper title, but Roland did not mind that. As far as he was concerned he was going into battle and it was one he might enjoy, considering no one was likely to be killed because of it.

'Miss Cartwright, 'tis madness,' Jacob Edwards told her the morning after her encounter with the Earl at Browhill. He had been summoned to Mandeville to be told she wanted to release funds for a new shaft to the Browhill mine. He was a young man of thirty, dressed in an impeccable dove-grey morning coat and pristine shirt. No one seeing him would have believed he had once wandered barefoot about the village lanes in torn breeches. 'It is not like you to go on beyond the point of a venture making a profit.'

'Profit is not everything.'

This statement made him laugh; it was so unlike her. 'If not profit, what do you hope to gain?'

'Gain nothing,' she said, 'but keep everything.'

'I am not very good at riddles. Pray explain.'

She began pacing the room impatiently, swishing her grey skirt about her as she turned at the end of each perambulation. He watched, admiring her shapely figure and striking features. He had admired her for years, ever since he had come across her as a child, but she gave no indication that she was aware of it or would consider an approach by him. In her eyes he was simply her factotum, someone to carry out her orders, occasionally to advise, never to look on with affection. He doubted she was capable of it.

'I do not want Amerleigh given the slightest opportunity to repossess it,' she said.

'The land might have been part of his domain, but he never mined it, nor did his father,' he said. 'The late Earl never established a claim to mining rights.'

'Would he need to, given he owned the land?'

'I do not know.'

'Then find out.'

'Very well, ma'am.' He bowed himself out and she soon followed. She had spent the morning at the Scofield Mill, supervising the loading of barges with bales of cotton cloth, to be taken to Liverpool by river and canal for loading on to the *Fair Charlie*. She hated the name, but as her father had chosen it to mark her birth, she would not change it. As soon as it was safely aboard, she had returned home to meet Jacob Edwards. Now, with an unaccustomed hour or two to fill, she decided to go for a ride. Not for a single minute did she admit, even to herself, that she hoped she might meet the Earl. The confrontation the day before had roused her in a way that nothing had ever done before. Accustomed as she was to making deals, striking a hard bargain, taking it for granted her orders would be obeyed, it was a refreshing change to have to fight for something. It was the battle itself that put the gleam into her eye.

She went to the kitchens, sent May to the stables to ask Dobson to saddle Bonny Boy, then, taking a basket, filled it with a can of milk, some eggs and a jar of cook's home-made preserve, all of which she intended to take to Mrs Biggs. The poor woman had recently had another baby and she was struggling to manage since her husband had lost his position as under-gardener at the Hall. The two oldest girls worked at the mill, but they could not earn enough to keep the whole family.

'It is the Earl's responsibility to look after his people, not yours,' Cook told her.

'Yes, but Beth and Matty work for me. I must do what I can to help them. Besides, I doubt the Earl has had time to see to such things and from what I have seen of him, his pockets are to let.'

'How can that be? He is an aristocrat, is he not? They always find money from somewhere for what they want. If not, they fall into debt and think nothing of it.'

Charlotte knew this to be true, especially of

the late Earl. It was why his heir had come home to desolation. She could almost feel sorry for him. Almost. But that did not mean she was prepared to see the villagers suffer. She had been helping them and would continue to do so. She went up to her room to change into her riding habit and put on her boots, then went back to the kitchen to pick up the basket. Five minutes later she was walking her horse down the drive and out of the gates in the direction of the village, balancing the basket in front of her on the saddle.

Mrs Biggs, who had seven children, lived in a little cottage near the church. Until he had been turned off by the late Earl's lawyer, her husband had been a conscientious gardener who did his best for the family, but since then he had become low in spirits and very bad-tempered. He did not like charity, but for the sake of the children was forced to accept it. Charlotte tried to go when he was not at home, in order not to embarrass him.

Mrs Biggs bobbed a curtsy and accepted the basket with gratitude. 'Will you stop and take some refreshment?' she asked, as she always did.

Charlotte knew that providing her with refreshment would mean others in the family going short and she would not have dreamed of allowing that.

'No, thank you, Mrs Biggs, I have other calls to make. How is the little one?'

'All the better for what you bring, ma'am. We all are. Do you think that now the new Earl has come home, he will re-engage the staff?'

'I am sure I do not know, Mrs Biggs. Let us hope so.'

She stopped to cuddle the baby, unmindful of her expensive clothes, and to talk to some of the other children before leaving, telling Mrs Biggs to send one of them back with the basket another time and she would give him a penny for his pains. She loved children and longed for some of her own, but to do that she must marry and, as she had forsworn to do that, she must put all thought of being a mother out of her head.

Leaving the cottage, she decided to ride further afield and set off through the village along the lane that ran beside Amerleigh Hall, intending to go up through the wood and on to the hill. She reined in when she saw workmen mending a broken wall beside the road. One of the men looked up at her approach and she was surprised to discover it was the Earl himself in overalls. 'Good afternoon, my lord,' she said coolly.

'Miss Cartwright,' he answered and waited.

'My lord, I am surprised to see you mending walls.'

'It needs doing,' he said, wondering what censure was coming next. 'Mr Frost's sheep have been straying onto the road, so he tells me, and I enjoy working with my hands. It is calming.'

She slipped from the saddle and, picking up her trailing skirt, walked towards him, leading Bonny Boy. 'I can understand you need something to calm you, my lord, and building walls is certainly a creditable occupation, but there are men in the village without work. Their families are suffering because of it. Could you not have employed one or two of those?'

His face darkened with annoyance. 'Whom I employ is my affair, madam.'

'Of course.' Antagonising him was not the way to influence him, she realised. 'But I am concerned for the people who once worked on the estate, and because you have but lately returned, I thought you were perhaps unaware of their desperate plight.'

He wiped his hands on his overalls and walked over to stand in front of her. 'I would not have made a very good officer if I remained blind to what went on around me, Miss Cartwright. I am very well aware of the state of affairs in the village.'

'Then you will think about re-employing the men? There is one in particular, a man called Biggs. His wife has recently been delivered of her seventh child and they are at their wits' end.'

'When circumstances allow I will do what I can.'

His words confirmed her suspicion that he was pinched in the pocket; no wonder he wanted her mine and the profits it made. 'Thank you. Does that mean you intend to stay?'

He laughed. 'Would you have me gone again so that you may ride wherever you like, acting Lady Bountiful?'

'That is not, nor has ever been, my role, Lord Temple. But starving people do not work well or willingly.'

'I am aware of that, Miss Cartwright, I do not need a lecture.'

He could not explain to her, of all people, that it was not callousness that held him back from helping the villagers, but the necessity to conserve his resources. He wondered why she had not married; she was still young and her wealth must surely be a great inducement. Could it be that prospective suitors were put off by her habit of saying what was in her mind and interfering in their affairs? If she had been anyone but who she was, he might have enjoyed working with her to help the villagers. As it was, enjoyment was the last thing on his mind.

She was about to remount when she became aware of a carriage being driven very fast along the lane towards them. She hesitated, waiting for it to pass, at the same time realizing that there was a small child on the road. She let out her cry of warning, but Roland had seen him too and dashed into the road to rescue him.

Charlotte watched in horror as the coachman tried to pull the horses up. They reared over the man and boy. The coach slewed round and toppled over and Roland and the boy disappeared. The coachman was thrown down beside the wall, which knocked him senseless, and the screams of the vehicle's occupants filled the air as it turned over.

Charlotte dashed round the overturned coach to the spot where she had last seen Roland and the boy, but was overtaken by Travers, who had been working on the wall with his lordship. The horses were struggling to stand and he quickly released them from the traces, but there was no sign of the Earl or the boy. 'Major!' he shouted.

'Over here.' The voice, though breathless, was surprisingly strong and came from the ditch on the other side of the carriageway. A moment later, his lordship's head appeared, followed by the rest of him, carrying the senseless boy in his arms. 'Had to pull him into the ditch,' he said calmly, laying the boy gently on the grass beside the unconscious coachman. 'I think he might have a bump on the head. He'll come to his senses directly.' He looked up and saw Charlotte standing uncertainly beside him. 'Are you hurt?'

'No, my lord. Are you?'

'Nothing but a bruise or two.'

She knelt down beside the boy, aware that a portly man dressed in a coat of blue superfine and nankeen pantaloons was climbing from the over-turned carriage. He had lost his hat and his hair was awry and he was very angry. 'Imbecile!' he shouted, addressing Roland. 'Letting your brat wander about the public road like that.'

'I think he is but slightly injured, sir,' Roland said coolly. 'But I do thank you for your kind concern.'

'Yes, well, he should not have been in the road,' the man said, recognising the put-down for what it was. 'Did he not hear us coming?'

'No, he could not,' Charlotte put in. She had recognised the six-year-old Tommy Biggs, who had come round from his fright and was looking from one to the other, trying to understand what was being said. 'He is deaf. But your coachman has no business to be going at such a speed he was unable to stop in time. Tommy could have been killed.'

'Are you his mother?' The man reached in his pocket and withdrew a purse.

'No, I am not, but that is not to say his mother would not appreciate some recompense. She is poor and doctor's fees will come hard.'

The moans coming from the coach grew into a wail. 'George, am I to stay here all day while you bandy words? Help me out.'

The man gave Charlotte a handful of coins and turned back to the coach. A head had appeared in the door of the vehicle, which now lay on its side, one wheel still gently spinning. The woman's round face was bright red, her hair such a vivid orange Charlotte could not believe it could be its natural colour. And it soon became apparent, as her husband struggled to haul her out, that she was exceedingly fat.

'Can you look after the boy?' Roland asked Charlotte. 'See that he does not move until I can examine him properly. I had better see to the passengers.'

'Of course.'

He left her to lend the fat gentleman a hand and

together they pulled the lady free with a great display of petticoats and set her upon her feet on the road.

'You are unhurt, ma'am?' Roland asked.

'I am bruised black and blue,' she retorted. 'And will undoubtedly suffer considerably, but I do not expect you to concern yourself with that. Be so good as to send for another conveyance to carry us forwards. We are in haste…'

'That much I had deduced,' Roland said wryly. 'But you know what they say, "more haste less speed". The delay will undoubtedly outweigh the advantage of the speed you were driving. I am sure your coachman will agree with that. When he regains his senses, that is.'

'And a little less of your impertinence, if you please. If you had kept your child under control—'

'The child does not belong to his lordship,' Charlotte said and watched with a broadening smile as the woman's mouth dropped open in astonishment.

'His *lordship*?' she managed at last.

'You have been directing your abuse at the Earl of Amerleigh,' Charlotte went on, throwing a glance at Roland, who had turned away to hide his laughter.

The woman swivelled round to look Roland up and down as if unable to believe this rough-looking man in the faded overalls could possibly be a member of the aristocracy.

'The lady ain't bamming,' Travers put in. He had been busy catching the horses, which, apart from a tendency to take fright, were unharmed. 'So you'd be wise to address his lordship with more respect, especially if you want him to help you.'

'Oh, I do. My lord, I cannot think what came over me. The shock, I suppose. Please forgive me. I took you for—' She stopped, not daring to put into words what she had taken him for.

'It is no matter, ma'am,' Roland said, doing his best to be serious at the woman's complete volte-face. Then, to Travers, 'Do you think we can right this coach?'

'Don't see why not.'

The two men, both exceptionally big and strong, strode over to the coach and, with a great deal of heaving and pushing and rocking of it, managed to turn it back on to its wheels. Roland went all round it, examining it carefully. 'I think it could be driven,' he said. 'If you take it slowly, it will carry you to the next posting inn.'

'Thank you, my lord,' the woman's husband said. 'But Greaves is in no case to drive. Perhaps your man…'

'What about it, Travers?' Roland asked. 'Fancy tooling a coach, do you?'

The corporal, busy harnessing the horses again, looked up and grinned. 'Very well, sir, but what about the wall?'

'We will finish it tomorrow. Miss Cartwright and I will carry the boy home and deliver him safely to his mother. I am sure Mr…'

'Halliwell,' the man said. 'James Halliwell, at your service, my lord. I will furnish your man with the wherewithal to return home.'

'Then I suggest you help Mr Greaves into the coach, and off you go.'

'Inside?' Mrs Halliwell squeaked, looking at her coachman, who was now sitting up, but still looking decidedly dazed. She obviously thought it was beneath her dignity to ride inside with a servant.

In the event Greaves disdained the comfort of an inside seat and insisted he would be perfectly at ease sitting beside Travers on the box and proved it by getting shakily to his feet and climbing up there. Mr and Mrs Halliwell clambered in and Roland secured the broken door with a strap and they set off, walking the horses very slowly and carefully.

Charlotte, still kneeling beside young Tommy, watched them go, then turned back to the boy, who was moaning softly.

'Do you think he is hurt anywhere beside his head?' she asked, stroking the boy's muddy cheek with a gentle finger. 'I do not think he can speak because of his deafness.'

Watching her, he suddenly realised he was seeing a very different woman from the one he had hitherto encountered and could not help gazing at her. Gone were the strong features, the firm jawline, the glittering eyes, the coldness of the hoyden, and in their place was a mouth that was tenderly soft and eyes full of warmth, as she comforted the boy. It was most disconcerting. He pulled himself together to answer her. 'A doctor will be able to tell,' he said. 'We must send for one at once.'

'I will fetch Dr Sumner. It will only take a few minutes on Bonny Boy.'

'Very well. I will carry the boy to his home if you tell me where that is.'

'The thatched cottage beside the church. His name is Tommy Biggs.'

'Biggs?' he queried, as he helped her to mount. 'That is the name of the family you mentioned, is it not?'

'Yes, it is,' she said, surprised that he had remembered it. She had not thought he had even been listening.

Unfortunately, Dr Sumner was out on a call, but

his housekeeper promised to give him a message as soon as he returned and Charlotte had to be content with that. She emphasised the urgency and rode back to the Biggs's cottage where she found Roland sitting on a stool beside a dilapidated sofa on which the boy was lying. Mrs Biggs, her face white and drawn, admitted her and then went to stand beside his lordship to look down on her son. Two toddlers hung on to her skirts.

'How is he?' Charlotte asked.

'He seems confused. His lordship has said it often happens after a blow on the head, but it should not last. I do not know what would have happened if his lordship had not been there, ma'am. He could have been killed. He should not have been so far from home, I don't know what got into the little devil.'

'He is like all small boys, Mrs Biggs,' Roland said. 'Into mischief, and the fact that he is deaf does not alter that.' He smiled at the boy and was repaid with a brave grin in return. 'He is a plucky little fellow.'

'The doctor is coming,' Charlotte said. 'I left a message.'

'Oh, but, ma'am, I ain't sure tha's necessary. He'll be his old self by and by…'

'Better be on the safe side,' Charlotte said, knowing the reason for the woman's reluctance and producing the coins Mr Halliwell had given her from the pocket of her habit. 'The man with the coach was most apologetic and anxious to do what he could to help. He gave me this to pay for a doctor and anything else Tommy needs.'

'Oh, thank you, ma'am. Perhaps it would be best to have him checked over…'

Again she offered refreshment and again was politely refused and Charlotte and Roland left soon afterwards, with Charlotte promising to return to find out what the doctor said and if there was anything else Tommy needed.

'You do care for those people, don't you?' Roland said, taking up the reins of her horse and leading it, obliging her to walk beside him.

'It would be a callous person who did not.'

She was still on her high ropes, he realised, trying to teach him his duty, to make him feel guilty. He decided not to rise to the bait. 'Enough to take on their welfare?' he queried.

'The two oldest girls, Beth, who is fourteen, and Matty, who is a little over a year younger, are my employees. You met them. I am told you gave them half a crown.'

'So I did. Your mill hands, shut out because they were too polite not to answer me when I spoke to them.'

'One cannot let tardiness go unpunished,' she said. 'But I have told Mr Brock that, in future, anyone who arrives late will not be locked out, but will lose half an hour's pay for every five minutes. After all, I am the loser when their looms stand idle all day.'

He laughed. Her good deeds seemed to be tempered with self-interest. But was that really true? She seemed genuinely concerned about the boy, and the look of tenderness on her face when she had been comforting him had showed a gentler side to her nature that stayed with him.

'There is nothing wrong in that,' she said, stung by his laughter. 'Everyone must do the work they are given.'

'Even me,' he said.

'Yes. It was fortunate you were working or you would not have been in a position to save Tommy's life. It was a brave thing to do.' It choked her to say it, but it was nothing but the truth and she was always one to give credit where it was due.

'I am a hardened soldier, Miss Cartwright, used to carnage, but you did not flinch when I handed the boy over to you. Other young ladies would have swooned away.'

She laughed. 'And then you would have had

two patients instead of one and no one to ride for the doctor. I am not such a fribble, my lord, and I never have been.'

He could readily believe it. He stopped and bent to cup his hands for her foot. She sprang astride the saddle, giving him a glimpse of a well-turned ankle, settled her feet in the stirrups and took up the reins.

'Good day to you, my lord,' she said, trotting away, leaving him standing looking after her, stroking his chin in contemplation.

He could not make her out. Was she still the spoiled, imperious chit of his earlier acquaintance or had she changed? Until this afternoon he would have said she had not changed one iota, but would the spoiled hoyden have concerned herself with the problems of a poor family? While they had been waiting for her, Mrs Biggs had sung her praises, telling him how generous she was and how without her they would be in dire need. He was unsure if the woman was deliberately trying to make him feel guilty or was too simple to realise how her words sounded. While his father had been ill and his mother too mortified by their straitened circumstances to go out and about, Miss Cartwright had been free to act the lady of the manor and perhaps she was not inclined to let that go. He chuckled to himself. If he had married her when his father suggested it, that was just what she would have been.

The devil of it was that their paths were bound to cross, living so close, and it was wearying to be for ever sparring, especially if they both wanted to do good by the villagers. They had to find some kind of harmony to their day-to-day encounters. He would do well to adopt a soft approach and avoid argument, leaving that for when the real battle began.

He turned and strode back to the Hall. There was a little more furniture in the house now, a proper dining table, a few chairs, a desk and some beds, but it was still minimal and the marble-floored entrance hall contained nothing but a small table and a faded Sheraton chair. He had instructed builders to make repairs to the roof where it let in the rain and to make good broken window sashes, but he had not yet put in hand a full-scale refurbishment. He wondered if he ever would. There he was, an aristocrat who had to watch every penny, trying to do justice to all his people, while that hoyden had more money than she knew what to do with. Paying lawyers would not trouble her at all, but it would drain his own minimal resources. His head told him to let it go, but his own stubborn pride resisted. The profits from that mine would make all the difference, not only to the restoration of the Hall, but to the tenants and villagers who looked to him to keep their dwellings in good repair. Was ever a man in such a coil?

Chapter Three

Charlotte, riding home, berated herself for a traitor. She had sworn the man was her enemy and yet there she was, conversing with him as if he had never said those hateful words six years before. Six years was a long time to hold a grudge, but what had he done since returning to make her think he had regretted his outburst? Nothing. He had accused Papa of cheating the Earl out of his land, had intimated he meant to continue with that ridiculous lawsuit, and had even gone up to the mine and poked about as if he owned it. It was enough to make Papa turn in his grave.

Papa. Had he realised the storm he would unleash the day he had said to her, 'It is time we found you a husband, Charlie'?

She knew him well enough to know that he had not said that on a whim, but had been thinking about it for some time. 'I hope, Papa, you are not thinking of sending me to London for a Season,' she had said. 'I tell you now, I should hate it.'

'Why so?'

'Mincing about in lace and ribbons, fluttering a fan and making foolish remarks about the weather to coxcombs with no more than a hen's brain between them. Besides, it would only be the prospect of my dowry that would persuade them to address me at all.'

He had laughed at that. 'I can see it would not serve, but we do not need to go from home to find just the fellow. Young Viscount Temple is a well set-up young man and, according to his father, on the lookout for a bride.'

'The Viscount! He would never consider me.'

'On the contrary, I am assured he has already expressed an interest. According to the Earl, he has been admiring you ever since he came back from university. In any event, the Earl is of a mind to hold a ball and we are invited. Play your cards right, my dear, and one day you will be a countess.'

In those days a ball at Amerleigh Hall was not to be missed if one was lucky enough to have one of its gilt-edged invitations. The grand ballroom, the music and dancing, the food and wine were always of the highest order. Her father had sent her off with his sister, her Aunt Harriet, to buy a ballgown and all the fripperies needed and no expense spared. The trouble was, and she had realised it as soon as she entered the ballroom and seen all the other ladies, was that her aunt's idea of fashion was sadly out of date. She had tried to make a mincing, blushing doll out of her, covering her in pink lace and silk rosebuds and having her wayward hair forced into tight corkscrew curls, which did not suit her at all. She had stuck her head in the air and pretended not to mind, but, at seventeen, it was a pose difficult to maintain. After stumbling over a gavotte with a pimply youth whose name she could not remember, she had, as soon as the music ended, excused herself and left the room. It was then, standing in a dim corridor, she had heard those dreadful, never-to-be-forgotten words.

They had clouded her life. From simply being a little tomboyish, a young girl who enjoyed the countryside, but who was ready to be courted, to fall in love in the prescribed manner, looking forward to being a wife and mother, she had become the woman she was: a hard-headed, determined businesswoman who had no time for the niceties of social intercourse, especially with the likes of the new Earl of Amerleigh.

Damn him!

She left Bonny Boy with Dobson and went into the house through a side door, intent on regaining her room without meeting any of her servants. She knew she looked a pickle. Her hair had escaped its pins and there was dirt and blood all down the bodice of her habit and she did not feel like being questioned. Once in her room, she crossed the floor and stood looking out of the window towards Amerleigh, hidden from view by the ridge of Browhill. Meeting the Earl again was making her question her whole life.

Roland's new clothes arrived the following afternoon. He had Travers trim his hair before changing into a double-breasted coat of dark blue superfine, a pale blue waistcoat and a plain white shirt with a neat muslin neckcloth. His biscuit-coloured pantaloons were tucked into his new Hessians. Thus transformed, he set off for the dower house.

He had almost reached the drawing room door when he heard ladies' voices. His mama was receiving visitors. Remembering she had told him no one called on her nowadays, he paused, smiling.

'I am sure you must be relieved to have his

lordship home again,' he heard one say. 'It is so difficult to know how to go on when there is no man about the place.'

'Yes, to be sure,' another said. 'But the new Earl is not living here, is he? I heard he has taken up residence at the Hall.'

'Yes,' his mother replied. 'That is as it should be.'

'Of course, I did not mean to imply otherwise. No doubt he is settling in well.'

'I believe he is. I do not interfere, naturally.'

'No, I agree, no mother should, but he must confide in you and take note of your remarks, dear Lady Temple.'

'He is a dutiful son.'

Roland, who was about to enter, stayed his hand. He was smiling so broadly they could not fail to notice if he joined them.

'No doubt,' a third piped in. 'But he has been away so long, he has perhaps forgotten all his old friends. We have been thinking that we ought to welcome him home more formally, introduce him to other young people. I know my Faith would be delighted to renew acquaintance with him.'

While Roland was racking his brains to remember someone called Faith, he heard Lady Brandon chime in, 'And I am sure Martha would be honoured to stand up with him.'

'Stand up,' the Countess echoed.

'Yes, a little soirée in his honour. A little conversation, a dance or two, perhaps, nothing elaborate. What do you think, Countess?'

'I am sure I do not know,' she said. 'I must ask Roland what he thinks. We are in mourning, you know.'

Roland, straight-faced once more, opened the door and made his entrance. Four pairs of eyes turned towards him. They belonged to his mother, Lady Gilford, Lady Brandon and Mrs Trent. He was glad he had changed out of his uniform into something more befitting the aristocratic owner of Amerleigh Hall. He bowed. 'Ladies, your obedient.'

'Roland, there you are.' His mother valiantly overcame her astonishment at his changed appearance. 'We are about to have tea. You will stop and take some?'

He lowered his long frame into a chair. 'Thank you. I hope I do not interrupt the latest *on dit*.'

'Not at all, my lord,' Lady Brandon said. 'We decided it was time we came to welcome you back among us and to suggest a small reception in your honour.'

'Ladies, I am flattered, but we are in mourning.'

'We know that,' Lady Gilford put in. 'But it is not to be a grand affair and I am sure your late father would wish you to venture into society. In his day, he was a great one for entertaining and being entertained. I remember one ball he gave that had the whole county by the ears.'

Roland, guessing she was referring to that disastrous evening six years before and was fishing for information that would set her high among her bosom bows when recounted, decided to cut her short. 'My lady,' he said, 'when circumstances permit, there will be balls again at Amerleigh Hall, then I shall be pleased to number you among my guests, but I cannot contemplate such a thing while we are in mourning.'

'No, naturally not,' Lady Brandon rescued her. 'We only came to enquire if you would attend a modest function at Scofield Place. I am sure there can be nothing unseemly about that.'

He caught sight of his mother, who nodded imperceptibly. 'I shall be delighted.'

Highly satisfied with their afternoon's work, the visitors took their leave. As soon as the door closed on them, he burst out laughing. 'Mama, what am I to make of that?'

Lady Amerleigh smiled. 'You are going to be feted whether you like it or not, and every mama of every single young lady will be trying to outdo the others in entertaining you.'

'Heaven help me! I am not in the marriage mart.'

She laughed. It was the first time he had heard her laugh since he came home and the sound lifted his spirits. 'One of these days, a young lady will come along who will capture your heart and you will sing a different tune.'

'I hope she may, but not before I have set the estate to rights. Today I have made a beginning.'

'That is good news.'

'Papa was not as profligate as we thought and I have some money of my own. But there is no need for anyone to know that. Let them think my father left me in good standing and the only reason he let the estate run down was because he was mortally ill.' He paused. 'It is not a massive fortune, so I cannot go mad, but there is enough to refurnish the main part of the house. Would you take charge of that for me, Mama? I have not the least idea what is necessary.'

She clapped her hands in delight. 'Oh, I should love that above everything. When shall I begin?'

'As soon as may be. Now I am going to visit the little deaf boy and see how he goes on. If you can spare me time tomorrow, I will come and we will make plans.'

Charlotte, faithful to her promise, returned home that afternoon in good time to visit Mrs Biggs and see how well Tommy was recovering, taking more milk and eggs and a jar of Mrs Cater's plum preserve. She was taken aback when Mrs Biggs admitted her to find the Earl of Amerleigh, dressed in the pink of fashion, sprawling on the floor beside Tommy, playing spillikins with him. Both were laughing at the Earl's ineptitude. His lordship looked up as she entered. 'Miss Cartwright, how do you do,' he said, scrambling to his feet and towering over her.

'My lord. I am well, thank you.' Her voice sounded normal, but it belied how she felt, for inside her heart was beating at twice its normal rate. If she had known he would be here, she told herself, she would not have come. But that was foolish, they were near neighbours and she could not avoid seeing him occasionally. She had to remind herself sternly that he meant nothing to her, except as an irritant she could well do without.

'I came to see how this young fellow did,' he explained, smiling as if they had never had a cross word and were amiable neighbours. 'He appears to have made a full recovery.'

'I am very pleased to hear it.'

He looked about him; there was clearly no room in the tiny cottage for both of them, especially as the rest of the children were all crowding round to see the great lord on the floor playing with their brother. 'I will leave you to talk to our young hero and satisfy yourself as to his recovery,' he said to Charlotte, then turned to face Tommy so that the boy could read his lips. 'I must go.'

Tommy's face was a picture of disappointment. He seemed to be trying very hard to speak, but the words were unintelligible to Charlotte. Roland bent down and ruffled the boy's hair. 'You may give me a chance to get my own back another day. Now I must go. Miss Cartwright is come to talk to you, so you will have company.'

He bade Mrs Biggs goodbye and was gone, leaving Charlotte feeling inexplicably flat. Their conversation had been mundane, as if each were repeating, parrot fashion, the niceties custom demanded, when what they really wanted to say remained unsaid. But perhaps that was best. Politeness cost nothing.

'His lordship is a fine man,' Mrs Biggs said, after thanking Charlotte for the provisions she had brought. 'He has told Alf he may have his job back, so we are all cheered by his coming.'

'I am glad of that.'

'And you have been good to us too, Miss Cartwright. The milk and eggs have made all the difference these last weeks.'

'Think nothing of it, Mrs Biggs. How is the baby?'

'Thriving, I am thankful to say. And my Hannah is old enough to work now and has been taken on by his lordship to work in the kitchen at the Hall, and with Matty and Beth both working too, we are well content.'

Charlotte had stayed a little while to nurse the baby and talk to Tommy, using signs and lip reading, which he seemed to manage very well, before taking her leave to return home. She had walked past the church and was making her way along the lane by the village green when she saw the Earl standing beside his mount, which was drinking at the trough. She was about to carry on, when he picked up his reins and led the horse over to her. 'Miss Cartwright.'

She stopped. Had he been lying in wait for her? She did not feel like another argument with him, but why else would he have addressed her? 'My lord.'

He fell into step beside her as she walked on. 'Not riding today?'

'No. I have been too busy.'

'With good works in the village?' He knew that was the case. Everyone spoke highly of her, praising her for her compassion, her generosity and her down-to-earth character. 'For all her money, she ain't haughty, not a bit of it,' they said. But did they really know her? Did they know she was as bad as her late father, that her fortune, on which she lived and which she used to bestow her largesse, was founded on slavery, not only in the Indies, but closer to home? The mills must make their profit; if it needed little children to do it, then she had no compunction about employing them. Perhaps she had had no hand in the blow her father had dealt his, but she seemed determined to keep the enmity alive.

'Among other things.' She paused. 'Mrs Biggs tells me you have given her husband his job back.'

'Yes. As you so rightly pointed out, I need him. The grounds are in a terrible state. They used to be admired for miles around. When I was a boy, my mother was always giving tours of the garden and sharing her knowledge with others of like mind. I doubt I can get it back to that condition, but with my mother's help I will do my best.'

'You mean to stay, then?'

'Why would I not? Amerleigh is my home.'

'Of course.'

'But you would wish me otherwhere?' Roland pressed lightly.

'No, why should I? I only meant you might not wish to go to the trouble of restoring it.'

'But I do wish it. It is a good solid house, the home of generations of my family and not easily abandoned.'

'The late Earl abandoned it.'

'He was ill, Miss Cartwright. The worry of it…' He stopped; he did not want to pursue that argument. 'I wanted to ask you, since you seem to know the family well, has anything been done to cure Tommy of his deafness?'

'I do not think so. I think they are all resigned to the fact that he will never hear and he does marvellously well with a few signs and facial expressions.'

'Yes, I saw that.'

'He has an old ear trumpet someone gave him, but he does not use it. It is almost as big as he is and is too much trouble carrying around when he wants to play.'

'But one day he will have to work.'

'If he finds nothing else, I will employ him. Being deaf might be a positive advantage in a room full of clattering looms.'

'Yes, and a more dangerous occupation for a child I cannot imagine.'

She had spoken without thinking, almost as if there was a little devil sitting on her shoulder goading her into making outrageous remarks, just to see what he would say, and she had been hoist on her own petard. 'I do not like employing children, my lord, but if I did not, my business would sink without trace and that would mean the adults would be without work too, not only in the mill, but those who work the barges, the crew of the *Fair Charlie*, even the servants and outdoor workers at Mandeville. It is the lesser of two evils.'

'So it may be, but children should be allowed to enjoy their childhood for as long as they can.'

'I do not disagree with that, but needs must when the devil drives.' Why, when she was in his company, did she make herself sound harder than she really was? Why compound the bad impression he already had of her? It was a question of pride, she supposed, pride and stubbornness.

'Nevertheless, I should like to see what can be done for the boy. I have come across deafness among soldiers due to the noise of the battlefield and it is a considerable disadvantage to them. There was a medical officer with our regiment who interested himself in deafness, and he was teaching them to communicate with signs.'

'Tommy already does that.'

'Yes, but this is more formal. By using the same standard, deaf people can communicate with others…'

'Who must also learn the same signs.'

'Yes. But if Tommy's mother and siblings were to learn it, they could translate what he is saying.'

'A laudable, if ambitious, idea, my lord, but who is to provide the teaching?'

'That I need to discover. Do you think Mr and Mrs Biggs would agree, if I should find someone prepared to do it?' His expression was serious, but by no means malevolent; there was nothing of the objectionable man who had insisted Browhill was his. Beware! the imp on her shoulder warned her.

'I am sure they would like to see him overcome his affliction, my lord, but Mr Biggs is a proud man and hates to be beholden to charity. I have to take my little contribution for their comfort when he is not at home or he would throw it in my face.'

'I thought that as the family's welfare interests you, you might use your influence to persuade them.'

On the surface his suggestion was a simple one, but underneath she detected undercurrents she did not know how to deal with. But how could she say no? How could she refuse anything to improve the lot of the villagers? It was the squire's prerogative to do that, of course, but the old Earl had done nothing and after they had moved to the dower house, the Countess had hardly been out and about at all. Charlotte had taken it upon herself to distribute largesse and give employment, and she had taken the Biggs family to her heart. 'You are asking for my help?'

'Yes.'

'But we are…'

'Sworn enemies?' It was said with a crooked smile.

'No, but we are in litigation.'

'Then let the lawyers get on with it. They will take an age and in the meantime there is work to be done.'

'That is very philosophical of you, my lord.'

'So?'

'Naturally, I will do all I can to help. But it is not just Tommy Biggs—you are needed by everyone in the village who has been waiting on your coming, hoping their lives will improve.'

He knew that and did not like it being pointed out to him, but he had made up his mind not to quarrel with her. To have two influential people warring in a small village would not make for harmony. 'I hope they will, Miss Cartwright. I am making a beginning.'

'And if the task proves too much, will you disappear again, back to the war and your comrades?'

'Ah,' he said, laughing. 'I knew you wished me otherwhere.'

She refused to be drawn by that. 'I read in the latest despatches that Lord Wellington is outside Bordeaux and the allies in the north are marching on Paris. Does that mean the war will soon be over?'

He might have known she would keep abreast of the news by reading the papers. 'Let us hope so.'

'And then the army will come home. The soldiers will need to find work.'

'Those that are not sent to America or other conflicts will be discharged and will certainly need gainful employment. I am thankful that I have something to come home to.'

'And different battles to fight,' she said with a smile.

He laughed. 'Battles I shall win, Miss Cartwright.'

She did not answer because they had arrived at the gates of the Hall. He halted and turned towards her, doffing his hat. 'Here we must part. Good day to you, Miss Cartwright. I will let you know what I can discover about the deaf teacher.' He sprang into the saddle before she could reply and cantered up the weed-infested drive.

'We shall see,' she murmured to herself, as she continued on her way. 'We shall see.'

* * *

Lady Brandon, full of self-importance, delivered Charlotte's invitation to her soirée herself two days later and was taken aback when Charlotte said she did not think she would go. 'What have you against the man?' her ladyship asked.

Charlotte was certainly not going to tell her. 'I find him top-lofty in the extreme.'

'Goodness, he has a right to be proud. He is an Earl, after all. I found him very civil and he has such an amiable manner. When we called on the Countess to ask her what she thought about a little soirée in his honour, his lordship arrived while we were there and he was politeness itself...'

'Who is "we"?'

'Lady Gilford, Mrs Trent and I. We asked him directly and, though the Countess declined on account of being in mourning, he was pleased to accept. You know, if he manages to come about, he will be the catch of the year. It will be amusing to watch all the mamas buzzing round him, trying to catch his eye.'

Charlotte smiled to herself. She had no doubt that Lady Brandon herself was one such mama. Poor Martha would be pushed and pulled and goaded to make herself agreeable to his lordship. It would be interesting to see how successful she would be.

'You will come, won't you?' her ladyship went on. 'If you do not, people will gossip and that would look ill, do you not think?'

Charlotte considered this for a moment and decided that gossip about why she was not pleased to see Roland Temple come home was something she could do without. 'I suppose you could be right. Very well, I will come.'

Her ladyship clapped her hands. 'Good. I want the occasion to be perfect. I want everyone to say it could never be bettered.'

'I thought it was only to be a simple soirée.'

'Oh, we can do better than that. Now I must leave you, I have much to do to have everything ready in time. I look forward to seeing you on Saturday.' And with that she took her leave.

Charlotte spent some time considering what to wear and finally decided on her brand-new gown. It was amber, deeper than gold, but not quite brown, with a rounded neckline and puffed sleeves and finished with coffee-coloured lace at the hem and a matching ribbon under her bust.

On the evening of the soirée, Meg, her maid, discreetly powdered Charlotte's face to subdue the tan, and dressed her hair in a Grecian style which even the usually modest Charlotte agreed made her look well. She had a drawer full of expensive jewellery which she never wore, but tonight she picked out a pearl necklace given to her by her papa on her twenty-first birthday. Taking up a matching silk shawl, a chicken-skin fan and a small beaded reticule, she went downstairs and out to her carriage.

The affair at Scofield Place, put about as a simple soirée, had grown out of all proportion. Anyone who was anyone in the county had been invited and had accepted. The food, produced by outside caterers, was sumptuous and would have fed a poor family for a year, if its taste were to run to the rare dishes, rich sauces and exotic fruits that weighed down the table in the wainscoted dining room. There were flowers and an orchestra and hired footmen in livery.

Lady Brandon, clad in a full-skirted gown of burgundy taffeta, which made her look rounder than ever, took both Charlotte's hands and looked her up and down. 'My dear, you look lovely. I would never have attempted that colour myself, but I do declare it becomes you.' Sir Gordon, in a black superfine evening coat and matching breeches with white stockings, made her a bow and said she looked very well.

There was a huge crush in the large drawing

room, stripped of its carpet and furniture, where an orchestra played for dancing, though that could hardly be heard above the noise of conversation as friend greeted friend and everyone enquired of everyone else if the Earl had arrived.

'I was right,' Lady Brandon told Charlotte triumphantly. 'The Earl is like to be the catch of the season. Just look at Dorothea Manton preening herself like a peacock, as if she were not already well and truly on the shelf, and if Mrs Barnard thinks he will take any notice of her plain Jane, then she is a greater fribble than I took her for. Why, our Martha has a better chance of being noticed than any of them.'

Charlotte did not think these comments required an answer; besides, she was too busy looking round herself. If his lordship were looking for a bride with a good dowry, then he was unlikely to find her here. Dorothea Manton's parents were well bred, it was true, but like many aristocrats, they lived outside their means. Faith Trent's dowry would certainly not suffice if the point of the exercise was to refurbish Amerleigh Hall. The same could be said of almost everyone else in the room. Charlotte smiled to herself; she was the only one with sufficient resources and she was the only one who would not drop the handkerchief for him. She became aware that the murmur of voices had died and everyone was looking towards the door, where Roland Temple, Earl of Amerleigh, had just arrived.

He stood inches taller than any other man present, dressed in a black evening suit, relieved by a pale blue embroidered waistcoat and snowy white cravat, skilfully tied. His dark curls had been trimmed into the latest windswept style and barely touched the high collar of his coat. Unlike the other men in the room, he wore no jewellery, but he did not need it. No one could deny he had a commanding presence and there was a concerted sigh from the ladies. His physical attraction was so strong and his character so compelling, he could, if she were the susceptible kind, make Charlotte go weak at the knees and forget they were mortal enemies.

Lady Brandon hurried to greet him and proceeded to lead him round the room, introducing him to those he had not met before and reminding him of others he might have remembered from his boyhood. He bowed and smiled and passed on to the next, convinced that everyone who was anyone in Shropshire must surely be crammed into the room in all their finery for his benefit and he wished it were otherwise. If they had been giving him a true welcome, he would not have minded, but he knew most of it was curiosity to see if he would do something outrageous and confirm their worst fears. And if he did not, if he turned out to be perfectly abstemious and polite, then every mama of an unattached female would work herself silly to have her daughter noticed.

He smiled quirkily as he bowed over Dorothea Gilford's hand, which made that poor child blush to the roots of her mousy hair. And it was not as if the smile was directed at her, but his own stupidity for allowing himself to become a party to it. He moved on quickly to the next group, noticing that the next in line was Miss Cartwright. So used to seeing and picturing the hoyden, he was completely taken aback by her changed appearance and for a moment could not pay attention to Lady Brandon. Pulling himself together, he murmured a greeting to the couple to whom he was being introduced and then moved on to Charlotte. Standing before her, he was obliged to amend his original perception of her—she was not plain at all. Here was a beautiful woman with the figure of a goddess. Even her wild hair had been tamed. He swept her a flourishing bow. 'Good evening, Miss Cartwright.'

'Good evening, my lord.' She was fully aware

of the effect she was having on him and it gave her a wonderful sense of gratification as she dipped a slight curtsy. She would teach him to call her plain and a hoyden!

He did not want to move on, but Lady Brandon was already approaching the next group and he had perforce to follow. It was not until he had perambulated round the entire room, smiling at the young ladies, kissing the hands of the matrons and bowing to their husbands, that he was able to relax a little. And even then it was not for long.

The orchestra struck up a country dance and he was induced to join a set with Miss Jane Trent. And after that it was another dance and another young lady and then another and he was just about to make his way over to Miss Cartwright when he became aware of Miss Brandon standing only a few feet away and looking at him, half-shy, half-expectantly. He bowed. 'Miss Brandon, will you do me the honour of joining this country dance with me?'

She smiled and curtsied and he raised her to her feet and led her into the dance. But his thoughts were on the other side of the room where Charlotte stood beside Lady Brandon.

'They make a comely pair, do they not?'
'Who?'

'Why, Martha and the Earl, of course. He is bound to look favourably on her, considering I have been at such pains to make him welcome.'

Charlotte watched the two dancers. The Earl was smiling down at Martha and had obviously paid her a compliment, for she was smiling back at him, eyes shining. It gave Charlotte an uneasy feeling in the pit of her stomach that she could not explain. 'You think he will offer for her?'

'I do not see why not. We will bring him round to it. She will make a splendid Countess.'

'Yes, but Amerleigh Hall is in a ruinous state.'

'Martha has an inheritance from my aunt and she has never had to spend a penny of it, I am thankful to say. It has been growing with interest ever since the old lady died five years ago. Sir Gordon will ensure his lordship is aware of it.'

'Do you think he would marry for money?'

'It must be a consideration. If his pockets are to let, it must mean his title is up for sale.'

Her words thrust Charlotte back six years to a time when the late Earl was ready to sell the title and Roland had refused absolutely to consider her. It stiffened her resolve; she would make him pay for that humiliation in whatever way came to hand.

'I think he will make an excellent husband,' her

ladyship continued, unaware that Charlotte was no longer giving her full attention. 'I have been hearing fine reports of him.'

'From his servant, no doubt.'

'From everyone. Why are you so against him?'

'I am not against him. I have no interest in his affairs. I was thinking of Martin Elliott. I am sure he has hopes of Martha.'

'Pooh, what is he? Nothing but a parson's son and he hasn't even found a living yet.'

Charlotte felt sorry for the poor man, but she refrained from saying so, because the dance had ended and the Earl was escorting Martha to them, smiling and speaking to her in what, to the highly sensitised mamas, was a most intimate fashion. The roomful of people watched their progress and sighed, many with disappointment.

He thanked Martha with an elegant leg, surreptitiously looking sideways at Charlotte as he did so, but she would not look at him, being engrossed in examining her fan.

'My lord,' Lady Brandon said. 'It is gratifying to see you mingle with us all so amiably. We are glad to have you among us again.'

'That is very kind of you, my lady.' There was a pause which to Charlotte, still studying the picture of a shepherdess and her swain on her fan, seemed interminable, before he added, 'Miss Cartwright, may I have the pleasure of the next dance?'

She looked up at him, fluttering her fan, as if she had only just discovered what the accessory was meant for.

'Come.' He was holding out his hand.

She stood up and put her hand into his and allowed him to draw her onto the floor for a waltz.

Waltzing had been in favour for two or three years in the capital, but had only recently been considered a suitable dance for the country. Lady Brandon was being greatly daring in asking the musicians to play for one, but she was determined that no one should think her behind the times and it might give the company some indication of whom his lordship might favour. And he had picked out Charlotte Cartwright! She was beginning to wish she had not tried so hard to induce Charlotte to come.

The warmth of his hand on her back through the thin silk of her gown seemed to spread right through Charlotte until she was quite breathless. For a big man, he was surprisingly light on his feet and she found herself wondering where he had learned to dance in that expert way, for he guided her unerringly. And for the first time in her life, she did not regret those dancing lessons. She chose not to notice that Lady Gilford and many of the other matrons were murmuring among themselves, nor the dagger looks of the young ladies who had hoped to catch his eye; she was immune to everything but the enjoyment of the dance, of doing something she had not done for years. Six years, in fact—the last time she had danced with him. She wondered if he remembered it.

The music came to an end with a triumphant flourish and Charlotte dropped into a deep curtsy. He bowed and took her hand to raise her up and then offered his arm to escort her back to her place and they found themselves the target of all eyes as they made their way slowly down the length of the room. She felt she had to make an effort at conversation, something safe, something not contentious.

'Have you made any progress about a teacher for Tommy?' she asked.

'I have made one or two enquiries, but so far nothing definite. With the war coming to an end, the medical officer I spoke of might be coming home and I might wait to see what he has to say.'

'If he is used to working with soldiers, he may not wish to teach a child.'

'Then he will not be the man we want and we must find someone else.'

'We, my lord?'

'You and I, young Tommy and his parents.'

'You include me?'

'Of course. You are very necessary to the success of the project.'

She laughed. 'Could it be that the help you need from me is monetary?'

'Not at all,' he said huffily. 'I am sorry I mentioned it. I might have known you would reduce everything to pounds, shillings and pence.'

'Pounds, shillings and pence are very useful things to have, my lord.'

'Is that all you can think of? Do you have no heart?'

'What has my heart to do with anything? It is a beating organ, necessary to life, just as yours is.' That little imp was on her shoulder again, making her say outrageous things, egging her on to produce a reaction out of him.

'True, but sometimes it can beat a little faster, someone says something or does something that sets it pounding. Have you never had that happen to you, Miss Cartwright?' He paused to look down at her and she felt the colour flare into her face and, what was more, her heart was beating nineteen to the dozen. She was sure he could hear it.

'That is neither here nor there. We were talking of Tommy and how he could be helped.'

'By all means, let us talk of Tommy.'

'I doubt a trained teacher would consider teaching one child a full-time task.'

'Perhaps not. But it set me wondering how many other deaf children there are in the neighbourhood.'

'I have no idea. Several I should think. You surely do not intend to teach them all. You would need premises and equipment and specialist teachers. It could not be done on half a crown.'

She was referring to the half-crown he had given to Beth Biggs, he knew. She never let slip an opportunity to have a prod at him. 'I know, but it is worth a try, don't you think?'

He did not know why he was even asking her. He did not need her permission or co-operation. The trouble was he had not been able to banish her from his thoughts. She was like an itch he could not scratch and yet this evening he had truly enjoyed her company. She made everyone else seem flat and colourless.

'Then rest assured, I will do what I can to help.' She paused. 'But that does not mean I have changed my mind about Browhill.'

'I did not expect you would,' he said with a faint smile, still unable to believe her transformation from hoyden to beauty. 'But we will leave that for another day. For the moment we can enjoy the respite of a truce.'

'Speaking of truces, do you think Napoleon can hold out much longer?' She had to say something, to make everything sound commonplace and polite, to maintain her dignity when every fibre of her wanted to thrash out at him, make her see her for what she really was, a person in her own right, not simply the daughter of her father. Why that mattered she did not know.

He recognised the change of subject as a way of diverting him from personal issues. 'Let us hope not, but he has so far refused all offers of peace.'

'Do you wish you could be with your comrades when they finally triumph?'

'In one way. On the other hand, I would not, at this moment, wish to be anywhere else.'

She must not allow herself to become susceptible to his flattery, she told herself, especially as she knew it was far from sincere. 'I know you are needed here in Amerleigh with your people, my lord,' she said, choosing to misunderstand him. 'But coming back to England must have been a wrench for you just when you were so close to victory.'

'It was necessary and if I could be sure of my welcome…'

She waved her hand at the crowded room. 'Tonight must have given you the answer to that.'

'It is gratifying, I own, but I find myself wondering how much of that is down to my being the Earl of Amerleigh and unmarried and how much to the returning soldier.'

'Time will tell,' she said, as they reached the end of the room.

He bowed and, taking her hand, put it to his lips, at the same time raising his eyes to hers. For a moment she could not look away and felt herself being drawn towards him, though she had not moved. Almost mesmerised, his eyes held hers. She thought she detected a message in their dark depths. Something like, 'I enjoy sparring with you, but we are not enemies, are we? We could be friends. More than friends.' Was he flirting with his eyes? Or was she being fanciful? And it came to her very suddenly that if she could encourage him, even make him love her, and then disdain him, that would be sweet revenge indeed! The trouble was she had no idea how to go about it. She had always been forthright and truthful, even if her hearers did not like what they heard. She could not be anything else. She snatched her hand away, making him smile.

He saw her to her seat, then took up a station near the door where a potted plant half-concealed him and from where he could watch the assembly, and particularly Miss Charlotte Cartwright. How could you dislike a woman you found desirable? And she was desirable, too much so for his peace of mind.

'Not dancing, my lord?'

He turned to find a young man, dressed in impeccable evening attire, standing beside him. 'I beg your pardon.'

'Jacob Edwards. You remember, we were often together as boys.'

'Good Lord! Jacob. Of course I remember. Many's the scrape we shared.' He held out his hand, which the other grasped and pumped up and down furiously. 'How are you?'

'Well. And you? I was sorry to hear about your father. He was very good to me.'

He remembered his mother telling him that Jacob had become Miss Cartwright's lawyer. 'And you have justified his faith in you. I hear you have done very well for yourself.'

'Yes, I give him credit for giving me a start.'

'But perhaps not enough to refrain from acting against him.'

'I assume you refer to Browhill?'

'Yes, unless there is some other villainy I do not know about.'

'I did no work for the late Mr Cartwright, my lord. I have only been in Miss Cartwright's employ just over a year, after she quarrelled with her father's lawyer soon after she inherited. I knew nothing of the business until recently and now, of course, I am obliged to act for her.'

Roland wondered what the quarrel had been about. 'So?'

'My lord, cannot the dispute be settled amicably? I am sure with a little goodwill…'

Roland was angry. Not five minutes before, he had been dancing with the lady and offering her compliments. He must have been mad. 'You may go back to your employer and tell her that when she shows a little goodwill over the matter, I might reciprocate. And, may I add, a country dance is not the place to air legal matters.'

'Then I beg your pardon. I spoke out of respect for our past friendship and a wish to prevent the expenditure of time and money that could be better spent elsewhere.'

Oh, how he agreed with that sentiment, but he had no intention of letting the other know it. 'How I spend my time and money is up to me,' he said. 'Now, if you will excuse me.' And with that he left him to join his hostess. The evening was drawing to a close and already some of the guests were taking their leave, so he felt justified in bidding his *adieus*. He knew he was being impulsive and erratic, but he did not seem able to help it. Charlotte Cartwright was making him like that.

The departure of his lordship caused something of a stir, and there was not a little consternation among the young ladies and their mamas, but Lady Brandon was quietly triumphant. He had danced with Martha and, having done that, there was no point in him staying and raising anyone's hopes only to dash them again. It was all coming about as she intended, so she told Charlotte, who had watched the Earl depart with a sinking heart. She was thankful when the evening was brought to a close and she was able to go home.

Chapter Four

Late as she had been in returning home and going to bed, Charlotte could not sleep and soon after dawn she rose and dressed. She had to be outside—the air indoors was stifling her. She went downstairs to the kitchen where May was raking out the fire ready to relight it. Mrs Cater had just appeared and was tying an apron round her plump middle.

'Miss Charlotte, you are never going out before breakfast.'

'I am not hungry,' Charlotte said truthfully, making for outside door. 'I am going riding.'

'But 'tis raining cats and dogs.'

'Is it?' She opened the door as she spoke and a gust of wind and rain blew in. Hurriedly she shut the door again. 'So it is.'

'Sit down and have some breakfast with us. You can tell us all about Lady Brandon's soirée. How many were there? Was it very fine? And the Earl, did he single anyone out?'

A real lady would not have dreamed of sitting down with the servants, but Charlotte had always been free and easy with Mrs Cater, who had befriended her when she was a lonely child and defended her against the governess of the day, and so she took her seat at the kitchen table.

'It was a very grand affair, much grander than a soirée,' she said, and went on to describe who was there and what they wore, who danced with whom as far as she could remember, the decorations and the food and drink. But they really wanted to hear about the Earl and her voice shook whenever she mentioned his name. It was going to be very, very difficult to live so close and meet him on almost a daily basis and yet maintain her cold dislike of him. He was not an easy man to dislike, with his innate good manners and cheerful disposition, except when he was talking about Browhill. Then he changed and became intractable. Why was she constantly thinking about him? Since he had returned to Amerleigh she did not seem able to think of anything else.

She picked at the ham and eggs on her plate and wished the rain would stop, but it was still raining at ten-thirty and she was obliged to go to church in the closed carriage. As everyone who owned a vehicle was doing the same, there was a jam about the church gate as they all endeavoured to get close enough to hurry into church under the shelter of an umbrella. The weather had brightened by the time they emerged and the Earl stopped with his mother to pass the time of day with other parishioners. Charlotte murmured a quiet 'good morning' and made her way to her carriage.

Pretending to pay attention to something the parson was saying to his mother, Roland watched her go, a proud, lonely figure, whom few people in his social circle even pretended to like. They had, almost to a man, sided with his father in his dispute with her father and it seemed the next generation were destined to follow the path of its sires, unless something was done to put an end to it. Last night, watching her at Lady Brandon's, he saw how she was cold-shouldered by the gentry and the only partners she had, besides himself, were pretentious young fops being bullied by their mothers into dancing with her. She was wealthy and that was enough for them. He had found himself feeling sorry for her, until Jacob came and spoke to him. Why that should have annoyed him he did not know.

* * *

During the next few weeks, Charlotte noticed the smiles he gave to all the other ladies and withheld from her and wondered why she did not explain that she had no part in what her father had done, that she did not hold with many of his methods and was trying to put matters right. But to do that would be disloyal to Papa and she was too proud to demean herself by appearing to beg for his lordship's good opinion. Jacob had relayed his conversation with the Earl and the sharp retort he had received to the offer to settle amicably. If that was how the man intended to proceed, then she could be obstinate too. She would open up that new level and it did not matter how much it cost.

When she had time she visited Mrs Biggs, but was always careful to make sure the Earl was not in the vicinity when she did so. But she heard about him, his name was on everyone's lips. He was a caring landlord and employer and was doing his best for all the people who depended on him. 'He has done wonders for Tommy,' Mrs Biggs told her on one occasion. 'He is going to see if something can be done for his deafness and, if not, to see if he can be trained to make signs and read people's lips.' To which Charlotte replied that she was very pleased.

Sometimes she would see him riding through the village and then she would call at one of the cottages or turn swiftly down the nearest lane, so that they would not come face to face when both were alone. Sooner or later, she knew she would find herself without a cottage or a lane to retreat into and there would be no avoiding him and it behoved her to be prepared, but when it happened she was not ready for it.

She was up at the mine, watching the carts pulled by two great Shires, bringing up the equipment, drills, gunpowder, ropes, pulleys and trucks, to start on the new level. It was quite an event and many of the villagers had walked up the hill to watch. Mining experts, who had located the seam, came to oversee the drilling into the rock of the hillside and the laying of gunpowder charges. When they were set off, the children squealed in delight and dodged the flying stones and clods of earth. Charlotte rounded them up and took them off to watch at a safe distance.

It was then Roland, being in the vicinity and hearing the explosions that seemed to shake the whole countryside, rode up to see for himself what was going on. He pulled up and raised his hat. 'Miss Cartwright, your obedient.'

She inclined her head. 'My lord.'

'Are you well?'

'Yes, my lord. I thank you.'

She was dressed in her grey working dress with the frogging on the jacket. Far from disguising her femininity it seemed to set it off, especially as she was hatless and her untamed chestnut-coloured hair blew about her face in curling tendrils. She had a habit of flicking them out of the way with a toss of her head, he noticed. He dismounted and looked round at the people milling about. 'Quite a spectacle. How far do you intend to drill?'

'As far as is necessary.'

'I wish you well of it.'

'Do you, my lord? You surprise me.'

'Oh, yes. The more you do, the less I will have to do when I repossess the land.'

'Surely you mean *if* you repossess it, my lord? I can tell you now that will not be until after I have extracted every last ounce of lead ore out of it.'

She was as intransigent as ever. Was it worth it, he asked himself, not only in terms of the cost of the litigation, but the bad feeling it aroused between them? He did not want always to be at loggerheads with her. If they could only work together, they could achieve so much more. He bowed. 'I thought we had called a truce.'

'So did I, but you seem intent on breaking it. Why have you come?'

'Out of curiosity, Miss Cartwright. I have never before seen a shaft drilled.'

She laughed. 'You think to learn from my endeavours how to go about it yourself?'

It came to him then that she was enjoying the battle, that there was no real acrimony, only a stubborn will to win. And he recognised the same thing in himself. It was like a strange courtship, a ritual dance, a showing off of one's attributes, as a peacock might preen its feathers before the hen, or the ducking and diving in the ring before a single punch is landed. He chuckled. 'Perhaps how *not* to go about it.'

She acknowledged the hit by waving a hand in the direction of the miners. Three worked together at the rock face, one holding a drill, the other two hitting it alternately with sledgehammers until they had a hole six inches deep. After making twelve such holes, they packed them with explosive. 'Then please avail yourself of the opportunity, but if you get your head blown off, do not blame me.'

He did not go, but simply stood beside her, while his horse nibbled the sparse grass, only moving back with her when Robert Bailey came and herded everyone farther away. The explosion, so close at hand, rocked the hill and made his horse take fright. His battle charger would not have pranced and neighed like that, would have done little more than flick an ear as if driving off a buzzing fly. He spent some minutes calming it and when he looked back again, there was an even bigger hole in the hillside and men with shovels were digging out the loose earth. Miss Cartwright was walking towards them.

He watched her go, saw her speak to the men and then turn towards him again, as if to say, 'What, are you still here?'

He swept off his hat with an exaggerated bow, mounted and rode slowly home again.

The next day he rode to Chester to buy lead for the roof of the Hall. He could simply have ordered it, but Charles Mountford had suggested it would be a good opportunity to inspect the lead works of Walkers, Maltby and Company. 'It might help you to make up your mind about pursuing your claim against Miss Cartwright,' Charles had told him. 'They will tell you how much ore has been supplied to them from Browhill.'

'Why should they tell me that? It is surely a confidential matter.'

'I have asked them to do so. You have a vested

interest and if the mine reverts to you, you must be in a position to deal with the company and know how much profit you are likely to make from it. They understand that.'

Having settled the matter of lead for the roof, Roland discovered that Charlotte's father had done well with the mine in the beginning, but the depth and frequent flooding of the mine meant it was costing a lot to bring to the surface. Would he be able to manage it any better? It was not simply the cost of it, though that formed a large part of his reasoning when his resources were so stretched, but that he did not want to fight Miss Cartwright. He would rather have her as a friend than an enemy.

News that the allies had entered Paris and Napoleon had abdicated reached the village in the middle week of April. It was the mail that brought it, the driver and passengers passing it on at every post at which they stopped. It arrived at the King's Head in Amerleigh in the early afternoon and by evening there wasn't a soul in the village who had not heard it.

Roland, busy with his accounts in the estate office at the Hall, learned it from Travers with mixed feelings. While deploring the loss of life that was inevitable in wartime, he had enjoyed the comradeship, the well-ordered routine, the regulation of army life, when his main preoccupation had been about a coming battle and how to win it, and finding food for his men. His opponents had been men with the same troubles and aims as himself, not a slip of a girl. How could one fight a woman? How could one rejoice in overcoming the frailty of the weaker sex? He laughed at himself. Miss Charlotte Cartwright could hardly be called weak; she did not even stoop to using her womanhood as a weapon, swooning and weeping, as other ladies might have done to get their way. She stood tall and defied him. And disturbed him.

He went with his mother to a thanksgiving service at the church, which everyone attended, including Miss Cartwright, sitting alone in her pew, and afterwards decided to wander over to the common where the villagers had built a huge bonfire. They had put an effigy of Napoleon on top of it, rejoicing in his defeat, though there were some, Roland among them, who did not believe he was beaten. He was not even to be punished, except by banishment to the island of Elba and that, in Roland's opinion, was not far enough, not by a long way. But he kept his opinions to himself and joined in the general celebration.

Charlotte, who had changed from her church-going clothes into a light wool skirt and high-necked blouse, topped by a neat-fitting pelisse, was there with Mrs Biggs and Tommy. She was carrying Mrs Biggs's baby.

He strolled over to them. Tommy turned to him, eyes alight with excitement. 'Hallo, young fellow,' he said, speaking clearly so that the boy could read his lips. 'How do you do?' The boy grinned and nodded energetically, but did not speak.

'He is well, my lord,' Mrs Biggs said.

'I have been making enquiries about a teacher for him,' Roland said. 'I am hopeful that someone will be found soon.'

'Your army friend?' Charlotte queried.

He turned to look at her. She was always surprising him and tonight was no exception. The baby was fast asleep in her arms. Her whole demeanour was gentler, her eyes softer, the reflection of the bonfire giving them a dancing light as if she were truly happy. It did not take much effort to imagine her as a mother. Would motherhood cure her of her hoydenish ways? he wondered. Was his mother right in saying she was only mannish because of the way she had been raised? 'Yes,' he said. 'I have discovered he has come home from the Peninsula and is working for the War Department in Horse Guards. I have written to him and await his reply.'

He stood beside them, watching the revelry until Mrs Biggs decided it was time Tommy and the baby were home in bed. Charlotte handed the baby back to her and then walked over to a crowd of young people, laughing and drinking and forgetting the hardship of their lives. Roland watched as she spoke to them and heard them raise a cheer for her. He joined her again as she turned and made her way back to the lane. 'Allow me to escort you.'

'I am only going to pick up my curricle from the King's Head, my lord. I am in no danger.'

'No, I did not think you were, judging by the hearty cheers I heard just now.'

'Oh, I told them they could take a day off tomorrow.' Then, lest he thought she was becoming soft, added, 'They will be in no state to work properly in any case.'

He was beginning to understand her a little. Her hardness was a shell, worn like a coat to protect her, and it was not a very thick one either. If he probed, might he pierce it? 'Under the circumstances, do you not think you could call me Roland?' he said. 'At least when we are alone…'

'We are not alone, we are surrounded by people.'

'Then I cannot address you as Charlotte.'

'No, my lord, you may not.' She was very firm about that.

They walked on in silence to the King's Head. There seemed nothing they could say that would not stir up dissent. He did not want to fight her and was toying with the idea of telling her he would not proceed with the lawsuit. It was only the memory of her defiance that held him back. If she would only meet him halfway, they could surely deal well together. He began to regret his sharp retort to Jacob Edwards.

Even in the dark, Charlotte was only too conscious of the man beside her. Tonight he was in uniform again as befitted the occasion. His physical presence was almost overpowering; he was taller than most men—broader too, and yet she knew he could be compassionate and gentle and little people like Tommy Biggs were not afraid of him. She did not fear him either, except that he could make her feel weak and helpless, and that she had to resist. She had to stay in control.

When they arrived at the inn, he waited with her while her pony was harnessed to the curricle, then handed her up. 'I will drive you, if you wish.'

She laughed. 'And then have to walk all the way back! No, my lord, I am used to driving myself and will come to no harm.' She flicked the reins. 'Goodnight, my lord.'

He doffed his shako. 'Goodnight, Miss Cartwright.'

He watched her drive away, competent as any man. It was four miles to Mandeville on lonely roads with nothing to light her way but moonlight. Did nothing frighten her? He went to find his own horse and, instead of going home, followed her at a discreet distance. As soon as she turned safely in at the gates of Mandeville, he turned back, laughing at himself for his foolishness.

Among the letters that arrived at the Hall the next morning was an invitation to a ball two Saturdays hence, to be given by Lord and Lady Gilford to celebrate the great victory and welcome their son, Lieutenant Thomas Gilford, home. How the young man was able to return so soon after the end of hostilities, Roland did not know. He put the invitation on one side and opened the rest of the post.

There were several quotations for work to be done on the house, which he proposed to go over with his mother, and an answer to his letter to Captain Miles Hartley. The Captain had not thought about extending his work with the deaf beyond his service, he said, but his lordship's letter had intrigued him and he would certainly consider it. He would come down and see him in a few weeks when his duties at Horse Guards was less hectic and they could discuss it. Roland was tempted to ride over to Mandeville to tell Miss Cartwright the good news, but his mother arrived and he decided it could wait.

They went over the quotations and spent some time deciding what was important and what could reasonably be left until he was a little more affluent, then he mentioned the Gilfords' ball. 'I suppose I shall have to go,' he said. 'But I have no one to escort. I wonder, would it seem very traitorous of me to ask Miss Cartwright?'

She laughed. 'I do believe you are coming round to like her.'

'In some ways I admire her, but that does not alter the fact that we are litigants and whenever we meet somehow or other the subject of Browhill crops up and we begin arguing. I would drop the whole thing if it wasn't for that fact that Papa was so badly cheated.'

She sighed. 'Roland, she could not help what

her father did, any more than you could influence your father, and she does a great deal of good. I will not think any the less of you if you drop it.'

'Then maybe I will. But what do you think about taking Miss Cartwright to the ball?'

'I do not see how you can. Lady Brandon and Lady Gilford called on me this morning to bring me an invitation and they were arguing about whether Miss Cartwright should be invited. Lady Brandon said she ought not to be left out, considering how influential she is, but Lady Gilford was very top lofty and said it was her ball and she could invite whom she pleased and if she did not choose to invite that daughter of a mushroom who thought she was a man, then she would not. The gathering would be very select.' She gave a little chuckle. 'Lady Brandon was silenced by that, probably thinking her own invitation might be in doubt if she made more of it.'

'Poor Charlotte.'

She looked at him sharply at his use of Miss Cartwright's given name, but decided not to comment. 'You could take Martha Brandon.'

'I could, but I won't. Lady Brandon is pushing the poor girl at me and Miss Brandon herself is against it.'

'How do you know that?'

'She told me so when we were dancing together

at her mama's soirée. She has her heart set on Mr Martin Elliott, but he is slow in coming forwards. She said she was only dancing with me to make him jealous.'

'What a strange conversation for a well-bred young lady to have with an unmarried man.'

'At least she is honest and I can admire her for it, but I do not wish to be used in that fashion. It is not fair on the young man for a start. I shall escort you.' He laughed. 'At least I shall be safe with you.'

'Roland, I am still in mourning.'

'You can still come, you do not have to dance or be gay, though I wish you would. It does not do to be always in the suds.'

'How can I be in the suds when you are home again and I have work to do making the Hall habitable again? How could I not be joyful?'

'Will you come with me? You can defend me from the mamas.'

'You are perfectly capable of doing that yourself, Roland. And I will not cause more gossip for this family by flouting the rules of society. You may tell me all about it when you come back.' And from that decision she would not be moved.

Charlotte heard all about the ball—Lady Brandon could not keep quiet about it, pretending she did not know Charlotte had not been invited. Charlotte herself realised very soon that she would not be among the guests and pretended she could not go on account of a prior engagement. Neither was deceived by the other. It left Charlotte wondering what the prior engagement could possibly be. And then it came to her; she would organise her own celebration on the same night. But not a ball, because everyone would be going to the Gilfords'. In any case, she did not think the *haut monde* would come to anything she arranged.

A party for her workers, that was it! She would invite every employee, high and low, to a grand occasion at the mill and make it a night to remember. The idea had the added attraction of proving to the Earl of Amerleigh that she treated her workers well and that they were all loyal to her. No expense would be spared. Food and drink would be the main expense; poor people were always hungry. There would be music and decorations, flags and flowers. And a brass band! If, led by the band and flags flying, they paraded through the streets of Amerleigh and Scofield, before entering the mill for the party, it would make a great deal of noise and drown out the oh-so-genteel orchestra playing at Gilford House. And fireworks. According to Lady Brandon, there were to be fireworks as a grand finale to the ball—then her fireworks would better, more noisy, more colourful. She would not be cowed and made to feel inferior, and set about the arrangements with a smile on her lips and a spring in her step.

Lord and Lady Gilford lived in a large mansion on the road between Amerleigh and Scofield, surrounded by a park and mixed woodland. The main part of the house was a hundred years old, but it had been added to in recent years and the whole of the inside refurbished and refurnished. Apart from the Temples, who ceased to count when the late Earl removed to the dower house, they were the *haut monde* of the area and an invitation to an occasion at their home was prized by local society. Lady Gilford had taken great pains with all the arrangements, the food and wine and music, only to find there was a shortage of fireworks. The supplier, who had a workshop in Shrewsbury, told her almost his entire stock had been bought up by another customer whom he declined to name. Her ladyship purchased what was left, hoping that her guests would be so mellow with food and drink by the end of the evening, they would not notice the Grand Finale was less than grand.

Roland, dressed in impeccable good taste, in a black evening coat, black trousers and a pristine white shirt, arrived only a few minutes late and was greeted warmly by Lady Gilford, who attached herself to him and took him round to make sure he knew everyone. When that was done, she invited him to join her party, which consisted of herself and her husband, her son, the lieutenant of the invitation; her daughter, Eleanor; and an elderly aunt. Eleanor was about eighteen, as plump as her mother was thin, with pale blonde hair, carefully dressed to make it look thicker than it really was. She was also painfully shy, which was obviously a source of irritation to her mother. Roland smiled at her and offered the usual politeness before marking her card for two country dances, which made the poor girl's cheeks turn bright pink.

After the first of these, she left him to dance with young Leonard Manton and Roland sat down to talk to Lieutenant Gilford, enquiring about his service. 'How did you manage to arrive home so quickly?' he asked him.

'I was in Lisbon with the Commissariat when the news came through and hopped on the first ship out. I saw no point in hanging about and Papa made it right with the Colonel.'

His mother, who had been busying herself with her guests, returned to them. 'My goodness, we cannot have two handsome young men sitting together and not dancing. Thomas, go and ask Miss Manton to stand up with you. As for you, my lord, I am sure I can find you a partner.'

'Thank you, my lady,' he said, with a smile. 'I think I can manage.' He left her and went to ask Martha Brandon to dance, realising as he did so that he was probably playing right into her hands, because he saw Martin Elliott scowling at him. After that, he found himself standing up with several other young ladies and then with Miss Gilford again. He escorted her into supper, much to the chagrin of Lady Brandon. He was beginning to feel decidedly uncomfortable, though not for a moment did his polite smile leave his face. Returning from supper, he stationed himself in an alcove to watch the dancers and found himself unaccountably wishing Miss Cartwright were present. He had enjoyed that waltz with her and the discovery that she was truly beautiful. If she were here, he might enjoy it more. The admission, if only to himself, surprised him.

'It must seem strange. Being home again, I mean.'

He turned to find Lord Gilford standing beside him. He had been a sea-faring man, which was evidenced by his weatherbeaten complexion and his way of standing with his feet braced apart as if still on the deck of a ship. 'Yes, it is a little.'

'Coming about, are you?'

He was annoyed at the impertinence of the question, but too polite to show it. 'I believe so.'

'Glad to hear it. Not married, though?'

'No time for it.'

'But thinking of it? After all, a single man with a title and a great estate must look for a wife at some point.'

'That goes without saying, but at the moment I am not contemplating marriage.'

'No? But if you are not, then there are going to be a number of disappointed mamas and their daughters. The little beauties are all in competition for you.'

Roland smiled wryly. 'I should hate to disappoint them, but there is no competition. I am not a prize to be won.'

His lordship gave a little snorty laugh of embarrassment. 'No, of course not. But you should perhaps be careful not to give the gabble-grinders fuel for their gossip.'

'What do you mean?'

'My wife tells me you are often to be seen in Miss Cartwright's company and she without a chaperon.'

Roland was furious and did not trouble to hide it 'That, sir, is my affair.'

'You may say so, but it won't do, you know. Your father and hers became mortal enemies and she is a chip off the old block, riding around as if she owned the whole village. I advise you to assert yourself before she rides all over you.'

Roland was taken aback by the man's impudence. 'No one rides over me,' he told him coldly.

'Of course not. But did you know her father was a mill hand before he rose to become manager and married the mill owner's daughter and became very rich through the *trade*?' His derogatory emphasis on the last word betrayed what he felt about that. 'She is very high in the instep, but not one of us, Amerleigh, never one of us, not of any consequence, at all. Apart from Lady Brandon, who hardly counts, she is not accepted in polite circles. You ought to bear that in mind.'

'What makes you suppose I have that particular lady in mind, or any lady for that matter?' Roland reminded himself that the man was his host and it would be ill mannered to be rude, but his voice betrayed the fact that he was angry, even while holding himself in check.

'Hold hard!' His lordship held up both hands as if to ward off an imaginary blow. 'I meant no disrespect. I told her ladyship it would not serve, but she would have me speak to you, to warn you…'

'I do not need to be warned,' Roland said icily. 'But thank her ladyship for me.'

And with that he walked away, out of the room and through a conservatory into the garden.

It was a clear, starlit night. Behind him the orchestra was playing a waltz and he found himself thinking of Charlotte Cartwright again. Did she mind being treated like a pariah? He had heard about her own party; Mrs Biggs had been full of it. The whole Biggs family was going, even young Hannah had been invited if he would be so good as to release her from her work. Of course he had agreed, almost wishing he could go too. Even from a distance he could hear the music.

Turning back to the house, he sought out his hostess, thanked her for her hospitality and took his leave, much to her chagrin. Then he walked out into the night again and, instead of turning for home, made for the sound of merriment coming from somewhere along the Amerleigh to Scofield road.

He came upon the procession just before it reached Scofield. There was a very noisy band playing a marching tune and it was followed by a great crowd, all dressed in their Sunday best, waving flags and singing. At the gates of the mill, which stood wide open, Charlotte was waiting for them. She was wearing a skirt short enough to reveal her ankles and feet clad in half-boots, and a dark-coloured burnoose with the hood thrown back. He watched as the workers, including, he noticed, Corporal Travers and others from his estate, marched past her and into the mill, which was blazing with light.

After they had all gone in, she saw him standing on the other side of the road in his fine evening clothes and wondered why he was there. She called out to him. 'What brings you here, my lord? Boredom or curiosity?'

He laughed. 'Both.'

'Would you like to join us? No one here is bored, I can promise you.'

He crossed the road and walked up to her. 'Thank you. I should like that very much, provided my presence does not spoil anyone else's enjoyment.'

'Shall we ask them?' She led the way into the schoolroom, which had been cleared of furniture. Already the musicians were playing a lively dance tune and the floor was crowded with dancers. A long table along one wall was so loaded with food there was no room to put another dish. At the end a man stood beside a barrel of beer, dispensing its contents. There was also cordial for the children.

Charlotte clapped her hands and the band fell silent and everyone turned towards her.

'Ladies and gentlemen,' she said, an address that raised a laugh and a cheer. 'His lordship finds the entertainment at Gilford House boring. We are not bored, are we?'

'No!' they yelled.

'Shall we let him share our party?'

'Yes!'

He knew they would have agreed to anything she suggested, considering she had provided all the food and drink and they were already merry on it. 'Thank you,' he said with a smile. 'Carry on, don't mind me.'

They took him at his word and the gaiety continued. The level of beer in the barrel went down and the loaded plates emptied and were refilled. The dancing became more boisterous and Roland and Charlotte were pulled into it, being grabbed and hauled round by mill workers. The estate workers were a little more restrained at first, but soon they, too, lost their awe of the Earl and began enjoying themselves, especially as he joined in with enthusiasm, dancing a gavotte with Mrs Biggs, while Charlotte danced with Corporal Travers, who was in uniform and very popular with both the men, who wanted to hear about the fighting, and with the women, who appreciated his rugged good looks.

In a pause in the dancing Roland found himself standing beside Charlotte again. He wondered why he had ever thought her cold. She was flushed and her eyes sparkled. She was truly enjoying herself and seemed to have forgotten they were at daggers drawn. And then she spoke and reminded him. 'In the ordinary way of things, this is the schoolroom,' she said. 'The law requires me to teach the children to read and little else, but some are quite intelligent enough to go further than that, so here they are taught not only to read and write, but simple mathematics, some geography, a little history.' She smiled. 'It is not only for the workers, but their younger siblings.'

'But they do not play.'

'This is a place of work, my lord, not a playground. It is all very well for the rich to play, they do not have to earn a living, but days like today put new heart into everyone and they are not unhappy. The only time they think about it is when some well-meaning philanthropist puts ideas into their heads or, what is worse, one of their own number with a grudge makes trouble.'

Was she warning him not to meddle? he wondered. 'Is anyone making trouble?'

'There are always troublemakers, my lord, though none that I know of here.'

Looking round at the joyful crowd, he could well believe it. She was such a strange mixture of benevolence and hardness, it was difficult to understand her. She could shut an employee out who was a few minutes late for work and yet she could take the trouble to distribute food to those in need. Her clattering looms kept her workers chained to them like slaves and yet she wanted to educate them, even though education gave people ambition, which might in the end not be to her advantage. She appeared not to care what people thought of her, but he had seen enough of human nature to know that she was susceptible. He would be her friend if only she would let him.

At midnight, the musicians put away their instruments and the leftover food was packed into little parcels so that everyone had something to take home, then they trooped out to the common for the fireworks, singing lustily as they went. It was a wonderful display, set out by Charlotte's mine manager, who knew a thing or two about explosives. Rocket after rocket shot skywards and exploded into the air, releasing a myriad of coloured lights. Roland, watching the faces of the children, alight with wonder, felt a tug at his heart. He would like children of his own, to nurture and love, someone to come after him, to keep his name alive, to look after Amerleigh so that it never again drifted into neglect. And to make that happen, he needed a wife. Sooner or later he would have to give some thought to it.

The trouble was that whenever that idea came into his head, he found himself thinking of the woman who stood beside him. He could not banish her from his mind. She invaded every aspect of his life, every decision he made, almost every word he uttered. She was with him every hour of the day and, worst of all, through the lonely watches of the night. Who she was, what she did, the life she led, made her entirely ineligible as a wife for him. That gabble-grinder, Gilford, was right, damn him!

When the last shower had drifted to earth and there was silence, someone called for three cheers for Miss Cartwright and the hills echoed to the sound. And then old John Bennett, bowed with a lifetime of working in the gardens at Amerleigh Hall, called for three cheers for his lordship and again the hills echoed. Roland wondered if they could be heard at Gilford House.

After standing about for several minutes, reluctant to call it a night, everyone slowly drifted away, many with a rolling gait that betrayed the amount of good ale they had consumed. Roland stood beside Charlotte, watching them go, as reluctant as they were to go home. If only everyone could always be as happy and cheerful as they had been this night, there would be no dissent, no quarrels, no need to resort to war. Or litigation.

'I have my curricle at the mill,' she said, as they reached the road. 'I can take you back to Gilford House, if you wish. It is not out of my way.'

'I am not going back there.'

'Then allow me to take you home to Amerleigh Hall.'

He laughed. 'When I suggested escorting you the other night, you disdained my offer.'

'But you did it anyway.'

'Oh.'

'Did you think I did not know you were behind me?' She was laughing up at him, enjoying his discomfiture.

'It must have been someone else.'

'Of course. Someone else, how silly of me.'

They had arrived back at the mill. The lights had all been extinguished except the lamp over the gates, which illuminated the horse and curricle being held in readiness by the night watchman. 'Now, do you come with me or do you walk home by yourself? The people might give you three hearty cheers, but your watch and fob might be too great a temptation if one or two of them met you alone in the dark.'

'Thank you.' He helped her up and climbed up beside her, taking the reins from her fingers. He'd be damned if he'd allow himself to be driven by a woman, however capable.

They set off at a walk. He was in no hurry to part from her. The air was balmy, the black velvet of the night sky was pierced with a myriad of diamond-like stars and, above the copse of trees on the slope of the hills, a new moon hung motionless. A faint shushing sound drifted on the air and he looked up to see a few red and green sparks flying skywards. They were passing Gilford House.

Charlotte laughed suddenly. 'Not up to mine, are they?' she said.

He knew she was referring to the fireworks. 'No, they are altogether more genteel.'

'Are you sure you do not want to go back?'

'Positive. At the moment I would not be anywhere else in the world.'

'Ah, I see you know how to frame a compliment.' He did not answer and she went on, 'What happened? Why did you leave the ball?'

'It was deadly dull and the efforts of the mamas

and their daughters too obvious for words. I felt I was walking on eggs not to give offence.'

'But you will have to choose one of them and that will offend all the rest.'

'I do not have to choose at all.' He turned to look at her, sitting beside him so composed, so cool, so in command of herself, he found himself wondering what it would take to rouse her. The only emotion she had shown him was anger, cool politeness and a willingness to bandy words, though she was soft enough with Tommy and the Biggs's baby. 'What about you? Do you not wish for a husband?'

'No, for I doubt I could find anyone to put up with me. I am too used to running my own life and doing as I choose, I should drive a husband to distraction.'

'You must have had offers?'

'From milksops after my wealth. They do not see me as a wife, but as the provider of an easy life. They do not stay about long.'

'Then we are both at an impasse. You have too much money and I have too much rank to find true love. What a pity!'

She was not sure whether he was bamming her or not, but decided not to comment. They rode on in silence until he turned into the gates of the Hall and trotted up the drive to the front door, where he stopped. Should he ask her in? The absence of a chaperon seemed not to have occurred to her, but then she went about on her own all the time. He had never seen anything remotely like a companion or even a maid with her, though he supposed she had one. And if she did go in with him, what could he offer her in the way of refreshment?

He jumped down and was about to hand the reins to her, when the front door opened and Travers came down the steps, having arrived back half an hour earlier. 'Shall I look after the curricle, Major?'

Roland turned back to Charlotte to find her standing beside him. He could hardly tell her to climb back in and go home. 'Yes, Corporal, if you please, and do you think you can find us some refreshment? I am sure Mrs Fields has gone to bed.'

'Yes, Major, she has, but she left something out for you. I'll bring it to the drawing room directly.'

He led the pony away and Roland put his hand under Charlotte's elbow and ushered her into the house.

It was only curiosity that made her leave the curricle, Charlotte told herself. She had not been in the house since that fateful night six years before and by all accounts it was very different now. It would be good to see how far the Temples had fallen since then, but it was difficult to convince herself they deserved it, when the man beside her bore no resemblance whatever to the stripling who had disdained her. If it had not been for hearing that rejection and knowing of her father's unmitigated hatred of the old Earl, who had so blatantly cheated him, she might have come to like and admire the present owner of Amerleigh Hall, might even have fallen in love with him. Fallen in love! What did she know of that? Nothing, nor ever would. Better not to think of it. But there was inside her an empty feeling, as if there should be something there that was absent.

She looked about her as they entered the inner hall. There were rugs on the marble-tiled floor. A table stood to one side and chairs were placed between the doors to the rooms. A solid oak staircase led up from the middle and divided on a half-landing before the two branches went up again to the first floor. There were no ornaments, no pictures.

He led the way into the drawing room. This was carpeted and properly furnished with tables and chairs and two sofas. The pale green paint on the walls was new and the curtains, drawn against the night, were of a rich ruby-red damask. A hand-painted screen stood before the empty hearth. Again there were no pictures or ornaments.

'As you see, we have not finished refurbishing,'

he told her. 'My mother is seeing to the interior while I look after the outside. It will take some time, I think.'

'But it is lovely house, so full of history. It seems to have an atmosphere of its own.'

'Yes, some of it goes back to Tudor times, but there have been additions over the years. It is something of a rabbit warren, but it has always been my home and I am very attached to it.'

'You would do anything to keep it?' she asked curiously.

'I suppose I would. Within bounds, of course.'

'Even to marrying one of those daughters of the wealthy whom you pretend to disdain?'

'I hope it never comes to that. I am not entirely without means.' His little nest egg was fast disappearing, but he would not admit that.

Travers arrived with a tea tray, which he set down upon one of the tables, and then went to fetch another on which was a plate of cold roast chicken legs, another of bread and butter and a third containing an assortment of little cakes. Roland and Charlotte watched in silence as he set them out. 'Thank you, Travers,' Roland said. 'We can manage.'

He indicated the teapot to Charlotte. 'Shall you pour?'

They sat at the table, she poured the tea and they

picked at the food, but the intimacy they had been enjoying had dissipated, blown away with the opening of the door. They conversed politely about the peace just concluded, about the wisdom of allowing Napoleon to live on Elba, about the squabbling of the allied powers as they set about carving Europe up between them, but Charlotte found herself thinking of what had happened six years before and wondered what on earth she was doing in that house. She must be mad! As soon as they had finished their meal, she said she must be leaving.

He stood up and rang for Travers to fetch the curricle to the door, then he accompanied her to the front door and down the steps. Travers stood at the pony's head, waiting. 'Shall I drive you home?'

She laughed. 'And then I should have to drive you back again and we could go backwards and forwards all night. I am perfectly capable, as well you know.'

He grinned. 'So independent. Is there anything you are not capable of tackling?'

'Oh, I am sure there must be something,' she said airily. 'I will let you know when I have discovered it. Goodnight, my lord.'

'Goodnight, Miss Cartwright. And thank you for an evening far more enjoyable than I ever expected it to be.' He took her hand and lifted it to his lips, lingering a little over the kiss, wishing he dare kiss her properly, but knowing he would be for ever damned if he did.

It was several seconds before she could repossess herself of her hand and by that time she was tingling with a sensation she could not describe. It was a feeling of being on the verge of something so exciting, she was shivering. Her stomach was churning, her heart beating so fast she could hardly breathe and her toes and fingers curled involuntarily. She climbed into the curricle without even knowing how she got there. This man was dangerous! He threatened everything she stood for. She must be on her guard, always on her guard, lest he undermine her confidence and the tenets by which she lived crumbled to nothing.

She flicked the reins and the pony started forwards, trotted round the circle before the door and out of the gate and she found herself murmuring, 'Remember whose daughter you are, Charlie Cartwright. And remember whose son he is.'

Chapter Five

In the next few weeks, the Earl of Amerleigh was seen everywhere, walking and riding round the estate, putting in hand the many repairs and improvements needed. The villagers' cottages were being repaired, window frames replaced, new doors hung, proper cess pits dug; up at the Hall, the builders were busy—bricklayers, plasterers, carpenters and painters swarmed about and every now and again a wagon loaded with carpets and furniture would draw up at the door and disgorge its contents. The Countess was in her element.

His lordship was also to be seen at musical evenings, at tea parties and picnics all round the county and all the hostesses praised his manners and all the hosts called him a fine fellow. He conversed intelligently, danced and played cards for negligible stakes and not by one word or gesture did he betray whom he favoured for a wife. It was being said that he could not make up his mind and everyone would know who it was when the refurbishment of Amerleigh Hall had been completed and he began entertaining himself. And so they waited for the invitation.

Charlotte did her best to avoid him. On the pretext of being too busy, she made excuses not to go to functions she knew he would attend. She had always pleased herself what she did and Lady Brandon, who might have tried to persuade her, was too busy trying to put Martha forward to miss her. 'He visits so frequently and is always punctilious in his attentions to Martha,' her ladyship told her one day when they met by chance in Shrewsbury. 'It must mean he is seriously considering her.' Charlotte smiled and said nothing, but wondered if Roland Temple visited because he was too polite to refuse her constant invitations or if he was seriously considering Martha as a wife. She ought not to have minded, but somehow she did.

Lady Brandon was not the only one; every mama of every single young lady was doing the same. Standing on the sidelines, Charlotte could see it happening, and wondered what the outcome might be. Thinking about it gave her a vague feeling of discontent, which she refused to acknowledge was anything but irritation with the man. Occasionally, she found herself face to face with him. She would smile politely and pass the time of day with him before moving on, doing her best to ignore the fluttering of her heart.

And he, surprised by her sudden coolness after that night of her party when he thought they had established a rapport, would answer her in like manner and watch her proud back retreating from him. He found himself remembering his half-jocular remark—'You have too much money and I have too much rank to find true love'—and wondered how accurate that was. She had built a wall around herself as impenetrable as the wall around Amerleigh Hall, determined to keep everyone out. And yet Tommy Biggs had found a way through her defences, along with other children in the village, which must mean she was not as hard as she would have him believe. If only he could crack that shell as they had.

'You know, you ought to do some entertaining,' Lady Brandon told Charlotte one Sunday afternoon, the only day of the week on which Charlotte did not go to Scofield or up to Browhill. It was the only day on which her ladyship could be sure of finding her at home. Sitting in the drawing room at Mandeville, sipping tea and nibbling cake, her friend evidently had something to say and was determined to say it. 'You have this wonderful house and no one ever sees it, except the outside and that from a distance.'

'I am entertaining you. And the Reverend and Mrs Elliott come and Mr Edwards…'

'Yes, but they are not society.'

'Neither am I.'

'But you could be, if you made the effort.'

'Why should I?' She knew she was being stubborn, but ever since the return of Roland Temple she had been feeling fidgety, conscious that there was something missing in her life and yet afraid to face up to it.

'You will become an antidote if you do not. A recluse. And for what? To acquire yet more wealth? What good is that to you? You have more than enough already.'

'My goodness, Catherine, you do not mince your words, do you?'

'I hope we have been friends long enough to speak plainly to each other, my dear. You used to go out and about, but I have noticed lately that you seem to prefer your own company. It cannot be good for you. You are still young. You should learn to enjoy yourself.'

Charlotte looked hard at her, making the poor woman blush. 'What has brought on this sudden interest in my welfare?'

'I have told you. You are working too hard and looking a little pale.'

'So I must work even harder to entertain people with whom I have nothing in common.'

'I will help you. You could give a concert, or a ball…' She paused. 'I have given a dancing soirée and Lady Gilford has held a Victory Ball—who else is there hereabouts to put on anything grand but you? Amerleigh Hall is not yet ready, though his lordship said he would hold a ball when it was. But we cannot wait for that.'

It occurred to Charlotte that her friend was running out of ideas for entertaining the Earl and throwing Martha in his path, and had suddenly thought of Mandeville. She smiled. 'I see. Who would come?'

'Why, everyone, especially if you invited the Earl. It would gain you an entrée into society if he were to accept.'

Charlotte laughed aloud. 'If I know his lordship, he will not consent to be used in that manner. He is not a fool, you know.'

'I did not say he was. But he seems to accept almost every other invitation. You are the only one who has not entertained him.'

It was obvious to Charlotte that her ladyship did not know about the party at the mill or else she discounted it. 'I will think about it.'

Having succeeded in her aim, her ladyship took her leave, and Charlotte sat on, thinking dreamily of making her name as a hostess, of being accepted in society, of being beautiful and sought after. And then she pulled herself up short. It was only a dream and dreams had no substance; she would do better to go over the report the mine engineer had sent her about the new level. She would never have begun it if the Earl of Amerleigh had not come back, poking his nose into her business. His long, handsome nose. Why could she not get him out of her head? Why did everyone have to keep talking about him, reminding her that he had kissed her hand and gazed into her eyes and something had passed between them that she could not define, something that kept her awake at night and would not go away?

She stood up and began pacing the room. It was a very large room, tastefully decorated and furnished. A collection of valuable paintings graced its walls and a display cabinet in the chimney alcove was full of the porcelain her father had collected. At the end of the marble-floored hall was a huge ballroom and opposite that an oak-panelled dining room. The dining room was only used when she gave dinner parties for her managers and other business people, otherwise she ate alone in a smaller room nearer the kitchens. As for the ballroom, that had never been used for its intended purpose that she could remember, though Mrs Cater had once said her mama used to give balls in the days before she was born. 'And very grand affairs they were too,' the cook had said. 'Your mother was so beautiful, so gentle and kind, everyone loved her, God rest her soul.'

'I wish I had known her,' Charlotte had said wistfully.

''Tis a pity you never did, but there, it was God's will to take her from us. You are very like her, you know.'

'Am I? How?'

'In looks and on account of caring for those less well off. She could not bear to see a child with bare feet and would buy up a whole shop full of shoes and boots and take them to the village for everyone to help themselves. Your papa used to laugh about it, but he always let her have her way.'

Papa laughing! That was something Charlotte had rarely witnessed. For the first time in her life she felt utterly alone. Catherine Brandon had unsettled her, as if she had not been unsettled enough as it was! She left the room, walked along the hall and entered the ballroom, all of eighty feet long and thirty wide, and stood looking round her. Empty. Huge and empty. Nothing but emptiness. Was that symptomatic of her life? Hurriedly she turned on her heel and went back to that mine report.

Roland was inspecting the new carriage horses, which had just arrived. Travers, who was knowledgeable about horses, had helped him choose them, a couple of well-matched sturdy greys with white tails and manes. The family carriage had been cleaned and repainted black with the Temple crest on the door, and now the horses were here, he could go out and about in a manner befitting an Earl. He did not mind so much for himself, but his mother had missed being able to order out the coach and pay calls and he wanted to please her. He had just watched the horses being led to their stalls when the sound of a rider trotting into the yard made him look up. A man in the uniform of a Captain of Hussars was entering the yard.

'Miles Hartley,' Roland said, coming forward to shake his hand as he dismounted. 'Why did you not tell me to expect you?'

'I was unsure of being able to leave until two

weeks ago and then I decided to take my time and see a little of the countryside on the way.' The Captain was tall, though not as tall as Roland. His face was tanned and his hair black. He had curly side whiskers and dark, humorous eyes.

'You are very welcome. Come indoors and I will order refreshment for you. Corporal, see to the Captain's horse, will you? And then ask Mrs Fields to come to me.' He led the way, taking his visitor in through the front door, across the wide hall and into the drawing room. They had barely seated themselves on the new sofas when his housekeeper appeared.

'Your man said you wanted me, my lord.'

'Yes, we have a guest. Please bring him some refreshment, then make up a bed in one of the spare rooms.' He turned to Miles. 'You will stay?'

'It will be a pleasure.' He gave Mrs Fields a smile that crinkled up his eyes and revealed perfect white teeth. She flushed with pleasure and bobbed a curtsy before leaving to obey her instructions.

'Tell me, what news?' Roland asked, as she disappeared. 'What have you been doing?'

'Administration work in the War Department, transporting troops home for discharge, bringing back unused supplies and armaments, making arrangements for Lord Wellington's return to the capital. He is in Paris at the moment, but there'll be a great to-do when he comes home, you can be sure. But until he does, there is a lull in the business and I decided to take advantage of it to come to see you.' He looked about him, taking in the newly refurbished room. 'Didn't know you had a place like this, Temple,' he said.

'I have only recently come into it. It has been run-down, but is coming round now. Still a lot to do, though.'

'What's this about deaf children?'

Roland told him about Tommy Biggs and his idea for teaching him signs. 'He was born deaf so I do not think he can be cured, but if only he could learn to communicate, his life would be so much better,' he finished. 'That is why I thought of you. I know you dealt with soldiers, but surely the principle is the same?'

'Yes, but a great deal depends on the receptiveness of the child. I should need to see him before I decide.'

'Of course. When you have eaten I will take you to meet him.' He paused, wondering how to go on. 'I have no idea what remuneration you would require. The family is very poor, but I could undertake a small salary.'

'Let us talk about that later,' Miles said as Mrs Fields returned.

'I've put everything in the dining room, my lord,' she said, bobbing.

Roland conducted his guest to the dining room. This was furnished with a table, six chairs and a sideboard and little else. They looked lost in that huge room. 'As you see, there is still much to be done,' Roland told him.

The food, though, was good and Miles did it justice before the two men set out on horseback for the village.

They had dismounted and were approaching the Biggs's cottage when they met Charlotte. She was wearing her strange riding habit, but as she was on foot, the wrapover skirt covered her breeches. She had a basket on her arm, evidently making for the same destination. They stopped and eyed each other warily, each wondering what the mood of the other might be. Avoiding the Earl of Amerleigh when she ventured into the village was almost impossible, she had discovered, but then why should she need to? Stiffening her shoulders, she smiled. 'Good afternoon, my lord.'

'Miss Cartwright, your obedient. May I present

Captain Miles Hartley. Captain, Miss Charlotte Cartwright, a neighbour.'

'Captain Hartley. Are you the gentleman who might be able to help Tommy?' Charlotte smiled and offered her hand, more the gesture of a man than a lady, who would have bent her knee and lowered her gaze.

Roland was used to her ways, but for a moment Miles was taken aback, then he grasped the hand. 'We shall see. I have come to meet the little fellow.'

'I do hope you can do something for him. I have promised the Earl my support in this, and as I know the family well, I shall be interested in what you think.'

'Then why not come in with us?'

'No, their house is very tiny, there will certainly not be room for three of us. I shall leave you to it. But come to Mandeville when you have finished examining the boy and let me know what you decide. I shall be pleased to offer you tea.' She was speaking to the Captain, but was very aware of the man standing silently beside him. The Earl might have caused him to come, but she felt every bit as involved, more so because the Biggs family had been a pet project of hers long before his lordship appeared on the scene.

The Captain bowed. 'I shall be delighted, ma'am.'

She handed the basket to Roland. 'Please give this to Mrs Biggs.' And then she left them to make their way up the garden path and knock on the door of the tiny cottage.

Charlotte had left Bonny Boy at the King's Head on the other side of the green, but she was soon in the saddle and riding swiftly back to Mandeville. Her exchange with the Earl had been minimal, but it was nonetheless disturbing. She really must learn not to let him upset her. She was not a simpering schoolgirl, not even a girl at all, but a woman of three and twenty and she ought to be able to control her feelings.

Once home, she changed into a plain silk gown and paced about her first-floor sitting room, wondering if Roland would come with his friend. She had not specifically excluded him, but neither had she included him in the invitation. She was answered two hours later when both men rode up the drive and dismounted at the door. She saw them from the window, though she was careful not to let them see her. Heaven forbid they should think she was watching for them! She went down to the drawing room and sat down with a London newspaper in her hand until a footman came to announce them. She put it down and rose to meet them, ordered tea to be brought in and invited them to be seated.

'Mrs Biggs asked me to return this,' Roland said, offering her the basket he had been carrying. 'She was effusive in her gratitude.' He had never been inside Mandeville before and was struck by the opulence, the sense that no expense had been spared in its creation. The furniture was of the very highest quality, the sofas well upholstered, the carpets thick and the curtains well hung, the pictures and ornaments priceless. But it was too perfect; there was no warmth, no feeling that the house was lived in. It was simply a showcase for wealth. But he could understand why she would look down on Amerleigh Hall, the sprawling mish-mash of styles, with its rattling windows and draughty corridors. He could not imagine children tearing about Mandeville, sliding down the banisters, playing ball in the vast hall, as he had done at Amerleigh as a child.

She put the basket on a table and sat down again and they seated themselves opposite her. 'How did you get on with Tommy, Captain?' she asked.

'He is very small,' he said.

'Of course he is.' She laughed. 'He is only six years old.'

He smiled ruefully. 'I am used to soldiers, ma'am, little children are strangers to me.'

'Oh, dear, then you do not think you can help?'

'I did not say that, Miss Cartwright. I am willing to try, but I shall be learning as well as the boy.'

'But you will need to teach his parents and siblings too, so they can understand him and he them.'

'Of course. I notice they comprehend much of what he is trying to convey already. I think the way forward is to incorporate the signs he has already developed—no sense in asking him to learn new ones for familiar things. He is not able to spell, so it is no good trying to teach him letters. That will come later, at a more advanced stage. I need to think about it carefully.'

'Surely many of the soldiers you taught could not read and write?'

'That is perfectly true, but the words they needed to use are very different from those of a child. It is a challenge, a very big challenge.'

'I am sure you are equal to it, Captain,' she said, as the tea things were brought in and she busied herself with the teapot.

Roland watched the two of them dealing together so amicably and a strange sensation of unrest came over him, as if something he had within his grasp was slipping from him. 'You will need a schoolroom,' he said to Miles. 'You cannot teach in the cottage with Mrs Biggs busy about her cooking and housework. You are welcome to use the schoolroom at Amerleigh. Kit it up with whatever you need.'

'That might do for the time being,' Charlotte said. 'But in the long term, my lord, you will want it yourself.'

'I am not about to go back to school,' he said, laughing.

'No, but you will marry soon and have children, then you will need it for them.' She did not know why she said that. It was impertinent and she deserved a put-down. Why did she always invite his ire? It was as if she needed to scratch an irritating itch and, having scratched, was left with a sore place.

'That is not imminent, Miss Cartwright.' He was being carefully polite and that goaded her to scratch again.

'No? I have heard you were about to make an offer.'

'Then will you please tell your informant she is mistaken,' he said firmly.

Bemused, Captain Hartley looked from one to the other and wondered how a simple conversation about a little deaf boy had suddenly become a cat-and-mouse game. 'I am sure the schoolroom at the Hall will do very nicely for a start,' he said.

They both turned towards him as if suddenly remembering he was there. 'That's settled, then,' Roland said. 'If all goes well, I should like to spread the word to other deaf children and their parents, make a little school of it.'

'Let us see how it goes with one pupil first,' Miles said.

The moment of dissension passed and they drank their tea and ate the bread and butter and the little cakes Mrs Cater had provided and Charlotte asked the Captain about his war experiences and showed herself to be far more knowledgeable than most ladies about the political situation. She agreed with Roland that a man like Napoleon Bonaparte would not be content with a life spent quietly on a little island. When he had capitulated, he had promised his followers he would return with the violets. 'Have the allied powers made sure he cannot?' she asked.

'I doubt it,' Miles said. 'He has been allowed to keep a regiment and a ship and that is madness.'

'Would you go back to the army, my lord, if he did show his face again?' she asked Roland.

He smiled, remembering their previous conversation on the subject of his leaving. 'It depends,' he said carefully. 'There is a great deal keeping me in Amerleigh at the moment.'

For once she did not rise to the bait, but sipped her tea and thought of Amerleigh without him. She would miss him if he ever left, but the reason she gave to herself, that she enjoyed their battles, was not the true one. Her thoughts went to that evening when he had kissed her hand and made her feel like a woman for the first time in her life. That was what she would really miss.

After the men had taken their leave and ridden away, Charlotte wandered into the ballroom and stood there a moment, then began humming a tune and dancing all by herself. But in her imagination she was not alone; the room was crowded and Roland was there and they were dancing together, hands linked, bodies moving in unison as they had at Lady Brandon's soirée. 'I will do it,' she said, coming to a standstill and speaking aloud. 'He will learn to rue the day he called me a hoyden.'

Organising her workforce, instructing men and women in their day-to-day tasks, was child's play to her. But organising an entertainment beyond a simple dinner party was something she had never done and the prospect daunted her. Nor had she any idea how to act the lady, to charm as a hostess. For that she needed help. There was Lady Brandon, of course, but she did not think her ladyship would serve; she had her own motives and they did not accord with Charlotte's. She went back to the drawing room and sat at her davenport to write a letter to her great-aunt, Lady Emily Ratcliffe.

'What an extraordinary woman,' Miles commented, as they turned out of the gate and, disdaining the road, made their way over the hill back to Amerleigh.

'Yes.'

'Wealthy, wouldn't you say?'

'Very.'

'I suppose you grew up together?'

'We were neighbours, of course, but I was at school and Oxford, then the army, and though I saw her about the village when I was at home, I cannot say I really knew her.'

'She's not a member of the gentry.'

'No, though I believe her grandmother on her mother's side came from a good family. Her mother died when she was born and her father brought her up. He died two years ago and left her everything.'

'Quite a catch for someone, then,' Miles said.

Roland looked sharply at him, wondering what was behind the remark. 'I suppose so, but too self-willed for my taste. She would want to wear the breeches in any marriage.'

'Depends how you go about taming her, I should think,' Miles said thoughtfully.

'You think you could do it?'

'If I wanted to, I could.'

Roland laughed and spurred his horse into a gallop to end a conversation that was making him feel decidedly uncomfortable. Miles smiled to himself and followed suit.

Miles left two days later to go back to Horse Guards where he intended to obtain his release and then return. He would be on half-pay and that, together with the small stipend Roland was able to provide, was enough for his needs, he said, especially as he was to live at Amerleigh Hall for nothing. He came back a week later to prepare the schoolroom for its new pupil. It was on the second floor of the oldest part of the house and every day he took himself up there and set about learning all he could about sign language.

One day Roland found him there, sitting on an old sofa, hands in front of him, moving arms and fingers this way and that, studying a book and drawing the signs on a slate. 'I think I should learn a little of that,' he said. 'I want to talk to young Thomas too.'

'I will teach you when I know enough myself.'

'I thought you invented it.'

'No. It was not invented, it grew. It was developed many, many years ago by monks who had taken a vow of silence and wanted to communicate with each other. I have no doubt it is still used for that purpose. Who decided it could be used by the deaf in the general population I do not know. I was sent to a Catholic school and learned some of it from the abbot who ran it and that fired my interest.' He smiled ruefully. 'I do not think Tommy would be interested in religious words and practices, so I must adapt it for a small boy.'

'You must not spend all your time up here, you know. What about coming out for a ride? I will show you round my domain.'

Miles put the book away. 'I shall enjoy that.'

Half an hour later they were riding through Amerleigh towards the hills, carpeted in red, pink and white heather, prickly yellow gorse and bright green bracken, with here and there the delicate blue of a harebell, so that the land was vibrant with colour. Familiar as he was with the sight, it always brought a lump to Roland's throat. Together with the house, it was what he had thought of most when away from home, especially poignant when he had not been sure if he would ever see either again.

They rode round in a large circle, taking in the boundary of the estate and finishing on Browhill. Here there was noise and clatter and dust. The new adit, which Roland had seen started, disappeared into the hillside. The big wheel was turning, which suggested men were working underground and a stream had been diverted and was running through the washing shed where two youths were working, separating the lead ore from the dirt and rubble that came with it.

'Is this part of your domain?' Miles asked.

Roland chuckled. 'I believe so, but Miss Cartwright has other ideas. We are in dispute over it.'

As he spoke, Charlotte herself came out of the building that served as an office. 'Good day, gentlemen,' she said. 'What can I do for you?'

Roland noted that she was in a benign mood; Miles noted that she was wearing a strange outfit, he might have called mannish if it were not for the skirt. 'Good day, Miss Cartwright,' Roland said, giving her a slight bow from the saddle. 'We were out for a ride…'

'And chanced to end up here.' She laughed. 'What is it about this place that draws you so, my lord?'

He was not going to rise to that bait. 'How is the new level going?'

'Very well, my lord.' She turned to Miles. 'Are you back to stay, Captain?'

'For a while, yes. I have been perfecting my signs ready to begin teaching the lad and his mother. His lordship has said he is going to learn them too.'

'Then may I join the party? I should think a skill like that might be very useful. You know, the mill hands have their own way of making signs when the clatter of the looms makes it impossible to hear anything said. I wonder if it is the same.'

Roland looked sharply at her, but she refused to meet his eye and concentrated on Miles, who was smiling at her in a way that made Roland remember that his friend had said he could tame her. Roland did not want her tamed, certainly not by anyone but himself. The thought came as a revelation. Charlotte Cartwright, tamed. That would be as cruel as trying to tame a wild tiger and just as impossible. 'I doubt your mill hands would appreciate your being able to understand their conversation,' he said with a chuckle.

'They probably have a language of their own,' Miles put in. 'As different from a soldier's or a small boy's as English is to French, but by all means join us. I plan to begin the lessons the day after tomorrow in the forenoon.'

'Yes, do come,' Roland said. 'That is, if you can be spared from all your other work.'

She smiled, but it was the smile of the untamed tiger and he almost recoiled from it. 'I shall manage it.'

As they rode away, Miles was chuckling. 'I think I am going to enjoy my time in Amerleigh,' he said. 'Something worthwhile to do and some fine entertainment.'

'Entertainment?'

'Yes, watching you and Miss Cartwright crossing swords.'

'I have no idea what you mean.'

'Oh, so you are the best of friends, are you? Whoever would have thought it?'

'Captain Hartley,' Roland said, trying not to smile, 'you are here for a specific purpose. Do not presume upon my friendship too far.'

Miles stopped laughing. He had hit upon something that mattered to his host, and, in Roland's eyes, it was not a cause for amusement. He hastily begged pardon and they rode on in silence. At the

Biggs's cottage they stopped to tell Mrs Biggs that Tommy could be brought to the Hall two days hence to begin his lessons, and then they called at the dower house where Miles was presented to the Countess and he explained what he hoped to do for Tommy.

'I am sure that is a commendable thing to do,' she said, dispensing tea in the drawing room. 'But I wonder how long you will be able to hold his attention. He is very small and has been thoroughly spoiled by his mother and sisters. He will want to play.'

'Then we must make the lessons seem like play,' Miles said. 'In any case, they will not last long, half an hour or an hour at the most. His lordship is going to be a pupil too. And Miss Cartwright.'

She laughed. 'Miss Cartwright and Roland, sitting side by side on those little schoolroom chairs, trying to talk without speaking. Oh, the wonder of it! I must come up and see this strange phenomenon. Have you met Miss Cartwright, Captain Hartley?'

'Yes, when I was here before and again today. We were out riding and came upon her at the mine.'

'What did you think of her?'

Miles looked from the Countess to Roland and back again. 'She is a very unusual lady,' he said carefully. 'Very forthright, though I imagine that is something she has learned; underneath she is vulnerable.'

'Vulnerable!' Roland exclaimed.

'Yes. Most women are, are they not?'

'Miss Cartwright is an exception.'

'Oh, I agree she is exceptional.'

'Talking of Miss Cartwright,' her ladyship put in, 'I heard she was going to give a ball at Mandeville.'

'Who told you that?' Roland asked.

'Why, Lady Brandon. She is in the young lady's confidence.'

'Who would go to a ball at Mandeville? You know Miss Cartwright is not accepted in society. Why, Gilford even tried to warn me off.'

'Goodness, why should he do that?'

'I have no idea—possibly because he has a daughter of marriageable age?'

'I would go and gladly, if she were to invite me,' Miles said.

'No doubt she will,' Roland said.

'And you,' the Countess told Roland with a twinkle in her eye. 'With you to grace it, it is bound to succeed and all those people who have always longed to see the inside of Mandeville will be glad to have a reason not to decline. If the Earl

of Amerleigh goes, then it perfectly proper for
everyone else.'

'If she thinks she can use me in that fashion,
then I am afraid she will be disappointed.' Even
as he spoke Roland realised that such a thought
would never enter Charlotte's head.

'Then I shall go alone,' Miles said, looking
meaningfully at Roland.

The thought of Miles flirting with Charlotte,
trying to tame her with his charm, was abhorrent
to Roland. Was she vulnerable? He felt a sudden
need to protect her, which was laughable. Miss
Charlotte Cartwright, mine owner, mill owner,
slave owner, needing protection was unthinkable.
And yet the thought had passed through his mind.
If it were not for those slaves and that disputed
land, if he had inherited a healthy estate, if she
had not been so obviously averse to him, things
might have been different. Why could he not get
her out of his head? Why, whenever he planned
something, did he imagine her at his side
advising him, encouraging him, and why did he
refrain from doing other things because he
thought she might disapprove? And why did the
prospect of holding her hand and dancing with
her again fill him with joyful anticipation? He
was behaving like a besotted schoolboy. 'Oh,

well, we shall see when the invitations come,' he said. '*If* they come.'

Charlotte had no idea that Lady Brandon was already spreading the word abroad that there was to be a grand ball at Mandeville. She was not even sure of it herself. Her doubts were centred on whether she could pull it off, whether she would remember everything that needed to be done— food, wine, music, flowers, invitations—and whether anyone would come. It would be dreadful to send out a hundred invitations and have only a handful turn up. Already she had written out a dozen lists and discarded them all. She had not yet had a reply to the letter she had written to her mother's aunt, asking for advice.

Great-Aunt Emily, the dowager Lady Ratcliffe, had never dealt well with her father and had never, to Charlotte's knowledge, visited Mandeville. According to her father, it was nothing but snobbery. 'She considered your mama married beneath her,' he had said one day when, as a child, she had asked him about their relations. 'I remember when we were first betrothed, she called me a fortune hunter.'

'Why?'

'Your grandfather on your mother's side was

already wealthy and had been knighted for his services to the cotton industry. Emily was his sister. She married Sir Bertram Ratcliffe and that made her think herself too grand for us.'

'She was wrong about you, wasn't she?' she had asked. It was important to be reassured on that point.

'Of course. I soon proved I could make more money than ever her brother did. All I needed was a start. Hard work did the rest.'

'No, I meant you really loved Mama and it was not her money that attracted you. You did, didn't you?'

'Of course. She was beautiful and kind. No one ever said a bad word about her.'

'I wish I had known her.'

'You do not wish it any more than I do,' he had said. 'The joy went out of my life when she died.'

She had found herself in sympathy with her father, but he did not invite sympathy and so she had said nothing and went back to her lessons. But it was strange how Papa had become so isolated. The gentry, who had hitherto tolerated him, would have nothing to do with him after he quarrelled with the old Earl, and even her mother's family looked down on him. His associates were all businessmen like himself. That isolation had been passed down to her, but she could not be easy with it as he had been. There was too much of her mother in her.

Mrs Biggs, in her Sunday best dress, brought a pink-scrubbed Tommy to the Hall as arranged. She was thoroughly overawed to be entering the big house and, once in the schoolroom, sat on a chair against the wall, while Tommy was beckoned forward to sit at the desk Roland had used as a child.

Miles began by talking to the child in signs, trying to find out how much he already understood. Having been told that he had to behave himself and pay attention, the poor child appeared more simple than he really was and the lessons did not go well. It was the arrival of the Earl and Miss Cartwright that changed that. He beamed at them and began making signs so fast that Charlotte had to stop him.

'Slow down,' she mouthed, laughing. 'I am not as quick as you.'

'We have come to join in the lessons,' Roland said, offering Charlotte a half-size chair and finding another for himself. They sat side by side and looked up at Miles expectantly.

Tommy giggled and his mother reproved him, putting her finger to her closed lips and he subsided at once.

'Ah, he knows the meaning of that,' Miles said.

After that the lesson went more smoothly. Tommy was asked what time he went to bed, what time he rose, what he liked to eat, all in signs. When his mother was tempted to answer for him she was gently told not to help him. An hour flew by.

'I think that is enough for one day,' Miles said. 'Bring the boy again tomorrow, Mrs Biggs. And help him to practise if you have the time.'

'I will find the time, Captain. And I'll teach the others what I've learned.'

'I think that went very well,' Charlotte said after Mrs Biggs and the child had left. 'Do you not think so, my lord?'

Roland had been amusing himself imagining Charlotte as a mother with a nursery full of children, beautiful, happy children, and her voice startled him. 'I am sorry, I did not hear the question,' he said.

She repeated it.

'Oh, yes, very well. So, what do you think, Miles, will you carry on with the lessons?'

'I think so. The trouble is, I have no notion how fast a child of that age should learn. I do not want to force him. He must want to learn. And later, perhaps, he could be taught to speak, though that is outside the scope of my expertise. We should have to consult others in the field. I have heard of a Dr Masterson who specialises in teaching deaf mutes to speak. I could write to him.'

'Then do so, my friend. Now, shall we go down and have some refreshment. You will stay, Miss Cartwright?'

Charlotte had, for the first time in her life, except when she was in Jamaica, absented herself from the mill, and she ought really to make up for lost time, but for some reason she did not want to, and that again was a first. 'I should be happy to,' she said, rising from the tiny chair and finding she had pins and needles in her legs and had to hop about to get the feeling back into them.

Roland watched her with amusement. The more he saw of her, the more he discovered of the woman she was beneath the severe exterior. He had been entirely wrong to call her a hoyden and plain, to boot. It was uncharitable and arrogant. How glad he was she had not heard him. But that did not alleviate his guilt. She was most definitely a woman with a woman's compassion and gentleness and the more he saw of her, the more he realised she was beautiful, not only her outward appearance, but her inner self. This was in spite of her upbringing, not because of it.

They went down to the drawing room where Mrs Fields served them with a light luncheon. 'How is your husband, Mrs Fields?' Charlotte asked her.

'Oh, he is much the same, but he keeps a cheerful countenance, ma'am, and since I have been working here he is much happier. He never did like me working at the inn.'

'I am so glad.'

The woman bobbed and disappeared.

'What is the matter with her husband?' Roland asked, wondering if there was anything Charlotte did not know about the villagers. Mrs Fields had been working for him over a month and he had learned nothing of her family.

'He had a stroke and is confined to the house. He feels helpless and was furious when Mrs Fields was roughly treated by one of the inn's clients and when she complained to the landlord, the landlord sided with his customer and dismissed her. Her poor husband could do nothing but rant.'

'How do you know so much about the villagers' lives, Miss Cartwright?'

'I hear things as I go about.'

'Then you are certainly not deaf,' Miles said with a laugh.

'No, Captain, my hearing is particularly acute,'

she said, looking hard at Roland as she spoke, but he was concentrating on the chicken leg on his plate and did not pick up on the implication of her words.

'I have heard you are going to hold a ball at Mandeville,' the Captain went on.

'Where did you hear that?' she asked in surprise.

'My mother had it from Lady Brandon,' Roland put in. 'Is it true?'

'I have been thinking about it, but have not yet made up my mind.'

'I hope you do,' Miles said, smiling at her in a way that irritated Roland, who assumed his friend was trying to make good his boast that he could tame her. 'And I hope I may be one of your guests.'

'If I go ahead, you will certainly be sent an invitation, Captain.'

'Will it be a society ball, with the men in breeches like they are obliged to wear at Almack's, or perhaps a *bal masque*?'

'I know nothing of what they do at Almack's. I am not, as you cannot have failed to realise, Captain, a society hostess. To me a ball is a ball. And my guests will not be confined to the upper echelons of society.'

'Then may I recommend the masked ball with everyone in fancy dress. It is a great leveller, is fancy dress. Do you not agree, Roly, my friend?'

'Yes, indeed.'

'I will certainly bear it in mind.' She stood up. 'I must be going. Would you send for my curricle, my lord?'

'I will go,' Miles said and disappeared, leaving Roland and Charlotte alone, facing each other awkwardly.

'Will you come again tomorrow?' he asked.

'I am not sure I can spare the time,' she said. 'I have much to do.'

'Of course. A woman who works.'

'We all work in our different ways, my lord. I am not ashamed of it.'

'Heaven forbid that you should be! I, too, have a great deal to occupy me, but I shall try to attend the lessons as often as I can. You are welcome to come whenever you can find the time. You do not have to send word in advance.'

'Thank you, my lord.'

'Would you be more comfortable if I provided some proper chairs?'

'No,' she laughed. 'Don't do that. Tommy likes us to be on his level and that is as it should be.'

'Brought down to size, eh?' He laughed too. 'Very well, I will leave things as they are and look forward to our next lesson together, whenever that may be.'

Miles returned to say the curricle was at the

door and she took her leave of both of them. Instead of going home, she drove straight to Scofield. She could not afford to neglect the mill, especially as she had heard there was dissent in neighbouring manufactories and she did not want it spreading to her workforce.

As she drove expertly along the lanes, she found herself thinking about her ball. Catherine Brandon had jumped the gun, telling the Countess, and no doubt every other of her bosom bows, about it, so if she wanted to save face, she must go through with it. If Aunt Emily accepted her invitation to come and stay, it would be a great help and give her a little standing in the community. Suddenly she wanted it to be a success. She had never minded her isolation before, but now it irked her. And for the first time, too, she realised that it was the Earl of Amerleigh she wanted to impress, not in a spirit of competition, but because, in spite of everything, she had come to like and respect him. And what an admission that was!

Having conferred with William Brock about their latest orders and made sure everything was running smoothly, she returned to Mandeville to find her great-aunt had arrived and made herself at home. Lady Ratcliffe was sitting on one of the sofas in the drawing room, with a tray on a low table at her side containing the remains of tea and cakes. She was in her late sixties, very upright in her carriage. She had on a full-skirted gown of mousseline, a short pelisse and a wide-brimmed bonnet with a huge curling feather. Her gloves lay on the arm of the chair.

'Why did you not let me know when you were arriving?' Charlotte asked, hurrying forward to kiss her ladyship's powdered cheek. 'I would have been here to greet you.'

'Your letter gave me to understand the matter was urgent,' her ladyship said, looking Charlotte up and down through her quizzing glass. 'I can see I was right. Wherever did you get that strange habit?'

'It is not a habit, Aunt, it is what I wear when I am doing business. I shall go up and change at once and then we will have supper. How did you come? Where is your luggage? I hope it has been taken to your room.'

'I came in my own chaise and I believe my trunk has been put somewhere. I have been waiting for an age for someone to conduct me to my room.'

'I am so dreadfully sorry, Aunt, but I did not expect you today.' She went to the hearth and gave a good tug on the bell rope beside it. 'I will take you up myself.'

A servant arrived promptly in answer to her summons and was instructed to take hot water up to the blue room and to tell Mrs Cater to delay supper for half an hour, then Charlotte conducted her ladyship up to the main guest room, apologising again as she did so.

The luxury of the room and its adjoining dressing room mollified her ladyship to some extent, especially as her maid was already there and had unpacked her trunk. Charlotte left her and went to her own room to change.

They had not made a good beginning, she decided, as she flung off the frogged jacket and grey skirt. She would have to work hard to change her aunt's poor opinion of her as a hostess, though why she should keep apologising, she did not know—her aunt should have sent advance notice. Perhaps she had been waiting for an excuse to come to Mandeville and do something about her motherless greatniece, and the arrival of the letter had brought her post-haste.

An hour later, they were sitting together in the small dining room enjoying a repast of roast lamb, pork cutlets and every kind of vegetable imaginable, followed by exotic fruits from Mandeville's own hot houses. Charlotte had changed into a green taffeta evening gown trimmed with bands of velvet and Meg had forced her hair into some sort of order, so that her aunt had looked at her with more approval.

'That is much better,' she said. 'I cannot think why you must wear that strange garb you had on when I first saw you. It was not even clean.'

'I only wear it for business and it was clean when I went out this morning. A mill is a dusty place, Aunt, and anything better would be ruined in no time. My workers would not respect me if I arrived in silks and furbelows.'

'Do you mean you actually go into the mill?'

'Of course. I must keep track of what is happening to the orders and oversee the work.'

'Nonsense, of course you don't. I never met a lady yet who would stoop so low.'

'I am not thought of as a lady.'

'Then it is about time we changed that. Why, you will never make a good marriage going on the way you do.'

'I am not thinking of marriage, Aunt.'

'Of course you are. Every young lady does,' her aunt contradicted firmly.

'No, Aunt. I simply want to give a ball, here at Mandeville, which is why I asked for your advice.'

'And I shall be pleased to give it, my dear, but surely you have had balls here before now?'

'I have been told Mama used to give grand balls, but it has never happened in my lifetime. I do not think Papa wanted to entertain after she died.'

'Have you not been brought out?'

'Not in the usual sense, no.'

Her aunt sighed heavily. 'I knew your father was an eccentric, but I did not realise he had so thoroughly neglected his duty as a father.'

'He did not neglect me,' Charlotte said, fiercely defensive. 'He simply had different ideas about how I should be brought up. I think he was disappointed I was not a son.'

'He should have married again and begot himself an heir.'

'I do not think he could bring himself to do so. In any case, he was always too busy.'

'Then we must set about a remedy. How old are you now, two and twenty?'

'Twenty-three, Aunt.'

'Almost at your last prayers! There is not a moment to lose.'

'Aunt, I am in no haste to marry.' Charlotte was beginning to wonder if she had been wise to ask her great-aunt for advice; she was liable to be given far more than was wanted or needed. 'I have yet to find the right man.' Even as she spoke, her mind's eye presented her with an image of Roland Temple, Earl of Amerleigh, sitting on the little nursery chairs, making signs at Tommy Biggs and laughing. That was the man she liked, not the arrogant youth, nor the proud owner of a failing estate. She could marry the gentle, caring man. She shook the picture from her. Whatever was she thinking of? She was not going to marry anyone, least of all Roland Temple, who had called her a hoyden!

'Nor will you, the way you are going on.' Great-Aunt Emily's voice broke in on her reverie. 'But I am here now and we may yet save the situation. Let us repair to the drawing room. You can tell me all about yourself over the teacups and we will devise a plan.'

Charlotte sighed and led the way.

Chapter Six

Lady Ratcliffe was decidedly put out when she discovered next day that Charlotte intended to go to the mill as usual and she was again wearing the strange dress that had so appalled her. 'I will try to come home early,' Charlotte said. 'We can talk over our plans for the ball then.'

'What am I to do all day?' Her ladyship was still in bed, sitting up drinking a dish of hot chocolate that Charlotte had brought herself. It was, she averred, an indecent time to be woken. 'Surely you can give the mill a miss until we have come to some decisions. You will never pass muster as a lady while you insist on racketing about in that dreadful outfit.'

'I must go, but I will be back in time for nuncheon and then I will change and take you round the village. We will call on Lady Brandon and the

Countess of Amerleigh. I am persuaded you will deal well with them both.'

'You are on calling terms with a Countess! Charlotte, you never told me that last night.'

'It must have slipped my mind. If you want something to do this morning, you could make shopping lists of everything you think we need for the ball and there is no necessity to spare my purse.' And with that, she kissed her great-aunt's cheek and left to drive herself to the mill.

They were getting low on some yarns, but as everything seemed to be working smoothly, she did not stay long. Instead of going up to the mine as she would normally have done, she went to Amerleigh Hall to take her place in the school-room alongside Tommy and Roland. Both expressed delight that she could join them again.

She knew she was being inconsistent. From doing all she could to avoid the Earl she now seemed anxious to seek his company. It might have been her interest in Tommy and the lessons, but that was not the whole of it. She had had a change of heart. She wanted to get to know Roland, to discover the man beneath the aristocrat, to delve below the facade and understand why he was the man he was and how much he had changed in the course of six long years of war. The lessons were a means of doing that; they had at least one thing in common and that was a love of children. When she was with children she felt different; she could relax with them and forget business for a little while. Roland Temple gave every appearance of feeling the same. He was not above sitting on tiny chairs or even squatting on the floor to be closer to them and they were not overawed by him.

'We are learning the signs for some useful daily phrases, Miss Cartwright,' Miles told her. 'Things like "I am hungry" and "Hurry up" and "It is time for dinner".'

'And "I am pleased to see you",' Roland added, pointing at his own eyes and then at her and smiling broadly.

'We will not speak aloud at all,' Miles admonished.

The lesson continued amid much hilarity, but they did not forget that it was Tommy who was being taught and he was included in everything they attempted. His mother had not stayed with him today; one of the little ones was unwell and she had returned to the sickbed.

'I will take him home,' Charlotte said when the lesson ended. 'I can ask after the sick one at the same time.' She turned to Tommy and successfully made him understand he was to go to the stables and have her curricle brought to the door. Grinning from ear to ear, he sped off to do her bidding.

'We are making great strides,' Miles said. 'Far better than I had hoped for, but I wonder at you both treating it so lightly.'

'You said yourself we must make it seem like play,' Roland said as they made their way down to the ground floor. 'He is happy about the lessons and learning fast. We shall soon be able to move on to teaching him to read and write. That will open a whole new vista for him.'

'You would make a scholar of him?' Charlotte queried.

'Why not? Every child, however poor, deserves an education. I know you agree with that, for you teach your workers.' He paused and gave her a smile that found its way to treacly brown eyes and crinkled the corners of his mouth. 'I am persuaded we have more in common than we have in dissent, Miss Cartwright.'

They had arrived in the front hall and she did not point out that he was the one causing dissent by insisting on continuing with that lawsuit. If he would only hint that he might drop it, she would gladly come to some accommodation with him, give him the title to the land and retain the mining rights perhaps. But he had to make the first move.

The door was open and Tommy stood at the head of the pony, waiting for her. 'Will you not stay for refreshment?' Roland asked. 'We could explore the common ground.'

'No, I am afraid I cannot. I have a guest and must return to Mandeville or she will think I have deserted her.' She paused. 'Do you know if the Countess is at home this afternoon? I thought of calling on her with my great-aunt.'

'I believe she may be. If not, she will be here. You are welcome at either place.'

'Thank you, my lord.'

She signalled to Tommy to climb into the curricle, bowed her head to Roland and Miles, and made her way down the steps to join the boy.

Roland watched her drive away, as capable as ever at handling the ribbons, and gave a huge sigh. Was he making any progress at demolishing the wall she had built about herself? She had seemed more at ease today and the fact that she wanted to pay a call on his mother must mean something. He had better go and see what Mama was doing that afternoon.

Roland was with the Countess at the dower house when Lady Ratcliffe and Charlotte, who was dressed becomingly in a pale blue muslin gown with a lace cape and puffed sleeves, were announced. His presence took Charlotte by surprise, but it was no greater than Lady Ratcliffe's astonishment on being presented and discovering that there was a handsome young Earl living not five miles from Mandeville. She quickly established he was not married and lacked nothing in manners. Whatever was Charlotte thinking of, not to cultivate so eligible a bachelor right on her doorstep?

'What do you think of Amerleigh?' the Countess asked her, dispensing tea.

'It is very pleasant, my lady, and the countryside is charming. At least it is at this time of the year. I collect it is not so agreeable in winter.'

'No, it was particularly bad in the early part of this year. We were cut off by snow for weeks.'

'How long do you stay, my lady?' Roland asked. He was sitting on a high-backed chair, while the ladies occupied the sofas. It made him appear even taller.

'As long as I am needed.'

'Needed?' he queried, looking at Charlotte with one eyebrow raised.

'Oh, yes. My great-niece is needful of my assistance in the matter of a ball and her come-out.'

Roland, who had been about to take a sip of his tea, spluttered with laughter. His mother looked anxiously at him and Lady Ratcliffe looked affronted. As for Charlotte, she was at first inclined to be angry, but then found her own lips twitching. 'I never said anything about a come-out, Aunt,' she said.

'You cannot have a ball without coming out first,' her ladyship insisted. 'It is not the thing. Am I not right, Countess?'

Lady Amerleigh appeared to be considering her answer carefully and her eyes were twinkling too. Charlotte wondered if her aunt was being made fun of, but decided the Countess was much too polite to do such a thing. 'In London, yes,' her ladyship said slowly. 'But we are far from the capital here and Miss Cartwright's circumstances are exceptional.'

'So they may be, but if she is to marry well, then we must do the thing properly.'

'I will not go to London,' Charlotte said firmly. 'I am far too busy to contemplate it; besides, I have no wish to marry and would look very foolish among all the young débutantes.'

'I think we may safely assume Miss Cartwright is already well and truly out,' Roland put in, looking at Charlotte with a teasing smile that told her plainly she had not heard the last of that particular topic from him. She must extricate herself somehow and take her aunt away before she made an even bigger fool of herself.

'Lady Ratcliffe has come to help me arrange a costume ball,' she said. 'I have been persuaded I ought to give one, but I do not have the time to devote to organising it.'

'When is it to be?' the Countess asked.

'I have not decided the date. It depends on so many things, but perhaps the last Saturday in June. Would that be convenient for you, my lady?'

'I am still in mourning, Miss Cartwright.'

'Yes, but it will be six months since your husband died—could you not go into half-mourning and grace it with your presence, even for a short time? No one will think ill of you for it.'

'Oh, go on, say yes, Mama,' Roland put in.

'I will think about it.'

Having successfully diverted attention from the matter of a come-out, Charlotte decided it was time they took their leave and rose to go. Roland accompanied them to the door and was surprised to see, not the curricle and its patient pony, but a grand carriage and four. First the feminine dress and now the carriage—did it mean Charlotte was trying to change? He was not sure he liked the idea. He bowed to Lady Ratcliffe as he handed her in and then turned to do the same office for Charlotte, taking her hand and giving the fingers a little squeeze, as he did so. The door was shut and he stood back as the coachman set the equipage in motion. Charlotte, leaning forward to look out of the window, saw him standing in exactly the same pose, feet apart, hand slightly uplifted, the wind ruffling his hair, until they turned out of the drive and he was lost to view.

'My goodness, Charlotte,' Emily said. 'I had heard of the Earl of Amerleigh, but I had no idea he was so young and handsome, nor that he resided in Shropshire. And so near to you too. I collect he is unmarried.'

'He has but lately come into his inheritance, Aunt. Before that he was in the army in Portugal. His late father let the estate run down, but he is busy setting all to rights.' She paused. 'And you may take that gleam out of your eye. I am not going to set myself up to snare him. We are at daggers drawn.'

'Daggers drawn! I saw no sign of that. He appeared good-natured and polite…'

'So he may be, but I have not always found it so. He can also be top lofty and obstinate.'

Her ladyship laughed. 'I think the kettle is calling the pot black, my dear.'

'Perhaps, but I do not want you matchmaking. There is enough of that going on in the village already and the poor man is besieged.'

'Ah, so he is a poor man, is he?'

'I have no idea of his wealth, but he is spending a great deal of money restoring Amerleigh Hall and the estate.'

'Ready for his Countess.'

'Possibly.'

'Would you not like to be a Countess?'

'I never thought of it, being ineligible.'

'On account of not being aristocratic enough? Wealth can overcome that, you know, especially if the young man is short of funds.'

'Not that young man, Aunt,' Charlotte said very firmly, reminded of his rejection of her six years before, just when she was beginning to push it to the back of her mind. 'Roland Temple will not be bought and I will not stoop to try it. I do not want to marry. If I did, I would have to hand over all I own to my husband, who could ruin everything if he so chose and I could not do a thing to prevent it. And I should lose my independence, the freedom to please myself what I do, where I go, what I choose to spend my money on. I would be no better than a chattel.'

'How hard you are, child. It is your father made you like that, for your mother never was. A gentler creature never breathed. But she could be stubborn too. We all told her she would rue the day she married your father, but she would not listen. Two years later she was dead, God rest her soul.'

'That was not Papa's fault. I believe he idolised her.'

'I am surprised he did not make a push to see you settled before he died. He should have given you a Season. I would have been pleased to have you stay with me and brought you out myself. Now, we must try to remedy the situation before it is too late.'

'Aunt, it is already too late. I simply want to give a masked ball. Everyone of consequence in the area has been getting up lavish entertainment to celebrate the end of the war and I do not want to be the odd one out. I want my ball to be the best, the most sumptuous, the most talked about in the whole county. And I do not care what it costs.'

Lady Ratcliffe turned to Charlotte in surprise and realised there was more to this than the holding of a ball. Her niece had suddenly become aware of what she had missed in her youth and her ladyship was prepared to gamble it had a great deal to do with the Earl of Amerleigh. She smiled to herself; she had not arrived a moment too soon.

* * *

Their next call was on Lady Brandon, who was a very different being from the Countess. She was a prattler, full of herself and her family, of Martha in particular who had so cleverly attracted the attentions of the Earl of Amerleigh. 'Have you met the Earl, my lady?' she asked Emily.

'Yes, he was with the Countess when we called. A very personable young man.'

'Oh, yes, he is, is he not? Somewhat pinched in the pocket, I understand, though that is of little account. Brandon has told him that Martha is an heiress in her own right. He is very particular in his attentions to her, you know, and we are hopeful of a happy outcome very soon.' She turned to Charlotte. 'Have you decided on the ball?'

'Yes, it is why I have asked my aunt to stay. She is going to organise it for me.' She kept her voice carefully controlled, though Lady Brandon's confidence was making her wonder how far matters had really gone between the Earl and Martha.

'Indeed, I am surprised, considering I offered to help you,' the lady said huffily. 'I would have taken all the hard work out of it for you.'

Charlotte realised her friend's show of hurt was on account of not being able to boast that Miss

Cartwright had no idea how to organise a ball and without her help it would have been a very sorry affair indeed. 'I am sure you would, Catherine,' she said carefully. 'But I know you are very busy yourself, but no doubt Aunt Emily will be glad of any help you can afford her.'

'Tell me, is the Earl really going to offer for her daughter?' Emily asked, when they were once more on their way.

'I have no idea. It is none of my business.'

'Then you must make it your business.'

'Certainly not!' Charlotte exclaimed.

'I shall make it mine to find out.'

'No doubt everyone will find out in due course. At the moment I am more concerned with making my ball a success.'

'Very well, let us talk about the ball, considering you have given me less that three weeks to have everything ready. If you want to have a full ballroom, the sooner you issue the invitations the better. Have you made a list?' Emily asked.

'I have made a start.'

'Good. Have you decided on any of the other necessities: musicians, food and drink, flowers, extra staff, your own costume?'

'No, that is why I asked you to help me. Apart

from choosing my costume, you may have the ordering of it all.'

'Then we had best go into Shrewsbury tomorrow and make a start,' Emily announced.

'You go. Take Lady Brandon with you. She knows all the best shops. I have to go to the mill.'

'Charlotte, I despair of you,' her ladyship said. 'Do you never think of anything but work?'

'Of course I do, but it is a particularly difficult time at the moment. We have a large order to fulfil and I am waiting on a consignment of cotton yarn from the spinners that is late. I must chase up our suppliers.'

She forgot all about the ball when she arrived at the mill next morning to be told that the yarn had still not arrived. 'I sent over to Langhams and they said the raw cotton had not arrived from Liverpool,' William Brock told her. Mr Langham, who conducted his business from premises just outside Shrewsbury, employed an army of spinners who turned the raw cotton into yarn, which he was contracted to pass on to Cartwright's for weaving. 'I am told the *Fair Charlie* is overdue. There have been storms at sea.'

Running short had never happened before, but

the *Fair Charlie* had never been delayed by more than a few days before, and she had taken on more orders than usual. She had been remiss in not making provision for such an eventuality and realised, to her chagrin, that she had allowed herself to become distracted by the Earl of Amerleigh and the social events in the village, which she had never previously bothered with, not to mention indulging herself going to Tommy's lessons when she should have been at work. 'There are always storms at sea. I came through one myself not three months since. The ship has always been able to weather them.'

'Then let us hope that it will do so this time.'

She mulled over the possibilities and remedies as she drove back to Mandeville. If the ship did not come in soon, she would have to find an alternative source of supply to keep the weavers busy.

At home again, she found Lady Ratcliffe entertaining Lady Brandon to tea and going over long lists of things they had ordered and others they still needed. As the money for it was not coming out of their purses, they had been more than extravagant, but considering she had said she did not care how much the ball cost, she made no comment on it.

'What about your costume?' Lady Brandon asked her. 'Have you given a thought to it?'

'Not yet.'

'We discovered a place in Shrewsbury that has all manner of costumes for rent. I have chosen mine and so has Martha. Why not go there?'

'I will see what they have to offer when I go into town next time.'

The next week was a worrying time and she could not give her mind to her costume or even to the ball, but as the two ladies more than made up for her deficiency, the arrangements were coming along nicely, which was more than could be said for the work at the mill. Rumours were flying round that the *Fair Charlie* had been lost and, when there was no more yarn to weave, all the workers would be laid off. It took all her time to reassure her workforce that such was not the case, especially as the supplies in the stockroom were dwindling to an alarming degree. Mr Brock had taken it upon himself to discharge one man, an overseer called Josh Younger, who was intent on exaggerating the rumours. 'He was making everyone discontented,' Brock told her when she questioned his decision. 'I had no choice.'

There was nothing for it but to go to Liverpool and find out what was happening herself.

'You can't go now,' Emily complained when she told her. 'You will not be back in time for the ball.'

'Of course I will. It is over a week away and you have everything in hand. I shall be gone no longer than I have to be.'

'Who is to go with you?'

'No one, except Talbot to drive the coach.'

'Charlotte, ladies do not travel around the countryside unaccompanied. Anything could happen.'

'I am not a lady, nor ever will be.'

She pretended not to hear her great-aunt's murmur, 'You will be if I have anything to do with it,' as she left the room to give orders for the coach to be readied and a groom sent ahead on horseback to arrange post horses.

Roland had not seen Charlotte for days. She had not attended the lessons, nor even been seen in the village. He missed her. He missed their wrangling, her chuckle of humour as she bested him in some argument. He missed her gentle care of Tommy, her understanding of the boy's needs, her fire when roused. And he enjoyed rousing her.

'Why not go and see if anything is wrong?' his mother suggested, when he voiced his concern. She had come up to the Hall to supervise the hanging of new curtains in the drawing room and they were enjoying a break for refreshment.

'Why would there be anything wrong? She is no doubt too busy organising the ball.'

'Then you have answered your own question. However, it is not only the ball, but her business that keeps her. I have heard rumours…'

'Rumours? What rumours?'

'The Cartwright mill is having trouble keeping the looms supplied with yarn.'

'Who told you that?'

'Lady Brandon, who had it from her husband.'

'Charlotte cannot possibly be in financial trouble, can she?'

His mother shrugged. 'I would hardly think so. This ball of hers must be costing a fortune and she is too level-headed to waste money on frivolities when it is needed elsewhere.'

'You do not think it can be Browhill that is draining her resources?'

'Who is to tell? If it is, you could put a stop to it in an instant. That is, if you want to. Or perhaps you would like to see her ruined.'

'Of course not. Mama, how could you think it?'

'Then give up this vendetta. I wish your papa had never started it.'

His mother did not wish it any more heartily

than he did. He and Charlotte seemed to have established a rapport, but if her business failed, those who decried women trying to do the work of men would make a laughing stock of her. He realised quite suddenly that he would hate that to happen to her. But he could not believe the rumours were true—she was too well established. 'I told Mountford an age ago not to proceed.'

'Did you?' she asked in surprise. 'Have you told Miss Cartwright that?'

'No, I left it to him to do so.'

'He might have an interest in forgetting his instructions. He was your father's man, you know, and he blames himself for advising your father to hand over the land. Perhaps he is hanging on, hoping to redeem himself.'

'I had not thought of that. I might as well go and see Miss Cartwright now, though if I know her, she will pretend complete indifference and tell me she never doubted the land was hers and she intended to open that new level notwithstanding.'

He left Miles teaching Tommy and set off for Mandeville, where he was received by a worried Lady Ratcliffe. 'I am so glad you came,' she told him, rushing forward to meet him. 'My greatniece has gone to Liverpool with no escort but the coachman. I cannot think that it is safe for her to go off alone like that, but she was determined and would not listen to reason. And by all accounts it is not the sort of place a lady should be wandering alone in, what with common sailors and all manner of foreign people who land there. You will go after her, won't you, dear Lord Temple? I cannot think of anyone else I can trust.' This was said in a breathless rush and she had put her hand on his sleeve to emphasise her words, but let it go to fish for her handkerchief in the pocket of her skirt and dab at her eyes.

'Of course,' he said, his head whirring with how it could be done. 'When did she leave?'

'First thing this morning.'

'Then she has a good start. Do you know whereabouts in Liverpool she was going?'

'To the docks. That is the worst of it. Her ship is overdue…'

'Do not worry, my lady. I will find her and see she comes to no harm.'

'Oh, thank you, thank you. That is such a relief to me.'

He took his leave and did not see her tears turn to smiles as soon as the door had closed on him.

He rode back to the Hall at a gallop, where he went over the route with Travers and sent him ahead to arrange the post horses, then he ordered

Bennett to harness the coach and went in search of his mother. She was in the schoolroom, watching Miles teaching Tommy. He put his finger to his lips and beckoned to her. She tiptoed out. 'What is the matter, Roland?'

'I hope nothing, but Miss Cartwright has gone off to Liverpool on her own and Lady Ratcliffe is in a stew over it.'

'So you are off to Liverpool after her,' she said, following him to his room and watching as he stuffed nightwear and a change of clothes into a carpet bag. She took them from him and started to pack it properly.

'Yes. I was planning to go in any case. We need new wainscot for the dining room. It is badly worm-eaten and there is no one locally who can provide the quality we need. If Miss Cartwright wants to know why I have followed her, I can say my being there is pure coincidence. If need be, I will rack up with Geoffrey.'

'Rack up—Roland, what a common way of putting it,' she said, laughing. 'You can hardly call one of Geoffrey's bedrooms a rack.'

His cousin, Geoffrey Temple, had made a fortune through the war providing uniforms for the army. He was also Roland's heir. But that was the last thing on his mind as he kissed his mother goodbye and hurried out to where Bennett waited with the carriage.

'Spring 'em,' he told him, as he flung his bag on the seat and himself after it.

He would need at least five changes of horses if he was to make good speed and he hoped the corporal's persuasive tongue and the hefty purse he had given him would ensure they were ready every time he stopped. Even then he did not expect to arrive before nine or ten that evening and Charlotte had half a day's start on him; he would have to look for her the next day, though what he would say to her when he met her, he did not know. He did not think she would welcome him with the same degree of relief that Lady Ratcliffe had displayed; she was far too independent.

But supposing she were in trouble, supposing her stubbornness to cut that new level at Browhill had been done simply to pique him? If it was, then she was not the hard-headed businesswoman she pretended to be. Miles had said she was vulnerable and perhaps he was right. Roland felt a weight of guilt that made him realise their bickering was not a game and could have direful consequences. His one aim now was to find her and reassure her. The journey seemed endless.

* * *

Geoffrey's mansion on the outskirts of Liverpool was a showcase for fine furniture, ornaments and pictures, but he was a good-natured man and received Roland enthusiastically, ordering supper for him and telling him he could stay as long as he liked.

'Thank you, but I think one night will see my business done.'

'Tell me about Amerleigh,' Geoffrey said, watching Roland eat. He had had nothing since breakfast and was hungry. 'How is your mama? I was there for the late Earl's funeral. A sad occasion and the Hall in a sorry state.'

'Yes.' He could do nothing about Charlotte until the next day and had to curb his impatience to answer his cousin. 'Mama is well and enjoying refurbishing the Hall.'

'Good. Tell me what you have done and what about the people? They must have been glad to see you again.'

They joined Geoffrey's wife, Elizabeth, in the drawing room and he spent the next two hours talking about Amerleigh and the villagers, and the longer he talked, the more he realised just how much it all meant to him. Everything. The Hall, the village, the people like the Biggs family, especially Tommy. And Charlotte, of course. He could not imagine life without her. Where was she? Would he be able to find her?

He rose early the following day and, leaving his carriage and horses in Geoffrey's stables, took a cab to the docks. Liverpool had become a very busy port, beginning to rival Bristol in the number of ships that put in there, much of it down to slave trading, though now that had been outlawed, the ships carried manufactured goods and the only human cargoes were emigrants. The dock basin was a forest of masts and several ships were loading and unloading at the quayside. The *Fair Charlie* was well known and he soon learned that it was more than two weeks overdue. Miss Cartwright had been there the day before, he was told at the harbour master's office, but they had no idea where she went after leaving them.

He stood looking about him at the throng of people—dock workers, sailors, voyagers. Where next? What would he do in similar circumstances? Keeping the workforce supplied with raw materials must be her first consideration. He set off for the dockside warehouses. After plodding from one to the other, he finally tracked her down. There was no mistaking her working dress and the chestnut hair blowing about her face. She was pushing it out of her eyes with her hand and talking fast and furiously to a man standing beside a stack of bales of cotton. Roland walked slowly towards her. She had not seen him and continued to argue with the man. 'How much will you take for it?'

'Naught. It's bought and paid for and only waits on the barges to deliver it.'

'I'll give you more, and you can take the cargo of the *Fair Charlie* when it arrives. Sugar from my plantation, cotton and tobacco from America.'

'*If* it arrives,' he said with heavy emphasis. 'I am not a gambling man, missus. Now, you go home to your husband and leave business matters to him.'

'Husband!' She was furious. 'Do you know who I am?'

'No, nor do I care.'

Roland stepped forward. 'Mind your manners, sir. You are talking to a lady.'

Charlotte swivelled round to face him, her face a picture of astonishment, quickly followed by an expression of irritation, while the cotton trader turned to him in evident relief. 'Ladies should keep out of what don't concern them.'

'This lady is the owner of Cartwright's mill.'

'I care not what she owns. I do not break a

binding contract for anyone—I'd never get another. Take her away, back to her embroidery, and explain to her it cannot be done, not for all the money in Christendom.'

Roland took her elbow and drew her away. 'Come, my dear, you will do no business with this fellow.'

'What the devil are you doing here?' she demanded as soon as they were out of earshot.

'I came to buy timber.'

'In a cotton warehouse! You are roasting me.'

'No, I am not. I was on my way to the timber yards when I spotted you. You seemed to be having some difficulty…'

'Not at all. I was simply bargaining for the cotton.'

'So I perceived, but if the man has already been paid for it, you can hardly expect him to sell it again to you.'

'No, I suppose not, but I have tried everywhere else, all my father's old contacts, the ships unloading at the quay, and none have cotton to spare. I suppose it is that damned war.'

'Shall we find somewhere to have some refreshment and talk?' he said, smiling a little at her unladylike language, but making no comment on it. 'You can tell me all about it.'

'Why should I?'

'Oh, do not be so independent, Charlotte. I only want to help.' He was conducting her along the busy street, making a way for them through the crowds towards the centre of the town. 'Where are you staying?'

She was too unsettled to notice his use of her given name. Unsure whether to hate him for his interference or to be thankful that he was there, his hand under her elbow, protecting her, she did nothing to pull herself from his grasp. 'I stayed last night with the family of my ship's captain. His poor wife is worried to death and I thought to comfort her. I hoped to have my business done and to start for home today.'

'It is too late to make a start now, you would be travelling through the night.'

'I do not mind that. I cannot impose on Mrs Scott a second night. Talbot is very capable.'

'So he may be, but anything could happen. There has been prodigious rainfall lately and the potholes are ruinous.' What he did not say was that if she insisted on going home in the dark, then he would have to follow. Bennett was considerably older than Talbot and could not be expected to do it. He could, of course, drive himself, but it would be safer if neither of them attempted it. 'Where have you left your coach?'

'At the livery stables next to the posting inn.'

'Then we will go and fetch it and then go to my cousin's. He lives but five miles out of Liverpool. He is a family man and I am sure his wife will make you comfortable. We will go home tomorrow.'

'I cannot do that!'

'Why not?'

'Because I cannot.' It was said with little conviction.

'Do you have a better idea?'

She did not, except to insist on Talbot driving her home in the dark. She might be able to doze in the coach, but he could not. He would have to keep all his wits alert to avoid the potholes and stay on the road, and supposing tiredness overcame him and he fell asleep? She hated admitting the Earl was right. 'You are not bamming me?' she asked. 'Your cousin is a respectable married man and his wife is at home?'

'I swear it,' he said, crossing himself, though he could not help laughing.

'It is not a laughing matter, my lord. I have two hundred workers who will be without employment in the next two days if I cannot produce some yarn from somewhere.'

'Have you tried asking nearer to home?'

'What do you mean?'

'Why, Sir Gordon Brandon. Surely as a friend he would help you out?'

'He may be a friend, my lord, but he is also a competitor.'

'Would you help him if he were in trouble?'

'Of course.'

'There you are, then.' They had arrived at the coaching inn where Talbot was enjoying a tankard or two of ale in the parlour, waiting for his mistress to return. He was relieved to see her and even happier to find her in the company of the Earl. He was told to order the horses to be harnessed and ready to leave while the Earl and his mistress had something to eat and drink.

They did not dawdle over it and were soon sitting side by side in her luxurious coach on their way to Geoffrey's. She was silent, her head full of problems that seemed insoluble, and all her senses alert to the man beside her. Why did he want to help her, when he held her in such contempt? What motive did he have except her utter humiliation? He had achieved that once before and though she was ready to concede that his father had perhaps driven him to it, since coming home he had given no indication that he was sorry for it. He was such a mixture of arrogance, obstinacy and old-fashioned chivalry, there was no under-standing him. They worked together in complete harmony when it came to helping the villagers and teaching Tommy, and yet there was about him a hidden reserve, as if he were afraid to let her see anything of the inner man.

'You have not done anything about your timber,' she said.

'It will do another time.'

'There never was an errand for timber, was there?'

'Indeed there was. I need new wainscot for the dining room at the Hall.'

'I would have expected the builders to deal with it.'

'That is the second time you have questioned my truthfulness, Miss Cartwright.'

'No, only your common sense. You do not seem able to delegate, but must do everything yourself.'

'It is as well I did on this occasion or you would have been in a scrape, thrown into a ditch some-where and your coachman injured, if not killed.'

She began to shake with laughter.

'I do not see how you can find such a prospect humorous,' he said stiffly.

'I was reminded of Mr Halliwell and his fat wife with the bright orange hair. She took you for a labourer and Tommy for your son.'

He found his own lips twitching. 'But it could have been much worse, you know.'

'I know.'

'Then concede I am right and we would do well to delay our departure until daylight.'

'I concede nothing. It would only puff you up.' She turned towards him. 'How did you know I was in Liverpool?'

'I never said I did.'

'No, but you were not surprised to see me. It was as if you had been on the lookout for me, and you gave up your own errand without a moment's hesitation. I have learned the hard way how to detect a dissembler, my lord.'

He gave a rueful smile. 'I should hate to be thought a dissembler, which is only one step above a liar. I went to Mandeville to call on you and found a distraught Lady Ratcliffe. She is not used to your ways, you know, and was quite convinced you would fall into a bumblebath of one kind or another.'

'So the knight errant set out to rescue a damsel who did not need rescuing.' She paused. 'Why did you go to Mandeville? There is nothing wrong with Tommy, is there?'

'No, I left him having his lesson. I went because I had something to say to you.'

'Then say it. You will never have a better opportunity.'

'Browhill…'

'What about it?'

'If it is causing you problems…'

'Now, where did you get that idea, my lord? I have no problems with Browhill. The seam is being worked and producing barytes at an acceptable rate.' Barytes was a heavy white mineral used mainly in the manufacture of paint and fetched a good price on the open market.

'Nothing has changed, then,' he said, leaning back in his seat. She was still as prickly as ever about that mine. He did not feel disposed to appear to capitulate. A man had his pride after all.

'No,' she said, unwilling to let him see how disappointed she was. That damned mine stood between them, like the rock in which it was worked. The past could not be wiped out, any more than she could wipe out the memory of his callous words six years before. And what did it matter anyway? They might work together for the good of the village, but they would never be more than neighbours.

They fell into silence and a few minutes later turned into the drive of Geoffrey's house and drew up outside the door. Talbot dismounted and beat a tattoo on the door, while Roland handed Charlotte down and, putting his hand beneath her elbow, guided her towards the entrance. In next to no time she was being introduced to Mr Geoffrey Temple and his charming wife, Elizabeth, in the elegant drawing room.

'We are at your mercy,' Roland told them. 'Miss Cartwright's business took longer than she thought it would and it is too late to start back to Amerleigh tonight…'

'Of course it is,' Elizabeth said, a little taken aback by Charlotte's grey skirt and military style jacket. 'Do please stay here. Roland is always welcome and any friend of his is welcome too. We are about to have supper. If you excuse me, I will go and alert Cook that we have guests and have a room made ready for Miss Cartwright. Roland was here last night and we thought he might return so his bed is still made up.' She bustled away.

'Oh, dear,' Charlotte said to Geoffrey. 'I fear I am imposing. After all, I am a stranger you never heard of before now.'

'Oh, but we have heard of you. Roland spoke of you last night.'

She looked sharply at Roland, who covered his embarrassment with a chuckle. 'Nothing bad, I do assure you,' he said. 'I was telling Geoffrey about

Tommy and our plans for a school for deaf children.'

'Yes, tell me more,' Geoffrey said. 'I might be able to interest others.'

While they waited for supper to be served and over the meal itself, Charlotte, who had not expected to be dining out and had therefore been unable to change, explained that she had come to take an interest in Tommy because his older sisters worked at her mill. From there, with gentle prompting from Geoffrey, she talked about the mill and the *Fair Charlie* and her fears that it might be lost.

'The *Fair Charlie*,' he said. 'I have heard of her. A good ship with a very good captain. I am sure he will bring her safely to port.'

'I hope so for everyone's sake. Captain Scott has a family who are very worried about him and I have hundreds of workers waiting for her cargo.'

'She used to be a slaver, I believe.'

'Yes, but my father gave up the trade years ago.'

'Do you still own slaves?'

'No, sir, I do not.' It was said very firmly. 'The workers on my plantation are free men and women working for wages. I do not believe any man or woman should be the chattel of another.'

Roland, who had been listening to this exchange

without interrupting, turned to her in surprise. 'I did not know that.'

'You do not know everything about me, my lord.'

'Evidently not. What next? I wonder.'

'I must say, I admire you,' Elizabeth put in. In order not to embarrass her guest, she had not changed from her day dress, a simple act of courtesy that Charlotte appreciated. 'To have so much responsibility at such a young age must be daunting.'

'I have been brought up to it, Mrs Temple.'

'You must have people around to advise and help you.'

'Of course. My father used to say the secret of good business was being able to trust the people around you and I have certainly found it so. But the final decisions are mine.'

'You have never married?'

'No.'

'A husband would surely take the weight from your shoulders.'

Charlotte laughed. 'He would take all of it and me with it.'

'Miss Cartwright enjoys her independence,' Roland said. He had learned more about her in the last two hours than he had the whole of the time he had been back from the war, and he wondered why she found it so easy to talk to his cousin and not to him. Why, when he accused her of owning slaves, had she not corrected him? Why did they strike sparks off each other? Why, when he wanted to make a concession, did she block it by saying something to stop him? Why, when she showed herself to be a compassionate and caring employer, did he have to goad her into proving otherwise? Why, when all he wanted to do was help her, did she disdain him?

'Independence can be an impediment if taken to extremes,' Geoffrey said thoughtfully. 'It prevents you from accepting help when offered.'

'Mr Temple, I hope you do not think I am ungrateful for your hospitality, because I assure you that is not the case at all…'

'Good heavens, ma'am, I never meant that. I was about to say I may be able to help you over the matter of the cotton. I am well known among the merchants of Liverpool and indeed further afield, and while my own expertise is in wool, I do have connections in the cotton trade.'

'If you can help, sir, I will most certainly accept it with gratitude.'

'How much do you need and how much are you prepared to pay for it?'

Charlotte became more animated, as if a weight had indeed been lifted from her shoulders. Roland watched as she answered his cousin, explaining the types of cotton yarn she needed to fulfil her most pressing orders, the amount and quality of each, and he marvelled. She was knowledgeable and astute—made that way by a father she did not always agree with—but, even in that strange garb, every inch a woman, young and beautiful and very desirable. He found himself suddenly wanting to tell her so.

The meal ended and the ladies retired to the drawing room, leaving the men to their port.

'An extraordinary woman,' Geoffrey said, handing Roland the bottle from which he filled his glass.

'Yes,' he said, giving the bottle back.

'Entirely unmarriageable, of course.'

'Do you think so?'

'Oh, no doubt of it. No husband worth his salt would put up with her ways.'

'Surely that depends on the husband,' Roland said thoughtfully.

'He would have to be a jackstraw, prepared to subjugate himself for an easy living.'

Roland laughed. 'There are plenty of those about.' He paused. 'Can you really track down cotton yarn for her?'

'Some, probably not all she needs, but enough to keep her going for a week or two.'

'You have my grateful thanks.'

'Your thanks? Does that mean she is more to you than a mere neighbour?'

'She is a delightful adversary.'

'Adversary? You mean over Browhill? Is it that important?'

'I thought it was because of what it meant to my father and also because it has always been part of the estate, but now I am not so sure. What do you think? You are, after all, my heir.'

'For now, yes, but what is that to the point? You will marry and have a nursery full of children.'

'Perhaps, perhaps not.'

Geoffrey looked searchingly at him. 'Oh, come, Roly, you are young and virile, of course you will marry. It is a man's duty, especially when he has an estate like Amerleigh to pass on. There must be any number of young ladies who would jump at the chance to become the Countess of Amerleigh.'

'I believe there are, but none I would feel comfortable with. And at the moment, recovering the estate is taking up all my time.'

'Well, I should forget Browhill, if I were you. Amerleigh is large enough without it and it does not do to be for ever at war with one's neighbours.' He stood up. 'Shall we join the ladies?'

Roland swallowed the remainder of his port and followed his host to where Elizabeth and Charlotte were enjoying a comfortable coze over the teacups. Charlotte was sitting on a sofa next to Elizabeth, her grey skirt and frogged coat a strange contrast to the green taffeta afternoon dress that her hostess wore.

Prompted by Geoffrey, who wanted to know what he had been doing the last six years, he spoke of the war. Bearing in mind there were ladies present, he did not go too closely into the cruelty and barbarity he had witnessed, but spoke of the daily routine, the long marches and the countryside.

'But you liked the life?'

'Yes. It has its good moments, and I do not mean the glory of victory, though that is exhilarating beyond anything you can find in civilian life, but the comradeship, the faith and trust we all put in each other. Every man's life depends on the man next to him.'

'What about the women who go to war?' Charlotte asked. 'How do they go on?'

He had smiled. 'Do you fancy yourself as a soldier, Miss Cartwright? I have known it happen on a very few occasions that women dress in male attire to fight alongside the men, but they are soon discovered.'

'I did not mean that. I meant wives and camp followers—that is what the women who follow the men are called, is it not?'

'Yes, and some are the most faithful, stalwart and courageous women I have ever met. They are often wet, cold and hungry and at other times hot and thirsty. And frequently they are very close to the fighting.'

'They walk?'

'Most of them. Some of the senior officers' wives have carriages, but the terrain is often difficult and frequently they are obliged to abandon them or fall behind and then they become prey to bandits. I would not recommend it, Miss Cartwright.'

'You evidently do not think a married man should take his wife on campaigns.'

'No, for if their husbands are killed, they are left entirely alone. Many marry again immediately in order to have some protection. I would never subject a wife of mine to that possibility.'

'How dreadful,' Elizabeth put in. 'They cannot love their new husbands.'

'I doubt love is even thought of.' He paused and smiled. 'Though you would be surprised at how often love does thrive in such unpromising circumstances. I have seen devotion of wives for husbands and husbands for wives, which is an example to us all. And liaisons made out of necessity that have stood the test of time.'

'But you remained immune?' Charlotte queried.

He looked closely at her, wondering what had prompted the question. 'Miss Cartwright, I am unwed, as you well know.'

'Unwed, yes, unloved—perhaps not?'

'Now that is something else entirely, and we were not speaking of me, but of soldiers in general.'

Realising she had gone too far with her questions, designed to learn more about the man himself, she quickly changed the subject and began to ask him what he thought the outcome of the allied deliberations might be, which led to a general discussion about the future, and that led to the state of the harvest and trade in general, and on that subject Charlotte was easily able to hold her own.

The harmony of the evening should have prepared Roland for a peaceful night, but in that it failed. He slept badly, his mind full of images of Charlotte: Charlotte comforting Tommy, cradling Mrs Biggs's baby in her arms, dancing wildly with her mill workers, sitting on a nursery chair, giggling like a schoolgirl over the signs they were making; Charlotte on horseback and driving the curricle to an inch, Charlotte in a temper, green eyes flashing; Charlotte, her face creased with worry about the *Fair Charlie* and its captain. How could he not adore her?

He woke late and went down to breakfast, only to discover that she was up before him and had left. 'She said she wanted an early start,' Geoffrey told him. 'She is anxious to reassure her workers that the yarn is on its way.'

'Why the devil did you not wake me?'

'She asked me not to. After all, you have your own coach.' He smiled. 'By the way, Elizabeth and I have been invited to a masked ball.'

'I had forgotten all about that. Will you go?'

'Of course. I would not miss it for the world.'

'Then you are welcome to stay at the Hall. I will ask my mother to join us; she will be happy to see you again and show you all the improvements we have made.'

'Thank you. I shall look forward to it. Now, help yourself to breakfast. I must leave if I am to do anything about that cotton.' He hurried away, leaving Roland looking down at the breakfast table where the used plates and crumbled remains of bread told of two people having breakfasted.

'Damn the woman!' he exclaimed. 'Damn! Damn! Damn!' He turned on his heel and went out to the stables to tell Bennett to harness the horses to his carriage. It suddenly seemed important to catch up with her.

Chapter Seven

It was not only her need to be at the mill that had hastened Charlotte's departure, but something within herself she did not want to face. It was the Earl, of course. He had been courtesy itself all the previous evening, chuckling at her jokes, smiling at her in a way that turned her stomach over and set her heart beating like a drum. She had watched the easy way he dealt with his cousin and Mrs Temple and realised being part of a family, however distant, was something to be envied.

And as they talked, she had learned more about the enigmatic man that was Roland Temple, seventh Earl of Amerleigh. What she could not do was relate the man she had come to know to the youth he had been. If she were truly honest with herself, could she blame him for not wanting to marry her when ordered to do so? Would any man with an ounce of pride do it? If he had meekly done as he was told, she would have despised him. What she found more difficult to explain away was the manner in which he had rejected her. He did not know she had heard him, so there was no reason why he should allude to it, and she would not demean herself by asking.

And now she was beholden to him for introducing her to his cousin, arranging a night's lodging and, what was more, helping her over her difficulty with the cotton. It was only a temporary reprieve and she would have to face it again if the *Fair Charlie* did not arrive with raw cotton for the spinners, but it was more than she could have hoped for the morning before when she was combing the warehouses. It had been a very long twenty-four hours, made bearable, even pleasant, by Roland Temple's intervention. And that galled her.

They accomplished the first three changes of horses without any trouble and Talbot, having been told to drive as fast as it was safe to do so, was taking them along at a cracking rate. The roads were rough and though the coach was well sprung, she was jolted from side to side until she thought she would be black and blue before they reached home. It was after the fourth stop that they encountered their first difficulty. The only horses available were an ill-matched foursome that pulled against each other instead of working in harmony. She endured it for half an hour, then put her head out of the door and called up to Talbot to slow them down. He must have taken his attention from the road in order to answer her because one wheel came down heavily into a pothole, which slewed the whole equipage round, but their speed was still carrying them forwards. Charlotte flung herself down with her head in her hands and waited for the impact as the corner of the coach hit one of the trees that lined the road. The sound of panicking horses, rending wood and Talbot's curses filled the air as the coach turned over into the wayside ditch. The padded seats tumbled about her head and dislodged her hat as she was thrown down on to the side now lying in the mud.

Talbot was at the door before she could extricate herself. He wrenched it open and peered down at her, his tousled head outlined against the branches of the tree and sky. 'Miss Charlotte, are you hurt?'

'No.' Dirty water was seeping in from the ditch, but she was laughing as she pulled herself upright and reached for his hand. 'Haul me up, there's a good fellow.'

It was not as easy as it had seemed when the Earl had helped Mr Halliwell to pull his wife out of their coach, but there had been two of them then and Talbot was on his own. Not only that, he had hurt his arm. There did not seem to be anywhere to get a purchase with her feet, but she managed it by stacking the cushions in the muddy water and climbing on those. Then, putting one foot into the shattered woodwork, and with Talbot's good hand to steady her, she emerged to sit on the top. It was an easy matter to scramble down from there, though her skirt was torn and muddy. Once out on the road, she helped the groom free the struggling horses and then turned her attention to his injured arm. 'Is it broken?'

'No, I do not think so, only bruised.'

'No more driving for you for a while,' she said, taking off his kerchief and using it to make a sling. 'How far is it to the next inn?'

'Four or five miles, Miss Charlotte. I could go and fetch help, but I cannot leave you here alone.'

'Then we had better both go.' She tried to cram her hat back on her head, but her hair was so dishevelled it fell off again and she gave up and flung it into the coach.

'What about the carriage?'

'It is no good to anyone, is it? Come on, let's round up the horses.'

'I should think they are in the next shire by now,' he said, looking about him for any sign of the animals that had bolted the minute they were freed.

She fetched her bag from the boot and though he went to take it from her, she would not relinquish it. 'Then let's be off, we can do nothing here.'

They had barely covered two hundred yards when they heard a vehicle on the road behind them, being driven at a furious pace. They stopped and turned towards it.

Roland, who had been dozing, woke up with a start as Bennett brought the horses to a shuddering halt, nearly catapulting him out of his seat. 'What's up?' he shouted.

'Miss Cartwright's coach is in the ditch,' Bennett called out, scrambling down to investigate.

Roland was out like a bullet from a gun. He peered into the coach and, finding it empty except for Charlotte's hat, looking decidedly squashed, searched about for any sign of her or her driver, becoming more and more concerned, imagining her unconscious in the ditch, hurt, even dead beneath the coach, and his heart almost stopped. He bent to try to move the vehicle, but it was stuck firmly in the mud.

'There they are!' Bennett said suddenly, making him look up.

Charlotte and Talbot were in the middle of the road, walking back towards them. 'Thank God!' Roland said. 'Come on, let's go.'

He set off at a run. Bennett returned to the carriage and walked the horses forwards until they were abreast of Charlotte, and stopped just as Roland reached her. He took her shoulders in his hands and looked down at her searchingly. There were smudges of dirt on her face and her hair was tumbling about her shoulders. He stroked it back gently. 'Are you hurt?'

'A few bruises, nothing more. Talbot has injured his arm.'

''Tis nothing, my lord,' the coachman said. 'I can ride beside your man, if you would be so kind as to look after Miss Cartwright.'

'It will be my pleasure.' He turned to Charlotte and guided her towards the coach. 'Come along. You can tell me what happened as we go. We will send someone back to fetch your carriage.'

She climbed in and settled herself, trying to hide

her torn skirt, wondering if she were destined always to be rescued by him. She might have saved herself the bother of rising early and hurtling through the countryside at breakneck speed; he had caught up with her, and now she would have to sit beside him in close proximity for hours and express her gratitude.

'Thank you, my lord,' she said, as he seated himself beside her and ordered Bennett to proceed. 'I believe there is a posting inn a few miles on. I can arrange for my coach to be fetched there.'

'Tell me what happened.'

'I believe we hit a pothole, the coach slewed round and turned over.'

'You must have been travelling at a prodigious speed,' Roland commented.

'I was anxious to reach the mill. And do not dare say it.'

'Say what?' he asked with a smile, guessing her next words.

'More haste less speed. I know it. I shall be delayed by hours.'

'No, for I will convey you to the mill, but not until after you have been home and changed your clothes. You will lose all authority if you are seen like that.'

She realised he was right, which only made her debt to him the greater. 'But my coach…'

'I doubt it can be repaired in hours. It will need to be taken to a coachbuilder and looked at properly, and that means fetching it on a flat wagon. We can arrange it once we arrive in Shrewsbury. There is a good man there who will effect repairs. I can do that after I have taken you home.'

'There is no need to inconvenience yourself, my lord. I can see to it myself.'

'Has no one ever told you it is discourteous to disdain a helping hand when freely offered?'

'I meant no discourtesy.'

'No, it is your infernal independence. What makes you like that? What are you afraid of? Is it simply me or are you the same with everyone?'

She found the question difficult to answer. 'I am not afraid of you, my lord. Why should I be?'

'There is no reason at all,' he said. 'But you seem unable to accept even the smallest service without protest. I do only what any gentleman would do given the circumstances.'

'But you are not just any gentleman, are you, my lord? You are the owner of Amerleigh and every-thing in it, my neighbour and my adversary.'

'That is only because you will have it so. It need not be. I should like us to be friends.'

'Friends?' she queried, trying not to let him see her hands were shaking and her face was on fire. She did not even have a bonnet brim to hide behind.

'Why not? We have much in common. I believe I have said that before. There is Tommy and the other villagers, for one, and our interest in improving their lives, and the more I come to know you, the more I realise that the hard exterior you show to the world is only a front, that beneath it beats the heart of a gentle woman.'

'You are being impertinent, my lord.' It was said with an attempt at severity, but she did not quite succeed and a small sigh escaped her.

He heard it and looked round at her. Captain Hartley was right; she was vulnerable. 'I beg your pardon. Perhaps I have been too long in the army and have forgot the niceties of polite society.'

'Did you ever know them, my lord?'

He looked sharply at her. 'Are you implying my manners were ever less than you would expect of a gentleman? If so, I might remind you we were only lightly acquainted before I went into the army. And you were only a schoolgirl.'

'So you *do* remember.'

'Yes, I remember. What a long time ago that seems.'

'What do you remember?'

'Let me see, a young lady in a dimity dress and pantaloons who could handle a shotgun almost as tall as she was and shoot ten ducks in a row.'

'Oh, yes, I did, didn't I?' she said, laughing at the memory. It had been very conceited of her to attempt it and she had been very relieved when she had made good her boast.

'What did you do with the pig? Did you eat it?'

'No, I could not bear to do that. It was a female. I bred from her and sold the litter. It was my first lesson in business.'

'Who taught you to shoot?'

'My father's gamekeeper. Papa was all in favour, but my governess was horrified.'

'I never saw you with a governess.'

'Oh, I was easily able to escape from them.'

'Them? More than one?'

'Yes, about one a year I should think. I am afraid I was not a very good child.'

He laughed. 'I can believe it. Who taught you to ride?'

'Oh, that was Papa, as soon as I could sit on a little pony. And the stable boy taught me to fish and swim, so you see my upbringing has been out of the ordinary. It was all to fit me for my role as my father's heir.'

'Were there no ladies in your life?'

'Only my governesses, though Mrs Cater—that's my cook-housekeeper—once told me my mother's sister came when Papa was first widowed, but he would not have her near him. She reminded him too much of Mama, I think, and he said he would brook no interference in the way he brought up his daughter.'

'You must have been very lonely.'

'I was never aware that I was, not until Papa died and I found myself owner of Mandeville and in charge of everything. By then, of course, my independence was part of my character. I could not change now, even if I wished to.'

'Oh, I think you could,' he said softly, reaching out and putting a hand over hers as it lay in her lap. 'You can learn to trust.'

'Trust, my lord?' She was aware of the warmth of his hand on hers, but made no attempt to withdraw hers. It was a new experience to be treated with tenderness. No one had done so before, not her father and certainly not the young men who paid court to her fortune and not to her. Was Roland Temple any different?

'Yes, trust your instinct. Instinct is a kind of sixth sense, more a woman's characteristic, I think. Where it comes from I do not know. The heart, perhaps. Listen to it.'

'And what should it be telling me?'

He reached out and put his fingers to the side of her throat, making her suck in her breath. 'Relax,' he said, half-jesting. 'I only wish to establish that it is in good order after all you have been through.'

She could feel her heart thumping as he took her chin in his hand and tipped her face up to his. She could not have pulled herself from his grasp even if she had wanted to and found herself looking up into his eyes and once again she felt the power in him, drawing her towards him, as if she had no will of her own. He searched her face and saw, not the harridan, not the wild woman, but the lonely girl who needed awakening, a girl with slightly parted lips and shining green eyes, tempting him. The temptation was too much to resist; he brought his mouth down to hers. He did not want to hurt her, but to arouse her.

He kissed her skilfully, pressing her into him, so that her body was held against his the whole way from shoulder to thigh. Her breasts were hard against his chest, her legs were pressing against his, her feet almost off the floor. The kiss lingered and deepened, making her squirm, no longer in an effort to resist him, but because what he was doing was sending little shivers of desire down through her belly to the secret places of her groin. She wanted him. She wanted him with an intensity that shocked her. His mouth moved from hers and found its way down past her ear to her throat, kissing, gently and insistently, and transporting her to a heaven she had never even dreamed of. She felt almost boneless, a quivering jelly that had no shape except his.

He drew away at last, holding her at arm's length to look at her. 'My God,' he said, grinning lopsidedly. 'You are all woman after all.'

If he had said anything else, if he had spoken tenderly, if he had shown some remorse for his behaviour, she would have been overjoyed at this awakening, but his words had reminded her of other words uttered in scorn six years before, words she could not forget. Her retort was for the girl she had been, not the woman she had become. 'How dare you! How dare you force yourself on me in that cavalier fashion and then mock me.' She was breathless from his kisses and her face was scarlet with mortification that she had given in so easily.

'I did not force myself on you, you were willing. As for mocking you…'

'Yes, mocking. You are a past master at that. I had a lucky escape six years ago, not that I would ever have considered marrying you .'

His teasing tone disappeared as suddenly as it had come. 'Six years ago?'

'Oh, do not tell me you have forgotten. "She is a hoyden and ought to have been a boy. She is certainly plain enough." *Your* words, Lord Temple.'

'Good God! You were never meant to hear them.'

'Then you should not have spoken so loudly, my lord.'

'If it is any comfort to you, I have regretted them ever since.'

'I do not need comfort, my lord. And my heart is still intact.' Her voice was icy. 'Now, I see we are drawing into an inn yard. I bid you good day.' She did not wait for Bennett or Talbot to open the door, but wrenched it open and jumped down, almost before the wheels had ceased to turn.

He watched as she marched into the inn, her hair bedraggled, her skirt muddy and torn, and he cursed himself for the biggest fool in Christendom. He was reeling from the knowledge that she had heard what he had said to his father, had not only heard, but had obviously been hurt, hurt enough to remember his exact words. While he did not think she had heard them, he could push them to the back of his mind, but now he was consumed with guilt, the more so since he had come to know her and realise how unjust he had been. He did not think she was plain at all, she was beautiful, and if she was a hoyden, it was a trait he could admire in her because she had had to step into her father's shoes with all the responsibility for hundreds of employees on her shoulders. Her burden was even greater than his. Too shocked to do anything else, he silently let her go.

Raised voices coming from the inn alerted him to the fact that something was amiss. He hurried inside to find her arguing hotly with the innkeeper who would not serve her, calling her a filthy gypsy and he wanted none of her like in his establishment. There was nothing for it but to intervene.

'The lady is with me,' he said. 'Her carriage has overturned and she requires assistance, not insults.'

She rounded on him. 'Assistance, not insults, my lord. How apt.' And she gave a cracked laugh.

'My lord?' the innkeeper queried, looking at Roland.

'Yes,' he said. 'I am the Earl of Amerleigh and this lady is under my protection. She requires a room in which to refresh herself, and after that we both require a meal.' He produced a pouch from his tail pocket and jingled it. 'Have fresh horses put to my carriage, ready for us to proceed as soon as we have eaten.' He paused. 'And you had better send someone back up the road to round up the horses from the overturned coach. I am afraid they bolted when they were released.'

'At once, my lord.' He bustled away.

Charlotte walked over to a settle against the wall and sat down, her hands in her lap. Her face was devoid of colour and for the first time he understood what her life was really like, fighting battles and having to win them, simply because she was a woman. He longed to fight them for her, to protect her, but he had forfeited the right. Going over to her, he sat down beside her. Neither spoke. A few minutes later the innkeeper's wife came to them. 'I have a room ready for you, my lady.'

Charlotte did not correct her form of address, but rose silently and followed her from the room and up the stairs to a bedroom that had been hastily made ready for her.

How she managed to answer the woman's questions about the accident and how the Earl had fortuitously come upon her, Charlotte did not know. She could not go downstairs again until she was calmer and once more in control of herself. She declined the help of someone to help her dress and arrange her hair, but, taking off her skirt, asked if it could be cleaned and mended. The woman took it away and she was alone.

She sat and shivered, though she did not know whether she was simply cold or whether she was suffering from the after-effects of that episode with Roland Temple. She had never intended to let him know she had heard his rejection of her and certainly not that she had been hurt by it, but the words in her head had escaped from her mouth. They had been getting along so well, chatting amiably, until his conversation had become a little more intimate. She might not have minded that if he had not so far forgotten himself as to kiss her and then to declare she was a woman as if he had only just discovered it! It had brought the past back as if it had been only the day before. Oh, she might pretend to be affronted, but she knew she was deceiving herself. Inside, inside the core of her, she had wanted him to kiss her, had revelled in the strange sensations that coursed through her, but in the end she had been left confused and unhappy.

Before today, no man had ever touched her, let alone kissed her, but Roland Temple had, and he had aroused a longing in her she could not account for, a longing to be held, to be protected and loved. Had she fallen in love? If she had, it was a foolish thing to do, especially as she had eschewed marriage and especially as the object of her turmoil was Roland Temple. He considered her a hoyden, way beneath him. Then why had he kissed her? To show his dominance? To prove he was her master? To amuse himself at her expense?

She was startled by a knock on the door. Brushing the back of her hand across her face, she discovered her cheeks were wet with tears. No one had ever made her weep, not since she was a small child, and then it had been out of temper and not misery. She made herself call out, 'Who is it?'

'Me.' The voice was easily recognisable even through the thickness of the door. 'How much longer are you going to be? Dinner is on the table and we must be on our way in half an hour.'

How she would have liked to tell him she would go no farther with him, but she was nothing if not a realist and knew there was no help for it. She stiffened her spine. 'I will be down directly.'

He had only gone up in order to satisfy himself she was still on the premises and had not fled, and hearing her voice had made him grimace at his fancies. She was not one to run away; she would always face her adversaries head-on. And to his sorrow, he was one of them. He returned to the dining room and she followed twenty minutes later.

Her skirt had been roughly repaired and her hair had been fastened back with a ribbon; she was, to all intents and purposes, the woman she had been before he kissed her. But there was a subtle difference about her. He could not quite make up his mind what it was. She seemed older, and though she had always been in control, there had before been a light-heartedness about her, a thumbing of her nose at everyone who decried her, an indifference to what people thought of her, which seemed to have disappeared. If it were possible, she was even more self-contained. He did not like or understand this new, cold Charlotte.

She sat down opposite him without speaking and made a pretence of eating. She answered his queries about whether she would have more vegetables, or a little more pie, or whether she preferred coffee or tea, but ventured nothing more than that. When the meal was finished, he conducted her out to the coach, being very careful not to touch her. If he intended to try to make things right with her once they were on the way again, he was thwarted.

'Talbot,' she said, as the coachman prepared to climb up beside Bennett. 'You may ride inside with us. I am sure it does your arm no good to be hanging on to your seat up there.'

He looked startled, shifting his gaze from her to the Earl and back again. It was an order he dare not question. 'Yes, Miss Cartwright,' he said, and helped her in.

Two can play at that game, Roland decided. 'I have a mind to drive,' he said, climbing up beside Bennett and taking the reins from the astonished man's hands.

And thus they arrived at Mandeville, having stopped only to change the post horses for his own at the last stage where they had been left against his return and then Charlotte did not leave the carriage.

Lady Ratcliffe came rushing out as soon as they stopped at the door and was astonished to find the Earl sitting on the box beside his old coachman, and Charlotte being handed down by Talbot, just as if he were the gentleman. 'Whatever has happened?' she cried out. 'Charlotte, just look at you!'

'I will tell you later, Aunt,' she said. 'His lordship is in some haste, so we will not detain him.'

Emily looked up at Roland, who tipped his hat to her. 'Your obedient, my lady. I must go and arrange for Miss Cartwright's coach to be fetched and repaired. Good day to you. Goodbye, Miss Cartwright.' And with that he drove away.

Charlotte stood and watched the coach disappearing out of sight, then with a huge gulp at what might have been, turned to go indoors with Emily fussing round her. 'What happened? Have you had an accident? Have you been set upon and robbed? Oh, you poor dear. Come up to your room and tell me everything. Meg! Meg!' And when the girl appeared, flustered at having been summoned in that peremptory fashion, 'Bring some hot water up to your mistress's room. And be quick about it.'

'Do not fuss, Aunt, I shall be as right as ninepence once I have bathed and changed and rested a little.'

'What was the Earl doing driving his coach? What has happened to yours? Oh, I knew nothing good would come of you rushing off on your own like that.'

'And so you sent the Earl hotfoot after me.' She was stripping off her clothes as she spoke.

'Someone had to save you from your foolishness.'

'Ah, but who was to save me from the Earl?'

'The Earl? Surely not?' She suddenly noticed Charlotte's bruises. 'He never did that?'

'No, of course not.' It might have given her some satisfaction to blame him for the marks, but she could not bring herself to lie. 'My coach overturned and I was thrown about. His lordship rescued me.'

'Oh, thank the good Lord. I thought for a moment—'

'No, Aunt,' she said, determined no one should

ever know what had happened in the coach. 'Nothing so fantastical. His lordship is, after all, a gentleman.'

The old lady seemed not to notice the irony. 'Yes, of course he is.'

The hot water arrived and Meg prepared to help Charlotte wash and change and they could not talk in front of her, so Emily left to tell Mrs Cater the mistress was home and required something to eat. By the time Charlotte had finished her toilette and sat patiently while Meg brushed the tangles from her hair and pinned it up, she was, on the outside at least, once more the Miss Cartwright everyone knew. She went downstairs and, over her meal, gave her aunt a carefully edited account of what had happened, which only confirmed the lady in her opinion that the Earl of Amerleigh was a gentleman of the first order and would make her great-niece a splendid husband.

The last stage of their journey had been made at a fair canter and Roland would not subject the tired horses to further work. He drove home and had his riding horse saddled, then he set off for Shrewsbury, leaving Bennett and Travers to see to the carriage. He had undertaken to arrange for the broken coach to be fetched and he would honour that undertaking, but he doubted Charlotte would allow him to do anything else for her.

Everything had been spoiled and it was his own fault for acting on impulse. If he wanted to live in harmony with Charlotte again, to share the lessons with Tommy, to work together for the good of the village, then he must somehow put things right. Could he explain himself to her satisfaction? Would she let him? And what could he say? 'Sorry,' or 'I did it because I love you', which would be the honourable thing to do, followed by a proposal. 'Sorry' was not enough and she would laugh in his face if he said he had fallen in love with her. And who could blame her for that?

Being on horseback, he could take the short cut over the hills and his errand was soon accomplished and he was on his way home, still musing over what to do about Charlotte. Dipping down into Scofield, he became aware of a noisy crowd outside the Cartwright mill, grouped around a man standing on a flat cart. 'I told you,' he was shouting. 'I told you no good would come of putting a female in charge. Now she has ruined the business and some of you are already without work. Tomorrow it will be a few more and the day after, a few more...'

'What would you have us do?' someone shouted from the crowd.

Roland dismounted and led his horse forwards to the edge of the throng to listen.

'Walk out. Every one of you, walk out and join your unemployed brethren. Without workers she will have to sell to someone who can manage the business properly. I know a gentleman ready to buy her out. Then you will be given jobs again.'

'Ain't goin' to do that.' Roland recognised Beth Biggs, about three rows from the front. 'Miss Cartwright hev always treated us fair. Ain't 'er fault if 'er ship's bin delayed.'

'A sensible employer would have made provision in case such a thing should happen, not let stocks run down to nothing. Proves she's not up to the job.' He turned to the men in his audience. 'Do you like bowing and scraping to a chit of a girl?'

Roland pushed his way forwards. Some, seeing who he was, parted to make way for him, while others continued the argument among themselves. Once at the front, Roland sprang up on to the makeshift platform. He was several inches taller than the man and his commanding presence silenced those near the front. He waited until he had everyone's attention. 'You have been misinformed,' he said. 'There is cotton on its way here. It will arrive tomorrow.' He prayed he was right in saying that. Geoffrey seemed sure that he could manage to find some.

'Too late,' someone called out. 'We've been stood off.'

'Not by Miss Cartwright?'

'No, Mr Brock.'

'That was a mistake.'

'What's it to do with you?' someone else asked. 'What do you know about it?'

'I saw Miss Cartwright in Liverpool yesterday when she arranged for the yarn to be delivered.'

'Oh, yes,' another jeered. 'I'll wager you were having a grand time of it too. Enjoy yourselves, did you, frolicking about while we went home with no wages?'

Roland's jaw tightened. He did not know how to answer that without having a verbal battle with the man and that he would not demean himself to do. His best defence was to attack. 'This man is a troublemaker,' he told his audience, indicating the man on the cart beside him. 'He has his own reasons for inciting you to break the law. I suggest you find out what they are before you listen to him.'

'And what reason do you have for interfering?'

the man demanded. 'This is a matter between Cartwright's and the mill hands.'

'You may think it is, but I am a magistrate, empowered to read the Riot Act, and I am telling you to disperse or face the consequences.' He watched as one or two drifted away. 'Report for work tomorrow,' he said. 'Miss Cartwright will confirm what I have told you.'

They murmured among themselves and began to disperse. Relieved that his strategy had worked, he jumped down and made his way back to his horse and it was then he came face to face with Charlotte, who had just driven up in her curricle. She evidently had two sets of her working apparel, for she was dressed once again in a grey skirt and a tailored jacket, both in pristine condition. He swept off his hat and bowed, stiffly formal. 'Your obedient, Miss Cartwright.'

She had seen him on the cart and her workers grouped round him, but had not been in time to hear all that was said. Could she go nowhere without him turning up? What was he doing addressing her workers? 'Can you not keep your nose out of my business?' she demanded.

'*My* business, ma'am. As a magistrate I am obliged to prevent riotous assembly. I was doing my duty as the law demands.'

She could not quarrel with that, but she had heard him mention her name. 'Riotous?'

'I believe so. One of the men was definitely inciting them to strike. At least they listened to me and dispersed.'

'And what is it I am to confirm?'

'That there is yarn on its way.' He picked up the reins of his horse, which was nibbling the wayside grass, and walked it over until he was standing beside the curricle. 'I gather Mr Brock put them off for lack of it.'

'Then I hope, for everyone's sake, Mr Temple is as good as his word.'

'I can vouch for that, ma'am.' He paused. 'I have just come from Shrewsbury. Your coach will be fetched tomorrow by Guthries. I have asked him to let you know the extent of the repairs and how long it will take. In the meantime, if you have need of a carriage, please avail yourself of mine. If my mother is not using it, that is.'

'Thank you, my lord, but I can manage very well with my curricle.' It was said politely, but there was no warmth there. She had obviously decided he was not to be forgiven and meant to keep him at arm's length.

He put his hand on the side of the vehicle,

preventing her from driving off. 'Miss Cartwright, I hope you will still come to Tommy's lessons. He—we—will miss you if you do not.'

'I am much occupied with more pressing matters at the moment—perhaps later, when I have more time.' She flicked the reins and he stood back to allow her to drive into the mill yard.

The evening was far advanced and in an hour or so it would be dark. He wondered if she would be safe. Would any of the mob wait around to waylay her? Leading his horse, he crossed the road and leaned against a tree where he could see into the yard of the mill. A pool of light from the upstairs office window spilled out onto the curricle and its patient pony. She would certainly not welcome his watchfulness, but he felt responsible for her. He asked himself why, but could think of no convincing reason.

Charlotte did not stay long talking to William Brock. She listened to his explanation of why he had laid off so many hands, then told him that in future he was not to do so without consulting her. 'We nearly had a riot on our hands,' she told him. 'If it had not been for the Earl, they might have come to violence. It is not unknown for a disgruntled mob to set fire to a mill. And it was all so unnecessary. You knew I had gone to buy cotton, you could have waited.'

He mumbled something about petticoat government, but she chose not to hear him, though he would bear watching. There might come a time when he would have to be replaced.

'Now, go home, Mr Brock, it is late. We will plan what to do tomorrow.'

She left him to secure the premises and drove out of the gate and made for Mandeville. She was aware of being followed by Roland and though she was tempted to turn round and send him on his way, she was strangely comforted by his presence. It did not matter what she did—he was determined to look after her. She laughed aloud and urged the pony onwards. It was a cat-and-mouse game, but who was the cat and who the mouse?

Charlotte was busy all the following week. The cotton mill was once again in full production, though she was still left with the problem of more supplies once those Mr Temple had sent were used up. A letter from the Liverpool harbour master had informed her that the captain of an incoming schooner had seen what he believed was the *Fair Charlie* dismasted and wallowing in heavy seas.

Struggling with his own vessel, he had been unable to get close enough to hale the stricken ship and had no idea what had happened, but she was so low in the water he could not think she could make landfall before sinking. Quite apart from the loss of the crew whom Charlotte genuinely mourned, it was a blow from which it would be difficult to recover and she would be at the mercy of independent importers for her cotton and exporters to take her finished cloth. She felt as if she were losing control, but she could not allow that to happen and spent days searching out contracts. For the first time she felt her gender was against her, but she persevered. Not to do so would mean throwing her mill hands out of work. In comparison to everything else, the coming ball seemed unimportant.

Lady Ratcliffe, of course, did not think so. As far as she was concerned, it was to be the event of the year and nothing less than Charlotte's betrothal to the Earl of Amerleigh would satisfy her. Charlotte had given up protesting; her great-aunt would see her error in the fullness of time.

When at last she found time to go into Shrewsbury to choose a costume, there was very little left; everyone had been there before her. She was offered elaborate gowns, which needed no end of corseting, and coiffures that would take hours to create—that is, if they could be created on her wild hair. She could just imagine Meg's dismay at being asked to do it. The alternatives were flimsy bits of nonsense that were hardly respectable. Or animals. She chose to dress as a black cat, hoping the disguise would be complete enough to hide her anguish. The anguish would be engendered by the sight of Roland Temple and the knowledge that, whatever happened, she must keep him at a distance. It was the only way to stay in control.

The week had been wet but the day itself produced thunderstorm after thunderstorm all day long and Charlotte wondered aloud how many of her guests would be put off by the weather. 'None,' Emily said. 'Everyone is agog to see Mandeville and as the Earl is coming…'

'Perhaps he will not.'

'Nonsense. Of course he will. He has accepted and I do not believe he is a man to go back on his word.'

Her great-aunt had no idea what had transpired between her and the Earl, that they were in a state of open warfare. And for what? A little strip of land? A grudge held for years? Or a kiss that had set her in such inner turmoil she could hardly go about her daily business for fear of coming upon him, or sleep at night for reliving it? 'No, I am sure he never does,' she said, thinking of other words spoken in the heat of the moment years before. 'And neither am I.'

Emily looked at her sharply, wondering what her great-niece meant by that. 'I hope you are not going to keep worrying about business all through the evening, Charlotte. The mill is not going to fall down simply because you take a little time off. If you want to be accepted in society, this preoccupation with business must surely stop. Ladies do not interest themselves in such things.'

'And who is to do it if I do not?'

'Your husband.'

'But I have no husband.'

'Nor will you have unless you observe the proprieties and learn to conduct yourself in a more fitting manner.'

Charlotte gave up the argument and her aunt was soon distracted by other things. Given a free hand, she had the servants scurrying hither and thither with vases of flowers and trays of glasses, urging people to do several jobs at once and scolding them when inevitably they failed. The maids, on hands and knees, had polished the floor of the ballroom until it gleamed like a mirror. The footman, even the temporary ones, had been given new livery, and the butler stood in his pantry, counting bottles of wine and champagne. Lamps had been strung up in the trees in the garden and a double row of them illuminated the drive.

Afraid that the weather would delay the musicians she had hired for the evening, her ladyship had sent a message requiring them to come early and they had to be fed along with everyone else and Mrs Cater was throwing a tantrum. How could she be expected to cook for the army of helpers at the same time as overseeing the caterers who were providing the elaborate supper to be served to over a hundred guests? she demanded to know.

'It is time you were going up to change,' her ladyship said, coming upon Charlotte in the kitchen with an apron tied round her business dress, helping Mrs Cater, an activity her ladyship deplored. 'Your guests must not find you unprepared to receive them.'

She went up to her room, stripped off her dress and lay down on the bed to wait for Meg to bring her hot water to wash. She had hardly slept the night before and had had such a worrying day, sleep overcame her. She was woken by the maid at seven o'clock.

'Why, you have not even taken your costume from its box,' Meg said, pouring hot water into the bowl.

'There was no reason to do so before I was ready to put it on.' Charlotte said, stripping off the underwear she had been sleeping in and washing before putting on a thin chemise and drawers and reaching out for the costume Meg had taken from its wrapping. It was of black velvet, very tight fitting, covering her from head to toe, far too daring for a country ball and, according to Lady Ratcliffe, to whom she had shown it when she brought it home, positively indecent and would horrify the Earl. That last remark was enough to strengthen her resolve to wear it.

There was a long black sarcenet pelisse to go over it, which would float around her and the mask would hide everything but her eyes and mouth and that was good. She did not want to betray what she was feeling to anyone, least of all the Earl of Amerleigh. It needed no jewellery, no trimming, no anything, except a small pocket for her handkerchief. Even her hair was covered by the velvet head and so all she had to do was brush it and push it up out of the way. She looked plain, simple and anonymous. Taking a deep breath, she left the sanctuary of her room and went downstairs.

Miraculously the rain had eased and the guests were arriving. Lord and Lady Brandon and Martha were the first. Sir Gordon was in ordinary evening dress, but her ladyship was dressed as Queen Elizabeth in a huge brocade farthingale with a stiff lace ruff around her plump neck. Martha was dressed as Columbine, making Charlotte wonder if the Earl might arrive as Harlequin. He would not be the only one, she realised, when the Reverend Mr Elliott, Mrs Elliott and Martin arrived. Martin was Harlequin.

'Now why did he have to go and do that?' Lady Brandon said in annoyance. Then, to Martha, 'Did you know he was coming as Harlequin?'

'No, Mama, but I told him I was to be Columbine.'

'Foolish girl!' her mother exclaimed.

Other guests followed them, kings and queens, knights and nymphs, strange animals, historical figures, maids and highwaymen, twittering and excited, exclaiming over the decorations as they made their way into the ballroom where the orchestra, replete on Mrs Cater's cooking, were tuning their instruments ready for the first dance. It wanted only the arrival of the Earl of Amerleigh to make the evening a huge success.

* * *

Roland had ridden to Shrewsbury to see Charles Mountford. The day before, poking about in the attics to find a costume for the ball, he had come across a chest full of very old documents. Some of them were crumbling to dust, others illegible and written in a script he could not decipher. One had a huge red seal and appeared to be signed by a Royal hand. Realising they might be the ancient deeds to Amerleigh Hall, he had decided to take them to Mountford at once.

'It will be interesting to learn if the old family story of the estate being given to my ancestor by Queen Elizabeth is correct,' he told him. 'Or perhaps it is a fairy tale.'

'If it is what I think it is, this will detail exactly what land is included,' Charles said, scrutinising them with a magnifying glass. 'Some may have been acquired later, during the war between King and Parliament, for instance. You need to show them to an expert who can decipher them. Professor Lundy would do it, but he lives in London.'

'I see. You cannot read it?'

'Only a few words here and there, not enough to be sure I was advising you correctly.'

'Then perhaps I'll take them myself when I have time.'

'Very well. Now you are here, have you time to go over the financial affairs of the estate? I think you need to reconsider your options.'

They had spent some time on the subject. The money he had brought back with him from Portugal was almost exhausted, though he did have his annuity, his half-pay from the army and the income from the tenants' rents, all of which would have to be carefully husbanded. 'Of course, if you had the income from the Browhill mine, it might help,' Mountford said.

'No, I have told you not to proceed with that litigation and I will not change my mind.'

'Then the best advice I can you give you, my lord, is to marry the present owner of Browhill. It would be the best way of repossessing it.'

'And that is advice I can well do without,' Roland said sharply, effectively ending the conversation. He took his leave and rode home with a great deal on his mind.

Tonight was the night of the ball. He had wondered if his invitation might be withdrawn, or, if it were not, whether to stay away. Charlotte would surely not wish to see him? On the other hand, his absence would cause comment. After telling himself over and over again he did not want to see her, he knew he did, that the hours and days when he did not meet her seemed barren and uninteresting. He must talk to her and make her understand that the youth who had so cruelly rejected her six years before was not the man who had come back to take up his responsibilities as Earl of Amerleigh, that he could not go on, day by day, doing his duty, looking after the estate, making plans for his deaf school, without her forgiveness. Or was that going too far?

He hurried into the house to find Geoffrey and Elizabeth with his mother and Miles ready to leave for the ball. Geoffrey was dressed as a Tudor gentleman and Elizabeth a lady of the same period, while a bewigged Miles wore satin small clothes and a pink brocade coat with enormous pockets, his wrists covered in cascading lace. The Countess was not in costume, but in a lilac evening gown trimmed with white lace. 'Roland, you will make us all late,' she said. 'Where have you been?'

'To see Mountford. You go on in the coach, I will follow in the gig.'

'You will get soaked.'

'No, the rain has stopped.'

He declined anything to eat, saying he would drink a dish of chocolate in his room while he changed. He had found a basket full of costumes in the attic; he supposed that many of the lavish entertainments his father had put on had included costume balls for which he had obviously provided the clothes. He had chosen to be a medieval knight, wearing a cross of St George on his jerkin. The imitation chainmail was knitted in some thick shiny material, but the effect was good and nothing like as heavy as the real thing. It also had a helmet with a visor, which would do away with the need for a mask. He pulled on his boots and fastened a sword belt about his waist. 'How do I look?' he asked Travers.

Travers grinned. 'Will I saddle your horse? A knight cannot go rescuing damsels in distress without his trusty charger, can he?'

'Corporal, I do believe you are bamming me.'

'No, sir, not at all, sir.' But his smile was almost enough to split his face.

'Then go and bring the gig round. I will drive myself. And there is no need for you to wait up for me.' He flung a cloak over his costume and went downstairs, wondering what the evening might have in store for him.

Chapter Eight

Because he arrived after everyone else had gone in, Roland's entrance was observed by the whole company. His costume was no disguise either; he was so tall and broad-shouldered, his figure could not be mistaken. He looked about him for his hostess among the costume-clad figures that crowded the room. Surely, even in disguise, he would know her? Lady Ratcliffe hurried forward to greet him.

'My lord, I am pleased you have come. The dancing has already begun. Miss Cartwright is about somewhere. I will go and find her.'

'Please do not trouble yourself, my lady,' Roland said. 'I will go and join my mother.' He had seen the Countess sitting with Lady Gilford and smiled to himself. So Lady Gilford had overcome her scruples over Charlotte's lack of breeding and

decided to attend, had she? There was no sign of
her husband. He crossed the room and made his
bow to the ladies and then stationed himself
behind his mother's chair to watch proceedings
and look out for Charlotte, though how he was
going to contrive to see her alone, he did not yet
know.

Charlotte had seen him and shrank behind Miles
Hartley with whom she was dancing, peeping over
his shoulder as the Earl spoke to her great-aunt
and then moved forwards into the room. He
looked magnificent in his costume; Saint George,
ready to do battle for a lady's honour, and all the
ladies present were sighing over him. She was not
sighing, she was crying inside, and if she were not
very careful the tears would come to the surface.

'Please excuse me,' she said. 'I must go and see
that supper will be ready on time.' And with that
she hurried away. She felt sick. And the reason she
felt so ill was that she had suddenly realised she
was in love with the Earl, hopelessly and irrevo-
cably in love with him. How could she have let it
happen? How could she have been so foolish as
to forget they were enemies, that he had cruelly
disdained her and they were at daggers drawn
over a piece of land that neither was prepared to
relinquish?

Roland saw her go and wondered what they had been talking about so earnestly, but he could do nothing about it because the musicians had begun another dance and the floor was crowded. He bowed before the young lady nearest to him and only then did he realise it was Martha dressed as Columbine. He smiled and held out his hand. 'Will you do me the honour of dancing with me?'

'Thank you, my lord,' she said, looking anxiously about her for her mother.

'Oh, it is all going according to plan.' Lady Brandon had come upon Charlotte in the dining room, where she was standing by the window looking out onto a damp garden. Behind her several tables were laden with food of every description: hams, chicken legs, fish, pastries, jellies, cakes.

'What plan?' She was still thinking about Roland and did not welcome the intrusion.

'Why, the Earl is dancing with Martha now. She will bring him up to the mark. I should not be at all surprised if he does not ask Brandon for an interview later.' When Charlotte made no response to this, she added, 'What is the matter with you, Charlotte? I never saw such a Friday face in all my life and there is no reason for it. The ball is a prodigious success and you will find yourself being invited to everything from now on.'

Lady Brandon had set her heart on making a Countess of Martha. Her daughter, of course, had no say in the matter. Would his lordship have any say either? Charlotte believed he was strong enough to resist, if he wanted to. But supposing he did not? Supposing he married Martha? Being a friend and confidante of Lady Brandon, she would be thrown even more into his company and it would be unbearable. But she was no simpering schoolgirl, she told herself sternly; she was a mature businesswoman who knew how to best an opponent. He was an opponent and she would get the better of him and of her own wayward desires, one way or another. She forced herself to sound bright. 'There is nothing wrong, Catherine. I was making sure everything is ready for supper.'

'You have servants for that. You should be mixing with your guests and making sure the young people have partners.'

'I know. I am just going back.'

She returned to the ballroom and set about her duties as a hostess with a bright smile, bringing young men and young ladies together to dance, chatting to the older men, laughing when they teased her about her costume, pretending not to notice the disapproval of the matrons. This was how it was going to be in future, this false brightness, this pretending, even with Roland Temple. Especially with him.

Roland was aware of her, but whenever he approached her, she found some reason to disappear, and just when he decided he would have to force the issue, he saw Lady Brandon crossing the room towards him, like an eagle bent on its prey. He looked about for a way of escape, but before he could do so, he felt someone pluck at his sleeve. Miss Brandon was looking up at him with an expression on her face he could only interpret as pleading. 'My lord, I must speak to you before Mama reaches us. Come with me, please.'

He had no time to demur, for Lady Brandon was very close and Martha, with a bright smile for her mother, took his arm and almost dragged him from the room, in full view of everyone. He groaned inwardly, but was too polite to resist, as she led him to the library and shut the door after them. She stood facing him, breathing heavily. 'My lord, it is important I speak to you.'

He bowed. 'I am at your service.'

'My lord, please do not let Mama bully you…'

'Bully me?'

'Bully you into offering for me.'

'Rest assured, Miss Brandon, she could not do anything that would influence me one way or another.'

'I am glad.'

He smiled ruefully. 'I thought you were intent on bringing Mr Elliott up to the mark. Is he still hanging back? I cannot think why he should be so dilatory. You are a charming young lady and just right for him.'

'The foolish man has decided I am above his touch, that he does not want people to think he is after my fortune and has told me he means to leave the field clear for you.'

'Good God! Miss Brandon, I hope that nothing I have said has led you to suppose…'

'No, of course not, it is all in Mama's head and of course she must boast of it in front of Martin. I truly do not know what to do.'

He must not appear too relieved, but how to answer he did not know. 'Can you not tell Mr Elliott the truth?'

'I cannot do that!' she said, aghast at the suggestion. 'In any case, while Mama thinks I have a chance with you, she will not entertain him.'

'Then what shall we say to your mama?' he asked.

'Nothing. I wish you would not accept Mama's invitations so frequently. You are filling her with hope.'

'Am I? I was only being polite and thankful to be received into society after my long absence.'

'I know that, but you know how people gossip and it has enhanced Mama's expectations. Could you not behave a little coldly towards me? Then perhaps Martin will see…'

The young lady was stronger than he had previously imagined, but she was also naïve and had not realised the consequences of taking him off to be alone with him. He was at fault for not resisting, but that would have caused just as much comment. 'Miss Brandon, I am afraid that would not serve. Everyone saw us leave the room and we have been talking together without a chaperon for several minutes. You cannot say, that in all that time, I did not make an offer. It would humiliate you and make me less than a gentleman.'

'Oh, I had not thought of that!' She gasped. Then her face fell. 'Do not tell me you feel obliged to offer for me after all?'

'I ought to.' He paused. Some way out of the dilemma had to be found. 'Shall we say I offered and you refused? Will that do?'

She smiled, obviously relieved. 'You would not mind?'

'No, it is the least I can do. But will your mama accept that?'

'I think so. I hope so. I hope Martin believes it…'

'Then, with your permission, I shall act the rejected suitor and take my leave. You may say I am heartbroken, if you wish.' He smiled, aware of the irony of the situation. 'If you like, I will act the part and take myself off for a few days to recover.'

'Thank you, my lord, but I wish you would not inconvenience yourself.'

Lady Brandon almost tumbled through the door as he was taking his leave 'Oh, there you both are! May I offer my felicitations?' She was so eager, she looked about to burst out of her tight pink bodice.

'No, Mama, you may not,' Martha put in, far more forcefully than Roland would have expected of her. 'Lord Temple and I have decided we should not suit.'

'Not suit!' her ladyship echoed, her mouth open in consternation.

'Your daughter has rejected me, my lady,' he said. 'Now, if you will excuse me.' He bowed to Lady Brandon and then turned to Martha, taking her hand and bending over to kiss the back of it. 'Miss Brandon, I wish you happy.'

He heard her ladyship's voice as he left. 'Martha, whatever were you thinking about? After all the trouble I have taken…'

He returned to the ballroom and made his way over to the Countess. All the ladies seemed to be whispering and looking towards him over their fans. They had seen him go off with Miss Brandon and had come to their own conclusions. He had been alone with her for several minutes so he must have offered and of course she had accepted. What young lady would not? Would Miss Cartwright allow the announcement to be made at her ball or must they wait for an official notice in the newspaper? He wondered wryly what they would say when they learned there was to be no wedding. 'I find I must leave,' he told his mother quietly.

'Why?'

'I cannot explain now. You stay and enjoy yourself. Geoffrey will see you home safely when you are ready. We will talk tomorrow.'

'Miss Brandon?'

'Yes and no.'

She sighed. 'Very well.'

A brief look about him ascertained Charlotte was not in the room and Lady Ratcliffe was in earnest conversation with Lady Brandon, who had followed him into the ballroom. He left the room and, instead of asking a footman to have his gig brought to the front entrance, found his way out of a back door and took a narrow path across the garden towards the stables. He would not say goodbye to anyone else; there was no one to whom he could bid *adieu* except Charlotte, and she was determined not to speak to him. The world would think he had left because of his disappointment, but that would not matter if it meant Miss Brandon could hold her head up in the community and not be laughed at for chasing him in vain.

Once he left the light shed on the garden by the lanterns close to the house, the darkness seemed absolute and he had to negotiate his way between bushes of buddleia and hibiscus, which was why he did not at first notice the dark shape on the path in front of him, a black, catlike shape. Not until she had bumped into him and he had his arms around her to save her from falling did he realise who it was.

'Charlotte!'

She had seen him go off with Martha and had come to the same conclusion as everyone else. That he should make his offer at her ball compounded her wretchedness and, finding the atmosphere of expectation in the ballroom too much to bear, had come out into the garden to compose herself. She was angry with herself for caring so much. And now she was even angrier for blundering into him. 'Let me go!'

He released her immediately, but as the path was narrow and he was going away from the house and she towards it, they had to pass each before they could continue. They stood facing each other, both undecided as to how to proceed.

'What are you doing out here?' he asked. The moon came out from behind a cloud and he could see her more plainly. The costume outlined every curve of her delectable figure and even the silly head that obscured most of her face only served to enhance its perfect contours. How could he have ever thought she was plain? 'The air is still damp. Are you not cold?'

'I am as warm as toast,' she snapped. 'I came out for fresh air.'

'I am glad you did. I need to speak to you, to explain…'

'Explain? I need no explanation. The truth is that in six years with the army you have not learned how to behave towards a lady. Oh, but I forgot, I am not a lady, I am a hoyden. Hoydens are tough as old leather, they do not have finer feelings, one may insult them with impunity…'

'You do not understand.'

'What is there to misunderstand? I heard you plainly enough.'

'And have held it against me ever since.'

'You are conceited if you think that, my lord. Until…' She paused and gulped. 'Until you were so ill mannered as to lay hands on me, I had forgot all about it.'

'Lay hands on you! Is that what you call it?'

'What else? No one has ever done anything like that to me before.'

'No, I wager they have not,' he said quietly, realising that in all probability she had always been deprived of physical contact, even as a child, and children needed hugs every bit as much as education and discipline. He longed to take her into his arms to try to make up for it.

She peered at him in the darkness, taken aback by his change of tone. How could he be so scathing one minute and gentle the next? He did not move out of her way and she stood undecided whether to ask him to stand aside or try to force her way past him. His very presence was upsetting her carefully managed composure. Inside the furry costume she was shaking and her breath was coming in great gulps. Anger was her only defence. 'I am surprised you had the effrontery to attend this evening.'

'I was under the impression I had been invited.'

'That was before…'

'Before what?'

'Before you insulted me.'

'I meant no insult.'

'No? To kiss one woman when intent on offering for another is an insult to both in my book.'

He could not deny that without humiliating Miss Brandon. 'You do not understand…'

'I understand perfectly well. It is permissible to kiss a hoyden because a hoyden cannot expect the courtesy and chivalry due to a lady of rank.'

He laughed softly. 'A *real* hoyden would not care so much.'

'You are mistaken if you think I care, my lord.'

'Oh, I think you do. Shall we put it to the test?'

Before she could do a thing about it, he had taken her chin in his hand and turned her face up to his and was scrutinising it as if committing its features to memory. She tried to struggle, but was powerless as his mouth came down on hers. His hand left her chin and went round behind her back, drawing her towards him, enclosing her in an embrace that was both powerful and tender. She felt herself slacken, felt her mouth open, felt her hands creep up around his neck, as if she had no will. He held her for a second, two seconds, a week, an age—she did not know how long it was before she suddenly came to her senses and started struggling furiously, hitting him about the shoulders and body with her fists, using words that were far from ladylike. Her hand came into contact with the hilt of his sword and she pulled it out of its scabbard and pointed it at him. 'Come a step nearer and this will be in your black heart.'

'Sharp as needles,' he said, laughing and taking it from her with little effort. It was, after all, not a weapon of honed steel designed to kill, but a toy for dressing up and she could never have used it in any case. 'You chose the right costume, I must say. A cat, a green-eyed, scratching feline. Sheath your claws, kitten, you are in no danger from me.'

'I wish I could say your costume was equally well chosen. But St George! The chivalrous knight, the slayer of dragons, the defender of womanhood. It is meant to be a joke, of course.'

He smiled crookedly. 'Of course.'

'At least you are honest.'

'Yes,' he said, his voice suddenly losing its edge and becoming soft. 'I am honest enough to admit my fault.' He stood looking down at her by the light of a pale moon, which had come out from behind one of the blustering clouds. Her lovely eyes beneath the catlike head-dress were huge and shocked. 'Charlotte, please listen to me…'

'Go back to Miss Brandon,' she told him. 'I wish

you happy. She will never know from me what a charlatan you are.'

He stood a moment longer, but he knew there was nothing he could usefully say, except a murmured, 'Goodbye, Charlotte.' Then he stepped past her and went on his way. He did not look back or he might have seen her, standing looking after him, her eyes swimming with tears. She brushed them away angrily. He had kissed her because he could, because it gave him a sense of superiority and put her in her place, no more than that. Thank goodness she had not been so foolish as to offer him Browhill. She scrubbed at her eyes and returned to the house.

How she endured the remainder of the evening, she never knew. The ball appeared to be a great success, there was dancing and laughter and gaiety and the supper was pronounced the most lavish anyone could remember, though she was aware of a certain tension in the air, as if everyone was waiting for something to happen. The matrons muttered behind their fans, while the men in little groups laughed a little too loudly, and Lady Ratcliffe was as busy as ever acting the hostess and urging Charlotte to look a little more pleased with the way things were going, which she made every effort to do. It was thanks to her father's teaching that she was able to achieve it. And when the time came to unmask, she stood beside her great-aunt as everyone revealed themselves, though most already knew each other. After that there were fireworks that rivalled even those she had put on for her workers. She smiled and received the congratulations of her guests as they departed and no one knew the misery in her heart.

When the last of them had gone, she did not stay to go over the events of the evening with her great-aunt, but pleaded a headache and went straight up to her room, where she dismissed Meg and stripped off that dreadful costume. It had not been a good idea; the Earl had made fun of it, as her great-aunt had predicted. And even in her grief she had been aware of the whispers about him and Martha. A gentleman did not take a lady off unchaperoned unless it was to propose to her. That he had done so at her ball added insult to injury as far as Charlotte was concerned. Martha had undoubtedly accepted him and in due course they would be married and live at Amerleigh Hall. How could she go on seeing him day by day, pretending civility and never tell him, or anyone, what was in her heart and mind? But there was no alternative and she must bear it. She had said she did not care, so now she must prove it.

* * *

Roland slept badly, his mind going over and over the encounter with Charlotte in the garden, the hurtful things they had said to each other, words, like those uttered six years before, which could not be unsaid. But words were not everything. He had not imagined it the first time he kissed her; she felt as passionately as he did, it had been evident in every move she made, the way her lips sought his even when he was ready to break apart, the way her arms wound round him, setting him on fire with desire. And her violent reaction—what was that but a very feminine fury at her own weakness? But apart from satisfying his curiosity on that score, what had he achieved by behaving so badly? Nothing.

He rose and was halfway through his breakfast when Geoffrey joined him. 'You are up betimes, cousin, considering the time you arrived back from the ball,' he greeted him.

Geoffrey sat down and helped himself to eggs and ham. 'Did we wake you?'

'No, I was not asleep.'

'Plenty to think about, eh?'

'You heard?'

'Heard there was something going on. Whispers all round and Lady Brandon flitting about like a bee, taking the news from flower to flower.'

'Did you hear what was said?'

'Only from Lady Gilford, and you know how things become exaggerated with repetition. I should pay no heed to it.'

'Come on, tell me the worst.'

'That Miss Brandon turned you down on account of your doubtful character.'

'My doubtful character!' he exclaimed. 'What did she mean by that?'

'Two nights away with Miss Cartwright, and her coming back in your coach for all the world as if she had been rolling around in the hay. Her hat lost and her dress torn…'

'You knew the truth of that and so did Lady Ratcliffe. Surely one of you said something? It is a vicious slur on my good name, let alone the reputation of Miss Cartwright.'

'I tried, but no one would take any notice of me and I never heard Lady Ratcliffe say a word on the subject, though I swear she heard it. It's my belief she would like to see you leg-shackled to the hoyden.'

'She is not a hoyden!' Roland almost shouted the words.

'Well, whatever her reputation was like before, it is certainly ruined now, unless you marry her and you can hardly do that, can you?'

Roland groaned inwardly. In trying to do his best for everyone, he seemed to have done just the opposite. He could not tell Charlotte he had not offered for Miss Brandon and the fact that the young lady had turned him down would carry no weight with her; for all she knew, Miss Brandon had been his first choice. As for the vicious rumour, what could he say to Charlotte about that, except to ask her to marry him? But Geoffrey was right, he could not do that so soon after having apparently offered for Miss Brandon. It would only add fuel to the rumours. He was in a cleft stick and his position in the village rapidly becoming untenable. He left his cousin munching toast, and set off for the dower house.

His mother had not yet put in an appearance downstairs, but on being told he was waiting for her, she slipped into a grey silk dressing gown and came down to join him. 'Come and have breakfast with me,' she said, leading the way into the dining room.

'I have had my breakfast.'

'Then come and sit with me while I have mine and tell me what happened last night. You told me Miss Brandon had her heart set on Mr Elliott.'

'So she has. Things were taken out of my hands somewhat.'

'So I noticed, and so did everyone else.' She seated herself at the table and indicated the chair next to her. 'Sit down, do, and at least have a cup of coffee.' She filled two cups from the jug at her elbow and pushed one towards him. 'I assume you offered for her?'

'Of course not. The silly girl dragged me off to beg me *not* to, but hadn't realized the consequences of her actions.'

'And Lady Brandon knows this?'

'She believes I offered and her daughter refused me. Miss Brandon and I agreed on this to save her reputation.'

'And you think that is an end of it, Roland? You must know it is not. She will not take that as her daughter's final decision, you may be sure. Young ladies often refuse a first time they are asked, only to give in later.'

'That is why I said I would go away to recover from my disappointment and give her time to bring her mother round to accepting her real choice.'

'Go away, Roland?' she asked in consternation.

'Yes. When she has accomplished that, I can return.'

'But that could take an age! Lady Brandon is the most stubborn and self-opinionated woman in the world. She will nag Martha to death.'

'But there is nothing she can do about it if I am not here, is there?'

'And what about all the work you have been doing here? You cannot abandon it.'

'No, but I am sure Geoffrey will keep an eye on the place for me and make sure everything runs smoothly while I am away.'

'Roland, these are drastic steps to take.'

'Drastic cures for drastic ills, Mama. It is for the best. I cannot bear another young lady to be hurt by me…'

'*Another* young lady? Roland, what do you mean? What other young lady has been hurt by you?'

'I have discovered Miss Cartwright heard me telling my father I would not marry her and the reason I gave, for which I am heartily ashamed.'

'But that was six years ago and you were only a stripling.'

'Nevertheless they were not the words of anyone calling himself a gentleman, as she has taken pains to remind me.'

'Have you not apologised?'

'Yes, Mama, but the lady is not disposed to accept my apology.'

'I see,' she said slowly, as understanding dawned. 'Then perhaps a week or two away might be beneficial. When are you going?'

'As soon as I am ready. There are one or two things I must clear up before I go.'

'I wish it had not come to this, Roland. I have been so happy to have you home these last weeks and the work you have done on the estate is beginning to pay off, everyone is more cheerful because of it. But if you have made up your mind, I will not attempt to dissuade you. I will try to see if I can influence Lady Brandon to accept Martha's choice of suitor, then you can come back the sooner.'

'I have been thinking about that myself. I believe the living at Scofield is in my gift and is due to become vacant shortly. Do you think it will help if I offer it to Mr Martin Elliott?'

'Oh, I am sure it will.' She rose and walked over to where he sat and bent to kiss each cheek in turn. 'Bless you, my son.'

She released him and he stood up and, with a parting embrace, left her. Returning to the Hall, he saddled his horse and set out for a ride, wondering if he might meet Charlotte doing the same thing, though he had little hope of it. The ball had not finished until nearly dawn and she was bound to rise late. Unless, like him, she could not sleep. If he did meet her, would she listen to what he had to say, any more than she had listened the night before? What was he going to say? That he was sorry his actions had led to gossip about her, that he had fallen deeply in love with her? Ask her to marry him? It might save her reputation, but it would certainly tarnish his in the eyes of Lady Brandon and the villagers who believed him smitten with Martha Brandon. Was ever a man in such a coil?

After days of rain, the air was fresh and clean and the meadows lush. Little rivulets of sparkling water found their way down between the stones on the hillside. In some places the ground was boggy and he picked his way carefully. The underground waterways would be rushing along in torrents, he mused, and that set him thinking of Browhill. The water in the lower levels would be higher than ever and unworkable. He still had not told Charlotte he was not proceeding with his claim and evidently Mountford had not. He turned his horse towards the mine, though he was sure no one would be working on a Sunday morning.

He was surprised to find the great wheel turning and several men hurrying about with ropes and buckets. Robert Bailey, the engineer, was directing some sort of operation. Roland dismounted and approached him. 'What's afoot?' he asked him.

'There's two men trapped underground, my

lord. They were working at the lowest level yesterday when a great rush of water broke through and filled the tunnel. It rises slightly towards the face and they are stuck there.'

'You know they are alive?'

'Yes, the spot where they are is just below a higher level and the men working there heard them banging, but if the water rises any more, they will undoubtedly drown. The pump is having little effect.'

'So what are you doing?'

'We are trying to break through from above, but we dare not use explosives. It is a question of hammering out the rock to reach them and the men have been going down in turns all night. The trouble is that we have no idea how much air they have. Time is not on our side.'

'Can I help?'

'I do not see how you can, my lord.' As he spoke two workers came up from below. They were stripped to the waist and glistening with sweat, and obviously exhausted. They sprawled on the ground. Bailey and Roland went over to them.

'We'll never do it,' one of them said. 'We've been down there three hours and hardly made an impression.'

'Are they still banging?' Bailey asked.

'I thought I heard them, but 'tis difficult to be sure. 'Tis not as loud as it was.'

'Who's next down?'

'Joe and Paddy.'

Roland was thoughtful, remembering boyhood adventures with Jacob Edwards exploring the holes and caves in the hills. Their parents never knew or they would certainly have been forbidden to go anywhere near them. 'There might be some way of diverting the water and draining the level, enough for the men to be able to wade out.' He went back to where the engineer had left his maps and began studying them. 'I remember when I was a child, we used to explore the underground caves. Some were dry, some had water in them. If we could find the source of the water and divert it…' He pointed. 'There. There is a sump there. I remember we used to dive through it.' He began stripping off his clothes until he was down to breeches and shirt. 'You keep on trying to reach them, I am going down to have a look.'

'My lord,' Bailey protested. 'It is too risky.'

Roland ignored him, grabbed a helmet with a candle on it and started to run up the side of the hill towards the smelting mill. 'Bring a rope,' he shouted behind him. 'A hammer, a drill and some explosive.'

A quick search about the tussocky grass and boulders that littered the hillside revealed a hole. It was smaller than he remembered it, but at the time he had been a boy, not a full-grown man. Robert Bailey followed with two men, one of whom carried a coil of rope. Roland took it from him and tied the end round him under his arms while another man lit the candle on the helmet and handed it to him. 'Pay it out as I go,' he said, lowering himself into the hole and taking the tools and explosive from the engineer. 'If I give two sharp tugs, that means haul me up, and three tugs means tie it off. I'll release myself before carrying on.'

'My lord, I do not think you should be doing this.'

He ignored the engineer's protests. 'Tell your men not to give up digging.' He was almost out of sight when he added. 'Has anyone alerted Miss Cartwright?'

'No, we did not want to worry her in the middle of her ball.'

'I think she would want to be told,' he said and continued to descend. He smiled grimly. Charlotte would be furious at being kept in the dark, especially if lives were lost and the rumour went round that she had been enjoying herself while her men were dying.

* * *

Charlotte, who had spent what was left of the night after the ball ended going over and over her predicament, tossing ideas this way and that to no good effect, emerged from her darkened room the next morning and told Emily her headache had gone. She had drunk too much wine, become too hot and gone outside in the damp air to cool down. Oh, she knew it had been a foolish thing to do and she had suffered for it, but now she was well again.

'Good,' Lady Ratcliffe said. 'I expect we shall have any number of callers today, paying their respects and complimenting you on the success of the ball, though I found it disappointing in one respect.'

'Oh, what is that?'

'The Earl did not stay and he was closeted with Martha Brandon alone for several minutes. It can only mean one thing.'

'So?'

'You have lost him.'

'I never had him.'

'You could have done.'

'I did not, do not, want the Earl of Amerleigh for a husband, Aunt, I wish you would believe it. Now I am going to get ready for church.' She was determined to go, if only to prove that what had happened at the ball had not in any way affected her. Determined to prove her un-hoydenishness, she dressed in a forest-green taffeta day gown, a short green velvet cape and a straw hat with a green ribbon.

If she had expected to see the Earl at the service, she was disappointed. The Countess and Mr and Mrs Temple and Captain Hartley took their places in the family pew without him, a fact that had the congregation looking at each other with raised eyebrows. Charlotte concentrated on the service and pretended not to notice. As she and her aunt were leaving, Lady Brandon and Martha joined them. Charlotte bade them good morning with a smile that she hoped would cover the cracks in her armour.

'I had to be the first to congratulate you on your ball,' Lady Brandon said, falling in beside her as she made her way to her curricle. 'And to tell you what happened between the Earl and Martha. It would be dreadful if tattlers like Lady Gilford came to you with the wrong tale. I want you to be able to tell them the truth.'

'The truth about what?'

'The Earl of Amerleigh offered for Martha, but she refused him.'

'Refused him?'

'Yes,' Martha put in placidly. 'I told him we should not suit.'

'But why?'

'I do not like him well enough—is that not reason enough?'

'The poor man is devastated,' her ladyship put in when Charlotte did not answer. 'He told Martha he would have to leave Amerleigh to make a recovery from his disappointment. Goodness knows where he has gone, but I heard he left this morning.'

'Oh.' He had obviously made the offer when he and Martha disappeared from the ballroom, and that was before meeting her in the garden. Had he kissed her again out of disappointment or to prove something to himself? Or her? Oh, if only she knew! But what would knowing what was going on in that complex brain of his avail her? 'But how can he be gone? There is so much he still has to do here.'

'No doubt someone else will do it. It is his mother I feel sorry for, that she should lose him again so soon after him coming home. And she was so happy too. I could spank Martha, I really could.'

'Mama, I told you, it would not serve. We should make each other miserable and he agreed with me.'

'I never heard such nonsense, you had him in the

palm of your hand, and you let him get away. I hope he realises it was your shyness over the honour he did you that made you answer in the negative and will ask you again.'

'He said he was going away.'

'So he did, but he won't be gone for ever, will he? When he comes back, we will arrange a quiet supper party, to welcome him back. He must know that young ladies do not always accept an offer on the first time of asking; it keeps a man on his toes to turn him down at first. He will ask again or I shall want to know the reason why.'

Charlotte did not want to talk about the Earl and was glad when they reached the carriages and went their separate ways. The sooner she forgot the Earl and what had happened, the better; the man was not worth her anguish. She would go for a ride and gallop herself into a better frame of mind.

She rode for miles, trotting, cantering, galloping, covering the green turf and the boulder-strewn slopes without noticing how far she had gone or how long she was out. It was only when she realised Bonny Boy was tiring that she halted and dismounted to rest him and realised where she was. It was here they had met, here he had accused her of trespass, here they had quarrelled over the ownership of Browhill. Had she begun to love him even then? Why had she not allowed him to explain? What was she afraid of? Of letting go, she decided, of letting go of her self-control, her independence, her dignity, of her father's influence. That most of all.

She was about to remount when she saw one of her mine workers riding towards her on what looked like Roland's stallion. Her heart went to her mouth. Something had happened to him, something dreadful. He had been thrown and killed. Her inclination was to run towards him, but she made herself stand still and wait.

'Miss Cartwright I am sent to tell you, there's been an accident…'

'Accident?' She felt the breath leave her body and had to hang on to her horse's neck to steady herself. 'When? Where is he?'

'He, ma'am?'

'The Earl. That is his horse, is it not?'

'Yes, but it ain't him what's hurt, leastways I don't think so. There's two men down the bottom level an' they've been trapped by rising water…'

She ought not to show relief that it was not Roland, though it was profound. 'What were they doing down there? I have never asked any of you to work on Sundays.'

'They've been down there since last night's shift.'

'Last night! Why was I not told?'

'Mr Bailey said not to worry you, what with your ball an' all.'

'Damn my ball!' she exclaimed angrily, then realised it was not fair to take her anger out on the messenger. 'Never mind that.' She hauled herself back into the saddle and began to ride up towards the mine. He turned to ride beside her.

'What are you doing on the Earl's horse?' she asked.

'It were the only one available. Mr Bailey came in his trap.'

'Where is the Earl?'

'His lordship hev gone down a hole. He reckons he knows 'ow to get at the men.'

'Down a hole? You mean down one of the levels?'

'No, down a hole up by the smelting mill, one o' them queer shafts.'

'Show me.'

He led the way past the main adits where the pump was still working and men were moving about in the last stages of exhaustion, to the smelting mill. Here several men were gathered, among them Robert Bailey. They had rigged up a block and tackle over a hole in the ground. She dismounted and went over to them and peered down. The hole was very narrow and she could see nothing. 'The Earl is down there?'

'Yes, Miss Cartwright,' the engineer said. 'I tried to stop him…'

'What does he think he can do?'

'He says he knows the underground passages. I knew of them; we have come across one or two when mining, but I had no idea they had been explored. His lordship hopes to divert the water by blasting a hole from one passage to another.'

'And drowning himself in the process.' She could hardly breathe for worrying about him. If he died… Oh, she could not bear it. She forced herself to sound practical. 'Is he alone?'

'Yes, he would not allow anyone to go down with him.'

'How long has he been down there?'

'Nigh on two hours, Miss Cartwright.'

'And no one thought to send for me?'

'We did not want to worry you, Miss Cartwright, and you could do nothing in any case.'

'So you sent for his lordship instead.'

'No, ma'am, he was out riding. He found us trying to reach the men from the second level.'

So, he had not given up wanting the land back. He had probably heard about the barytes and had come up to see how his mine was doing, and, finding it in trouble, must needs interfere. How could she be so angry with him at the same time as she was out of her mind with worrying about his safety?

'Are the miners still alive?'

'We think so. There has been no more rain since last night and the pumps are keeping the water at the same level.'

'But it is not going down?'

'No. We cannot know how much air the men have left and digging is taking too long.'

'Who are the men?'

'Daniel Biggs and Jake Salhouse.'

She would be concerned for any of her workers, but Daniel Biggs was one of her special protégés whom she had taken on when the new adit was opened. How she would break the news to his mother if anything happened to him, she did not know. 'Do you think his lordship can do anything? Or is he foolishly risking his own life?'

His answer was cut off by the sound of an explosion. It rocked the whole hillside and a few stones and boulders began tumbling down from above. They took shelter behind the smelting house and waited until the movement subsided and the loose stones stopped bouncing down towards them. What had happened below their feet? Had the explosive been set off on purpose or had there been an accident? The men looked significantly at each other. 'He's gone,' Job Bunty said and crossed himself.

Charlotte felt weak in the knees and it took all her self-control not to fall to the ground and howl. The man she loved was dead. She would never see him again, never watch his smile light up his face, never see his eyebrow lift as it did when he teased her, never hear his soft voice, never be touched by him, feel his lips on hers, his warm body pressing against hers, setting her on fire with desire. Never quarrel with him again. It was too much to bear and she turned away so that the men might not see her grief.

Chapter Nine

In the confined space of the narrow tunnel the force of the explosion sent Roland flying back against the wall, knocking him unconscious for a moment and putting out his candle. When he came to his senses he could not see, or breathe, because of the dust that filled the air. He felt in his pocket for the flint with which to relight his candle. It took several attempts before he had a glimmer of light and could see the result of the explosion. Apart from making a big hole in the wall, nothing had happened. The tunnel was still dry. His memory must have been at fault and he was not in the right place at all. He began to crawl forwards, feeling his way along until he came to the hole he had blasted in the rock. He had no idea what was beyond it and found himself looking into a huge cavern. Its floor was uneven and there was water in the bottom of it, caused by a stream running through it. Downstream it disappeared into a cleft in the rock and from there he had no doubt it found its way into the mine where the men were trapped.

He waded in and turned upstream, feeling his way carefully to where the water was coming in through a narrow tunnel that was almost full. There was a few inches from the surface to the roof, no more. He edged his way into it very slowly. It was back breaking because it was lower than his height and he had to bend and at the same time keep his head above water. When the roof became even lower, he took a deep breath and dived, knowing that if he could not find a way out he would surely drown. And he was once again in the dark. He kept reaching up for the roof.

Just when he thought his breath would give out, he felt air on his hand and came to the surface, blowing hard. Ahead of him was a tiny patch of daylight, enough to allow him to see that the water was coming through a fissure in the rock and was running down the tunnel from which he had emerged. When he moved forwards, he found himself in a smaller cave and there was another tunnel running almost parallel and on a slightly higher level, which was dry. Exhausted as he was, he clambered over the rock and set off to explore it. It lead to an old working of the mine, probably abandoned as unprofitable by Mr Cartwright in the early days of his venture. He turned back to the daylight and began the long, slow and difficult climb to the surface. He did not even have help because the men he had left at the top were watching at another hole, waiting for him to tug on the rope to be hauled up.

It was like a rough chimney and he inched himself up, using his back against one side and his feet against the other. He had no idea how long it took and several times he had to stop and rest, but at last he hauled himself out and lay on the grass, too exhausted to move. Knowing time was running out, he sat up and looked about him, wondering how far he was from his starting point. The men he had left were about two hundred yards below him and Charlotte was with them. He got up and staggered down to them.

Charlotte was sitting on a boulder looking despondently at her feet when one of the men yelled, 'There he is!'

She looked up and saw Roland stumbling towards them. He was soaking wet, his breeches clung to his muscular legs and his shirt was torn to ribbons and there was blood running down his arms and from a cut on his forehead to which his soaked hair adhered. She stood up and ran to meet him, wanting to throw herself into his arms, but she stopped when she realised he was so exhausted she would knock him over. 'So you could not keep away,' she said, relief making her voice squeaky.

He grinned lopsidedly, but did not answer. Instead he addressed himself to Robert Bailey who was right behind her. 'I think I've found a way. We need to divert the water into an old mine working. If you fetch the map, I'll show you where.'

Charlotte watched them poring over the map and talking quietly, then they folded it up and Robert Bailey began issuing instructions. Now the rescue was in other hands Roland sank to the ground, too tired to move. Charlotte went and dropped down beside him.

'You idiotic, headstrong man,' she said. 'You could have killed yourself.'

He reached out and took her hand. 'Would you have cared?'

'Of course I would. I would have cared very much.'

He lifted her hand to his mouth and kissed the back of it. 'Bless you for that.'

Embarrassed, she said, 'I could not have you dying on my land trying to save my workmen, could I?'

He let that go, which surprised her; he had never before failed to rise to the bait when she goaded him about the ownership of the land. If he gave up fighting for it, would she be glad or sorry? It had added a zest to their relationship while keeping her feet firmly on the ground. 'You ought to change out of those wet clothes before you catch a chill,' she said.

'I am not cold. I will stay here with you until the men are ready.'

'You are surely not thinking of going down that hole again?'

'Of course. I must show them the way.'

'They can find their own way. You are not to go, I will not hear of it.'

He chuckled. 'How will you stop me?'

'Like this.' She turned and pushed him back so that he was lying face up to the sky and pinned his wrists to the turf either side of his head, so happy to have him back in the land of the living, she did not care that she was exposing her feelings so blatantly.

He could easily have freed himself, but chose not to. Instead he looked up into her face, only inches from his, and searched for a sign, a sign that she had forgiven him and returned his feelings. 'Oh, Charlotte, why must we always fight when we should be making love?'

'Making love?'

'Yes. Love. It is what I feel for you and if I had had any sense six years ago, I would not have been so quick to turn my back on it. But I was young and foolish; the world was before me and I did not like being dictated to. My father was a tyrant and I was a rebel. Can you not forgive me?'

His words set her mind and heart in a whirl. Did he mean what he was saying? It was easier to answer his question than dwell on what he meant by making love, which she could not quite grasp. After all, he must have said something similar to Martha little more than twelve hours before. 'I might, if I thought you had truly repented.'

'Indeed, I do. I have done since the day I came back to Amerleigh. I was wrong to say what I did, not only because it was insufferably arrogant, but because it is palpably not true. You are beautiful. Even in that rig.' He chuckled and indicated the riding breeches and open skirt she was wearing.

'Then you are forgiven for that, but it does not explain why you offered for Miss Brandon and then kissed me last night.'

He sat up beside her. 'I kissed you because I

could not help myself, any more than you could help yourself and I will do it again, given the chance.' He freed his hands and pulled her face down to his and kissed her soundly.

It set her on fire again and she knew she had not mistaken her own feelings the night before, but what had changed? Their dispute had not been solved and he had still offered for Martha. She tried to regain some of her dignity by scrambling back to a sitting position and spreading her skirt demurely about her breeches-clad legs. 'You are an incorrigible rake.'

'No, just a man in love.'

'In love! You can't be.'

'Why not? Do you think I am incapable of it?'

'No, but—'

'I can and I am,' he insisted, sitting up beside her. 'I don't know when I recognised it for what it was. When I followed you to Liverpool, I suppose, but it was probably there, deep inside me, long before that, waiting for me to come to my senses.'

'But you proposed to Miss Brandon.'

'It would seem so,' he said laconically.

'What exactly does that mean?'

'Ask her what happened.'

'She told me. She said you offered and she turned

you down and what was more you would have to leave Amerleigh to get over your disappointment.'

He smiled crookedly. 'Was her mother present?'

'Yes.'

'Then ask her again when she is alone.'

'Oh.' There was more to it than was immediately obvious and her heart was so filled with joy she thought it would burst, but then she quickly sobered again. It did not solve anything. 'Roland, what are we to do?'

'Say it again.'

'Say what again?'

'Roland. It sounds good to me.'

'It just slipped out. So, what are we to do?'

'If I ask you, say, in a few weeks' time when the tattlemongers have run out of ammunition, will you marry me?'

'Marry you?' She could not hide her astonishment. 'You cannot mean it.'

'Why not?'

'Because you are who you are and I am who I am, children of our respective fathers.'

He knew what she meant, but he did not see why their differences could not be overcome. 'That is a silly answer, if it is an answer at all. You asked what we should do and I made a perfectly sensible proposition.'

'That was not what I meant. You once said to me that I had too much money and you had too much rank to find true love.'

'I seem to make a habit of making ridiculous and erroneous statements.'

'Perhaps you were right.'

'Do you mean by that you do not love me?'

'I am not sure I know what love is. I have never been brought up to consider it.' She might not have been brought up to think about it, but she was learning fast and she had discovered it was both wondrous and extremely painful.

'Then I feel for you.'

'I do not need your pity, my lord. I am content as I am. I have sworn not to marry.'

'Fustian! I could change your mind if you would let me.'

'According to my father, nothing is done for nothing and behind every offer there is a price to pay.'

'And what do you expect to have to pay?'

'My independence, everything I own. You know as well as I do that a married woman can own no property; it all becomes her husband's to do with as he likes, no matter what she wishes. How do I know you are not asking me in order to get your hands on Browhill?' It was said half-jokingly, but underneath was a core of real concern. Could a man who had so thoroughly disdained her suddenly discover he loved her?

'Damn Browhill! I told Mountford long ago not to pursue that claim.'

'Why did no one tell me?' She gave a strangled laugh. 'To keep me on my toes, I suppose.'

'Does it make a difference? To your answer, I mean.'

She was thoughtful, considering his question. 'If I agreed to marry you, you would get it anyway.'

'I do not want it.'

'But you have just risked your neck to save it.'

'I did that for two men trapped underground and they are still there, so if you do not mind, I will go back to helping fetch them out.' He rose and hurried to join the men, who had pulled up the rope and dismantled the block and tackle and were re-erecting it over the hole from which he had emerged. He was furious. It was her father's fault and he cursed him with all the invective of which he was capable for all the harm the man had done, the damage to a sensitive being that could not, it seemed, be repaired. And included in his condemnation was his own father. If they had left well alone, nature might well have done what they had plotted and failed to achieve.

* * *

She sat and watched the rescue efforts, but did not take in what she was seeing. He had left her so suddenly she was forced to the conclusion he was angry because she had dared to refuse him— him an Earl and the owner of an estate that matched hers in extent, if not in opulence. How had she come to make such a mull of everything? He had declared his love, asked her to marry him—was that not what she wanted? She remembered Mrs Cater once saying to her that she wanted to have her cake and eat it too. It had been over some trifling thing that she could not remember. But was it true now? She had sworn never to marry, but she wanted Roland Temple more than anything she had ever wanted in her life; material possessions meant nothing in the face of that. So why could she not give way?

It was the ghost of her father, of course. It would not leave her alone, lecturing her, telling her she was as good as any man, that she had the ordering of untold wealth and hundreds of people depending on her business acumen and her first duty was to them and to the profitability of the Cartwright empire. A husband would get in the way of that.

She sat on for hours, until the sun dipped over the horizon and the air became chill. She could not move, could not leave until she knew the men had been saved and no lives had been lost. That, too, would be her responsibility and the longer it took, the greater the chance they would already be dead when someone at last managed to reach them. Marriage was out of the question.

Roland made himself concentrate on what he was doing. With others to help him, they set off a carefully calculated explosion in the end of the water-filled tunnel, which filled it with rubble. Standing up to their knees in water, they watched the water rise slowly until it was up to their waists and then tip over into the higher passage. Slowly, achingly slowly, the water level in the lower tunnel dropped until it dwindled into a mere puddle. Roland returned to the men, waiting at the bottom the shaft. 'I think we've done it.'

They gave a loud cheer and scrambled to the surface, helped by men at the top with the tackle and it did not take a quarter as long as it had for Roland to do it the first time. Once on the hill again, they ran down to the mine workings and Roland volunteered to go down to see if their strategy had worked.

Charlotte tried to prevent him from doing so, but he insisted and so she watched him disappear down the adit and stood with her heart in her mouth, waiting impatiently for him to report what he found. The news of the disaster had spread in the way things like that did in a small community and there was a large gathering of miners and their families, including Mrs Biggs, Beth and Matty, and Jacob Edwards who had arrived from Shrewsbury. Everyone was praying, some audibly, some just moving their lips, some silent and watchful.

It seemed an age before they heard a voice echoing up from the depths. 'They're alive! Send down a bucket.'

A large bucket in which men and equipment were sometimes lowered was sent down and a few minutes later it was hauled up and a weak and only just conscious Daniel Biggs was helped out. Mrs Biggs and her daughters, all crying with relief, crowded round as he was carried off to one of the nearby cottages to be revived. The bucket went down again and the second man was hauled up, followed by Roland, for the second time, soaked to the skin. 'They were in water up to their chests,' he reported. 'Another half-hour and their air would have given out.'

'Thank God!' Charlotte breathed and her prayer was repeated all round. 'Now seal that level off. I will not risk another man's life down there.' She had sloughed off the mantel of the passionate woman as easily as taking off her clothes, Roland noted, and was again the practical woman, used to command, though she did seem to have a conscience about what she asked of her workmen.

'Miss Cartwright, that will put men out of work,' Jacob reminded her.

'I will have to find something else for them to do.'

'We owe a great debt to his lordship,' Robert Bailey said. 'Without him the men would never have been brought up alive.'

'I know,' she said, glancing towards Roland. His wet shirt and riding breeches outlined every contour of his body and increased her anguish. 'We cannot thank him sufficiently, but no doubt a way will be found to show our appreciation.'

'I want no thanks,' Roland said stiffly. 'I did what any man would have done in the circumstances. Now if you will excuse me, I will leave you.' He bowed to Charlotte, picked up his coat, waistcoat and hat from the ground where he had thrown them, and went to find his horse, quietly cropping the grass. He had done all he could, not only to help save the men, but to redeem himself in Charlotte's eyes. But it was not enough.

It was dark when he returned home and his hope that he might be able to gain his room unnoticed was dashed when he was met in the hall by Geoffrey and Elizabeth, coming down the stairs dressed for dinner. It was long past the usual hour and he surmised they had put off the meal to wait for him to come home, until Mrs Fields told them it would be ruined if it was not soon eaten.

'Roland, whatever has happened to you?' Elizabeth asked, shocked by the sight of him. 'You are soaked and covered in blood.'

'Am I?' He had hardly noticed that. 'It is nothing. I will go up to my room and clean myself up. Go in to dinner. I will join you later.'

'But you must have your wounds seen to.'

'Travers will look after me.' He toiled up to his room where Travers joined him, accompanied by two footmen carrying a bath, which they proceeded to fill from jugs of hot water brought up by maids. 'Lor, Major, you look as though you've been in a battle,' the corporal said as Roland stripped off and lowered himself into the water. Scratches and yellow and purple bruises covered his body.

'You could call it that,' he said, smiling ruefully. 'A battle with the elements. Two miners trapped below ground by rising water.'

'Did you get them up safely?' Travers, the bluff soldier, was as gentle as a woman, bathing his cuts.

'Yes, thank God.' He went on to give a succinct

account of what had happened and how fortuitous that he had been riding in the area and remembered the underground tunnels.

Half an hour later, refreshed and in clean clothes, with his scratches cleaned and dressed and his bruises anointed, he was ready to go down to join his house guests. 'While I am gone, you may pack,' he told Travers, as he went out of the door. 'We are going to London on the morning stage.'

'Very good, Major.' Travers smiled to himself, wondering if this sudden decision had anything to do with a certain young lady, but he could not ask. His master had been in a strange mood for weeks, up one minute, down the next. It was as if he had been waiting for something to happen, and now it seemed it had, if the expression on the Major's face was anything to go by. He was pale, his jaw rigid, but he was calm. Travers had always understood that strange and dangerous calm and knew it was not the time to question or comment.

Roland went downstairs for a belated dinner, and for a second time, gave an account of the rescue at the mine, this time to Geoffrey, Elizabeth and Miles Hartley, though he said nothing of his conversation with Charlotte. That was something he would never divulge.

'You will be the hero of the hour,' Elizabeth said, when he had finished. 'If you were not in demand before, you will undoubtedly be besieged with invitations now.'

'I should hate that. I intend to leave Amerleigh for a time.'

'Leave!' Elizabeth exclaimed.

'Yes, I have business in London.' He turned to his cousin. 'Geoffrey, could I prevail upon you to keep an eye on things here while I am away? You do not need to stay in residence if you do not wish to. My mother can send for you if you are needed.'

'Certainly, I will. How long will you be gone?'

'I do not know.' He was tempted to say he wasn't coming back at all, that he could turn his back on Amerleigh with no regrets, but he knew he was deceiving himself. There were regrets in plenty: leaving his gentle mother who loved him and whom he loved, and there were all the people who depended on him, the staff, so recently reinstated at the Hall; the Biggs family, little Tommy Biggs and all the other village children he had come to know through him; Miles Hartley and the proposal for a school for deaf children. Most of all his disastrous love for Charlotte Cartwright, who could not love him because she saw him as an enemy she must overcome. She would think she had won and he supposed she had, since he was leaving the field. He would forget her all the sooner if he never saw her face, never saw those appealing hazel-green eyes, the abundance of chestnut hair and that enchanting smile ever again. And suddenly that prospect was far from appealing.

'A few days, perhaps a week or two, time to let the furore die down.' He did not mean the fuss over his supposed bravery, but the gossip about Martha's rejection of him. Then perhaps he could face Charlotte again and begin courting her properly. He could not give her up. 'Miles, I will also try to see the doctor you spoke of, if you give me his direction.'

'Of course. I will come with you, if you wish.'

'No, stay here and continue your work with Tommy. That must not come to a stop because I am not here. Perhaps Miss Cartwright will resume sharing the lessons.' It almost choked him to say her name.

It was Dobson, saddling Bonny Boy that afternoon, who told Charlotte he had seen the Earl leaving on the morning coach when he had been taking one of the other horses to the smithy in Shrewsbury. 'Going to London,' he said. 'And staying, too, for he had a portmanteau with him.

And his servant was with him, carrying a knapsack. Smart as ninepence in uniform they both were.'

'Really, I cannot see what business it is of yours where he goes,' she said, still miserable over her inability to accept Roland's offer. She remembered thinking, when he first came home, that she should make him love her and then disdain him, just to teach him a lesson. She had not consciously tried to do anything of the sort, but in any case, it was she who had learned the lesson. 'He is a free agent and may go where he pleases, when he pleases and with whom he pleases.'

'Yes, miss. I thought you might be interested, considering what he did yesterday.'

'How do you know what he did yesterday?' she asked sharply, her mind still on her conversation with Roland.

'Why, everyone knows, Miss Charlotte. Half the village heard the explosions and went up to see what was going on. I heard tell there was going to be some kind of reception in his honour.'

'They can hardly do that if he is not here, can they? No doubt he found the idea distasteful and that is why he decided to leave.'

'Yes, miss.' He finished his task and handed her the reins before bending down to offer his joined hands for her foot. 'No doubt he will soon be back. There's still work on the estate and he would not leave a job half-done.'

'No, I am sure he would not.' She settled herself in the saddle and trotted out of the yard, down the drive and on to the lane.

She did not want to hear about the Earl, she did not want to know his reason for leaving the village, she told herself she had no interest in the time of his return and the sooner she forgot his existence and went on with the work that was her lot in life, the better. It was a life for which she had been trained, a life bequeathed to her by her father and she must accept it and hide the ache in her heart as best she could.

At Browhill, the men were worrying about their jobs, even while they obeyed her and tipped stones and rubble down the shaft. Mr Cartwright would never have closed the level down just because there was a bit of a risk, they told her; all mining was risky, they accepted that. She reassured them, telling them she would open more levels; the mine was still viable. Satisfied that all was well, she returned to Mandeville.

Home. She had known no other. As a child she had loved it, loved the building and its open spaces, where she could roam on foot or on horseback, with the wind in her hair and the smell of the heather in her nostrils. But now it meant nothing without Roland and, perhaps for the first time, she realised what loving someone meant. It meant being adaptable, talking problems over, sharing everything, the good and the bad, giving way sometimes. None of her riches could compensate for his loss. Oh, why had she not seen that before, when she could have done something about it?

She dismounted and handed her mount over to Dobson and went indoors to be greeted by a great-aunt who seemed to have come to stay, determined to make a lady of her. Too late. Much too late.

It was politeness for guests to call on their hostess after a ball, to express their appreciation and gossip over the teacups about what had happened, and Charlotte wondered why no one came, especially as they must be agog with curiosity about what had happened up at the mine. When she commented upon it to her great-aunt, Emily was reluctant to offer a reason—'I am sure I do not know'—in a way that made Charlotte realise she was hiding something.

'What are the tattlemongers saying now, Aunt?' she asked.

'Oh, they have nothing better to do than think up monstrous tales.'

'Go on. I insist on knowing.'

'Oh, it is something and nothing. They say Martha turned the Earl down because you spent two days with him in Liverpool and though you went in your own coach you came back in his and you were seen arriving in a state of undress… You do not want me to go on, do you?'

'No, I understand. Perhaps it is as well his lordship has gone away.'

'If he had an ounce of decency, he would offer for you and be done with.'

Decency! Did he know what they were saying? Was that why he had proposed, just to save her reputation? She did not know whether to be pleased or angry and anger won the day in the end. 'If he did, I should refuse him. I do not want to marry anyone, least of all the Earl of Amerleigh.' She said it firmly to convince her aunt, but she could not convince herself. 'I am going up to change.'

She had hardly had time to put on a light blue silk dress, tidy her hair and rejoin her great-aunt in the drawing room, when they heard the sound of a carriage arriving.

'I wonder who that can be,' Emily murmured,

going to the window to peep out. 'My goodness, it is the Countess. Charlotte, stir yourself.'

Two minutes later a footman came and announced, 'The Countess of Amerleigh, ma'am.'

Charlotte hurried forward to greet their visitor. The Countess, although always perfectly polite when they met, had never called on her before and she wondered if the visit had anything to do with the events of the previous day and her refusal of Roland. Surely he had not sent his mother to plead on his behalf? She dismissed that idea as ludicrous; he would never let anyone else fight his battles for him. 'My lady, you are very welcome. You will take some refreshment?'

'Thank you.'

Charlotte ordered the footman to see to it, and indicated a chair. 'Do sit down, my lady.'

The formalities dispensed, her ladyship ensconced in a chair and Emily twittering beside her, Charlotte sat down on one of the sofas and waited to be enlightened.

'I have come to congratulate you on the success of your ball,' the Countess began. 'And also to see if you have taken any harm from what happened yesterday. It must have been a very worrying ordeal.'

'I came to no harm, my lady. In fact, I did

nothing at all, and the worrying was done by the men. We have Lord Temple to thank that all ended happily.'

'So I have heard.'

The conversation halted as a footman brought in the tea tray and set it down beside Charlotte. 'You can leave it,' she told him. 'I will see to it.'

'I was worried to death when my niece was out so long,' Lady Ratcliffe said, as Charlotte set about pouring tea. 'I felt sure she had taken a fall from her horse and was lying somewhere on the hills, injured, or even, God forbid, dead. I sent servants out to search for her and was in total despair, especially when I was told there had been explosions up at the mine. You do not know the relief I felt when she returned safely.'

'I can imagine it,' the Countess said. 'I did not see my son when he returned, but I have been told he looked as if he had been in a fight. But he assured everyone he was unhurt and was able to leave this morning as planned.'

'He planned to go?' Charlotte asked in surprise.

'Yes, we thought it for the best.' She paused. 'It was an unfortunate business and a shame it had to happen at your ball.'

'Oh?'

'I refer to my son's interview with Miss Brandon.'

'It is of no consequence to me, my lady,' Charlotte said firmly.

'She is a very silly girl,' Lady Ratcliffe put in. 'I saw her drag him off myself. Being an honourable man, what could he do but offer for her?'

'Miss Brandon is very young,' the Countess said. 'I do not think she quite understood the implications of her actions.'

'Then her mother should have made sure she did,' Emily said sharply. 'If she were my daughter—'

'Aunt, I do not think we should speculate on what happened, do you?' Charlotte put in. 'There is enough of that going on already. And I am sure the Countess does not want to hear it.'

As she sipped her tea, Charlotte was aware that the Countess was looking closely at her and it made her feel uncomfortably transparent. How much did her ladyship really know? Did she know that a little over twelve hours later Roland had proposed to her?

'My son decided a little time away from Amerleigh might be beneficial to all concerned,' the Countess went on. 'But he has not gone for good. His roots are here and, whatever happens, he would not neglect his duty to his people.'

'I am sure he would not,' Charlotte said. 'No doubt you will miss him very much.'

'Yes, especially as he has not long been back after six years away.'

'Did you find him much changed?' Charlotte had not meant to ask that, but the words slipped out.

'He has grown much bigger,' the Countess said with a light laugh. 'And more self-assured.'

'I did not think he ever lacked self-assurance, my lady.'

'Oh, he did, you know, but as his father would have condemned it in him, he covered it with a certain brashness that made him appear unfeeling. But that was not the real Roland. The Roland I keep in my heart is gentle and courteous and affectionate...'

'I am sure he is,' Charlotte murmured, agreeing with every word.

'I would be distressed if you thought ill of him, Miss Cartwright. Whatever you may think, he holds you in high esteem. And so do I. I should be glad to welcome you at the dower house, should you ever wish to call.'

'Thank you.'

After a little more desultory conversation, mostly about the weather and the close shave the trapped miners had had and how thankful they were that they had taken no lasting harm, the Countess took her leave.

'Well, what do you make of that?' Emily asked after the door had closed on her.

'Nothing. She was just being polite.' It was more than that; the dear lady must have known how Charlotte was being vilified and had come to reassure her that not everyone condemned her. It was done so discreetly that Charlotte could not have openly thanked her, but she was grateful.

'There is hope for you yet.'

'Hope? Hope for what?'

'Being received into society. With the Countess of Amerleigh on calling terms you cannot fail and when the Earl comes back…'

'Aunt, I will have no more of the Earl, do you hear me? I have too much to do to waste time in idle gossip.'

She tried immersing herself in work, in an attempt to put Roland from her mind, but it was impossible when all around her were reminders of him: the new wall, the newly trimmed hedges, the new thatch on the rows of workers' cottages, the windows of the Hall, glinting in the sunlight, Mr Biggs bending over the flower beds and young Tommy Biggs, smiling up at her and asking her, in his mute way with hands and expressive eyes, when she thought the Earl would be back.

'I don't know,' she told him. 'Soon, perhaps.' She missed him. She missed his gentle chiding, she missed their arguments as much as she missed their harmony over things they both found important. She missed his warmth and understanding and the sheer joy of having him touch her and rouse her with his kisses. She wanted him to come back every bit as much as Tommy, though what she would say to him, if he did, she had no idea. He was too proud to repeat a proposal once it had been turned down, especially in the manner in which she had done it, and she was too proud to raise the subject herself. But if only they could *talk.* They were as uncommunicative as poor little deaf Tommy...

The capital was *en fête.* The great and the good, rich and poor, soldiers, beggars and thieves, thronged the streets and blocked the roads so that any vehicles caught up in the mêlée had to go at the pace of a snail. The crowds had been mostly good-humoured, shouting their approval of those in the carriages they liked, even making way for them, while they jeered those for whom they had only contempt, and that included the Regent. What they had really come to see was the return of the Duke of

Wellington, the architect of the victory against Napoleon, the saviour of the nation. Balconies, tree tops and even roofs were being used as vantage points to see him and cheer him as he arrived by carriage from Dover.

All the hotels were full to bursting and it was with some difficulty Roland managed to find a hotel to take him and Travers. It was run-down and not at all clean, but he had stayed in worse places. Having Travers looking after their belongings, he set off to see Professor Lundy, whose direction Charles Mountford had given him. The professor was away, but expected back within the week, Roland was told by his assistant, so he left the documents and said he would return. From there he made his way to Dr Masterson's at the top end of Piccadilly, where he had a thriving general practice, but he specialised in deafness and was making his mark teaching deaf mutes to speak.

Roland's title alone ensured him an interview and he lost no time telling him about Tommy. 'Teaching signs is not enough,' he told the doctor, who had invited him into his office and offered him a glass of Madeira. 'I should like the boy to learn to speak. Can that be done?'

'I cannot tell without seeing him and ascertaining if his vocal cords are intact...'

'He seems to be able to grunt and shout, but nothing intelligible.'

'That is a good sign. I am about to take my class—would you like to come and watch?'

Roland said he would and he was conducted down a corridor to another room where half a dozen boys sat at their desks. The room was silent except for the scratching of pens and the rustle of paper. They sprang to their feet when the doctor and Roland entered. Roland found a chair and sat on one side to watch proceedings.

He discovered that most of the boys were already proficient at reading each other's lips and it was this ability that was used to try to get them to say words. Some were better than others, but the doctor said that was because some had not been born deaf and their deafness was not absolute. Those to whom the world was a completely silent place, and always had been, were finding it more difficult. The words they uttered were unintelligible to Roland, though sometimes the doctor murmured 'good' when they tried.

After the lesson was over, he and the doctor discussed Tommy's case. 'I need to see the boy and discover just how much he can hear and if he is a suitable case to be taught,' Masterson said. 'Some never manage to speak at all and it is not good to give the boy false hope. You would have to bring him here and, if I decided to take him on, he would enter as a boarder.'

Roland had been expecting the man, like Miles, to go to Amerleigh, and he was not at all sure it would be a good idea to uproot Tommy. The boy was very young and he would miss his family. 'We must discuss it with his parents,' he said. 'They are poor people and ill educated and fees for boarding out would come hard, though I have no doubt they could be found.'

'Then I suggest you leave well alone. My fees are not inconsiderable, you understand. I do not do what I do out of charity. My boys all come from genteel families.'

'I see. Have you thought of passing your skill on to others? Captain Miles Hartley is interested in the subject and he is teaching signs, but if he could be taught your methods, he could take on my protégé, and others in the area of my home.'

'I am acquainted with Captain Hartley. We have had some correspondence on the matter. If he is willing, we can perhaps come to an arrangement for him to attend me here, as an assistant.'

Roland thanked him and left. Back at the hotel, he sat down to write to Miles and Charlotte. The letter to Miles was easy enough, but that to

Charlotte presented a problem. He wanted to write a love letter, to pour out his feelings, to tell her... What? Repeat his proposal? Was that so outrageous a suggestion? After all, his father and hers had not thought so. But they had not been thinking of the happiness of their children. Mr Cartwright had wanted a title for his daughter and his own father had wanted his debts paid; they had not expected, or even wished for, their offspring to fall in love. Nor had he when he had so outrageously rejected her. But he loved her now. She was always in his thoughts; distance had done nothing to ease his aching heart. Could they not put the past behind them and start again?

An hour later the carpet around him was littered with screwed-up pieces of paper as he had begun a letter and then discarded it. It was no good, the right words would not come. Either they made him sound as if he were grovelling or they were too arrogant. His love and his pride were doing battle and it seemed neither would give way. He gave up and went to White's, where he spent the whole night gambling, but as he was a skilled player and took care to remain sober and alert, he found himself winning. It seemed he could not lose, and by the time daylight was allowed into the room by the drawing of the curtains he was five thousand pounds richer. 'Lucky at cards, unlucky in love,' he murmured to himself as he pocketed his winnings. At least the money would go towards the school.

It was only a week since the Earl had left, but already his absence had left a void in the lives of everyone, most of all Charlotte's, and not even the news that the *Fair Charlie* had limped into Liverpool, badly damaged by ferocious storms at sea, but with everyone safe and most of the cargo intact, could cheer her up. The mill was busy, the mine's new seams were looking hopeful and her freed slaves were working happily, so she had been informed, and yet she felt so downpin, she could burst into tears at the drop of a hat. The hoydenish daughter of Henry Cartwright was a woman after all. It reminded her of Roland's comment when he had kissed her the first time; she would have laughed if she had not been so miserable. It did not mean she could neglect her work. Duty was all.

'You will work yourself into an early grave,' her great-aunt said, one evening when she was almost too tired to eat her supper. 'Ladies were never intended to work, their constitutions will not stand it.'

'Fustian! I am as strong as an ox.'

'That is nothing to be proud of. Your good name is more important. You really must take time to make a recover in society.'

'How am I to do that?'

'You could start by calling on the Countess. She has said she would receive you and yet you have never been. And Mr and Mrs Temple are still at the Hall.'

'I am to bow and scrape to them?'

'Do not be a ninny, Charlotte. You do not have to scrape to anyone. Dress yourself up and go in friendship. Ask the Countess if she has heard how his lordship is, show an interest in the refurbishment of the Hall.'

'Aunt, I cannot do that! You will have me as transparent as Lady Brandon.'

'Speaking of Lady Brandon, she called this afternoon.'

'Oh?'

'Yes, full of the fact that Martha has become betrothed to Martin Elliott. It seems he has been given the living of Scofield and finally plucked up the courage to propose. So all is well that ends well.'

All well, Charlotte mused. All was a very long way from being well, but she was glad for Martha's sake and wondered whether the Countess had heard of it and, if she had, if she would inform Roland. 'Please excuse me, I have some work to do on my ledgers before I retire,' she said and took herself off to her office where she made a pretence at work, but wherever she was, in her bedroom, the drawing room, the office or out of doors, she could not escape from her anguished longing for the man she loved.

She passed her hand over her aching brow and looked up at the shelves on the wall above her head. They were crammed with dusty files, she had never had time to investigate. Perhaps now was the time to do it. She might even find out if there was any substance to the Earl's allegation that there was something underhand in her father's acquisition of Browhill. She looked along the rows of boxes for dates and, finding one for 1808, pulled it down and began to read.

She had not expected to find anything but, after half an hour, she found it and her heart began to beat uncomfortably fast. What she had in her hand was a surveyor's report done on Browhill, a report that informed Mr Cartwright that he had been correct; there were large deposits of lead beneath Browhill that would repay mining. The dreadful thing about it was that it was dated after Roland's rejection of her, but before the land had changed hands. She had to look twice to confirm it, but it was there in black and white. She suddenly remembered riding home in the coach with her father after leaving the ball. He had been white with fury. 'He will pay for this night's work,' he had said. 'No one makes a fool of Henry Cartwright and gets away with it. You will be revenged, Charlie, have no fear of that.'

That was why he had refused the offer of the capital sum back and had instead slapped on that enormous rate of interest! He had not wanted the money repaid, he had wanted to crow over the Earl when the mine made him richer than ever. 'Oh, Papa,' she murmured. 'Do you know what you have done to me?' She sat with the document in her hand, her eyes blank, and reflected on her life, which could have been so different if it had not been for her father's ambition and his vengeful nature. The worst of it was she had genuinely believed she had a right to the mine.

What Papa had done had not been illegal, but it was certainly dishonourable. It was a wrong that had to be righted. It meant swallowing her pride, but her conscience would not let the matter rest.

The very next day she sent for Jacob and instructed him to send the Browhill deeds to the Earl.

He stared at her. 'Miss Cartwright, are you sure you are being wise? It forms a large part of your income and you have employees to consider.'

'I know that, but I am sure the Earl will wish to continue their employment. Get those deeds off at once.'

He bowed his way out.

The next day a letter arrived from Roland. Not that it raised her hopes, far from that, but it was a gesture of some sort.

'Dear Miss Cartwright,' she read. 'I have spoken to Dr Masterson with a view to having Tommy Biggs taught to speak. The doctor is not prepared to come to Amerleigh because of commitments in the capital, but says if Tommy were to go to him, he would assess whether he might be suitable for instruction and, if he were, to have him enrolled in his class. Naturally, I would pay his fees, but I am unsure whether it would be a good thing to take him from his home. The alternative is for Captain Hartley to come to London and learn the doctor's methods, which is the option I prefer. I would appreciate your opinion on the matter and also if you would be so good as to speak to Mr and Mrs Biggs and ascertain their views. I remain your obedient servant, Roland Temple.'

Not a personal word at all, cold as the hills in winter, but he need not have written at all. She let the letter drop on to her lap and gazed at the picture on the wall of the drawing room facing her. It was a portrait of her father, but she did not see it. She was miles away, sitting on the side of a hill talking about love and marriage, and reshaping the conversation in her head so that, instead of spurning Roland, she had accepted his offer. She allowed herself to dream a little, to imagine her family, boys and girls and husband, playing in the grounds of Mandeville on a brilliant summer's day, chasing each other in and out among the trees, laughing... She stopped her musing abruptly, realising she had placed her imaginary family at her home, not Amerleigh Hall. She was as entrenched in her ways as ever, if she could not, even in her dreams, concede the loss of Mandeville as her home.

Chapter Ten

Mr Biggs would not hear of allowing Tommy to go to London. 'I don' mind 'im being taught at the big house,' he said. 'But as for speakin', we know he'll never do that and it ain't fair to get 'is 'opes up.'

'You do not know that.'

'Course I do. He's my child, ain't 'e?'

Charlotte turned to Mrs Biggs, who was feeding pap to the baby. 'What do you think, ma'am?'

'I can't part with him. He's too little to go so far from home.'

Charlotte did not try to persuade them, knowing perfectly well that she would feel the same. She set off for the Hall.

'Miss Cartwright, it is a pleasure to see you again,' the Captain said when she was shown up to the schoolroom. 'Please sit down and let Tommy show you how well he is doing.'

She sat on one of the little chairs, reminded of happier times when the lessons first began and watched without speaking until the end of the lesson. Tommy was happy to come without his mother now and darted away like any reluctant schoolboy when he was dismissed.

'He seems to be doing well,' she told Miles.

'Yes. He is a very intelligent boy and deserves all the help we can give him.'

'I agree. I have heard from his lordship, have you?'

'Yes,' he said. 'He suggests I take Tommy to London.'

'In my letter he expressed concern about taking the boy from his home and asked me to find out what Mr and Mrs Biggs thought about it. I have done so and they will not agree and I cannot say I blame them.'

'They have a houseful of other children...'

'All equally important, all equally loved and cherished, Captain.'

He bowed, accepting the criticism. 'Tommy has to be examined to see if he is capable of speech and if Dr Masterson will not come here...'

'Then you must go and learn the doctor's methods, as the Earl suggested.' She paused, wondering whether to go on, then took a deep breath and continued. 'If you could also persuade his lordship to come home, I am sure everyone would be glad to see him back. You can tell him that Miss Brandon's betrothal to Martin Elliott has just been announced. There is no reason for him to stay away. He is needed here.'

'Is that so?' He smiled ruefully. He was to be her envoy, to bring her lover back to her.

She could almost read his thoughts, and added quickly. 'Yes, by everyone in the village, his tenants and workers and his mother. I know she wants him to come home.'

'And, unless I am mistaken, so do you.'

'Goodness, Captain, you must not tell him that!'

'Then I will not.'

She bade him goodbye and went to call on the Countess. It was time she returned her ladyship's visit.

Roland had gone to call on Professor Lundy, to see what he had made of the old documents he had left with him. The professor had only the previous day returned from his trip out of London and had not yet had time to peruse them. When Roland was shown in, he took them from the cupboard and unrolled the first one. Roland was unprepared for the man to become so excited about them; he wanted to sit down and begin translating them right away.

It took him a long time. Roland, who was not aware he had anything more important to do, sat down with him and listened as he read his translation aloud, sometimes quite fluently, sometimes haltingly and occasionally stopping to consult books and other documents. Tea was brought in to them, and later, claret, and both were consumed with hardly a pause. At noon, the professor sent a servant out for food from a pie shop and picked up the next document, unrolling it carefully and standing weights on the corners to hold it open. By this time Roland was becoming nearly as absorbed as the professor.

It was when he came to a mention of Browhill that Roland sat forwards, giving him all his attention. And then he laughed aloud. 'You mean when the land was given to the first Earl and his heirs, it specifically stated that any deposits found beneath it would remain the property of the Crown?'

'Yes, it is not unusual for such a thing to be specifically excluded. In simple terms, the surface belongs to the holder, the grass and scree and whatever the top contains, but nothing below it. To mine there, you would have to apply to the Crown for mineral rights.'

Roland was still laughing. 'Then we neither of

us had a right to the lead. Oh, what will she say about that, I wonder?'

'She, my lord?'

'The lady who owns the land.'

'I thought you did.'

'The Temple family did once upon a time. Now it belongs to Miss Charlotte Cartwright, a neighbour of mine.'

'Then I suggest you enlighten the lady before she does anything illegal.' The professor smiled, rolled the documents up again and handed them back. 'Take care of them, they are priceless.'

Roland was still laughing as he left the building and returned to the hotel.

'There you are, Major,' Travers said, nodding towards a tall figure standing by the hearth. 'Captain Hartley's here.'

Roland hurried forward to greet him. 'Did you bring the boy?'

'No, his mother would not let him come, but I mean to take up Dr Masterson's offer.'

'Good. Travers, go and order refreshments to be brought up.' And as Travers left to obey, Roland turned back to Miles. 'Sit down, please. I'm sorry for the poor state of my accommodation. It was all there was to be had.'

'You will be glad to go home, then.'

'Yes, when my business is done.'

'I should think it is done. I am to tell you that Miss Brandon is now affianced to Mr Elliott, and to give you this. It arrived at the Hall just as I was leaving.'

Roland took the brown paper package and quickly undid it. It contained a sheaf of official-looking documents. There was an accompanying letter signed by Jacob Edwards on Miss Cartwright's behalf and asking for his signature on the agreement. A swift scrutiny told him what the documents were. Deeds to Browhill. After all their fighting, all her intransigence and his obstinacy, she had simply sent them to him. He turned everything over. There was not a word of explanation, nothing from her personally at all.

'Not bad news, I hope?' Miles queried, watching the changing expressions flit across his friend's face.

He considered the question. Was it good or bad? What on earth had been in Charlotte's mind? If she thought he would simply sign as requested without asking questions, then she was sadly mistaken. Travers had come back into the room. 'Pack,' he told him. 'We are going back to Amerleigh.'

'Yes, sir!' Travers was grinning from ear to ear.

'I will have to leave you to see Dr Masterson on your own, Miles. I have urgent business at home.'

* * *

Two hours later he was in a coach going north, travelling at the pace of a snail on account of unseasonable fog. Nothing the passengers could do would make the coachman go any faster. 'I ain't risking my horses, for you nor nobody,' he said when they grumbled.

'At this pace, we'll be on the road a se'ennight,' Travers said gloomily, as the coach crawled along the dark roads. Once they nearly collided with the mail coming in the opposite direction and only the skill of both sets of coachmen averted a disaster, which proved how right their driver was to be cautious. Roland, as anxious as his servant to reach their destination, could only sit back and contain himself in patience, ruminating on what foolish notion Charlotte had taken into her head. After all, he had told her he had dropped the claim. Was she feeling smug because she could afford the grand gesture, that if he made a concession, then she could make a greater one? Was ever a woman more contrary!

On the second day, the fog began to lift and their driver, determined to make up for lost time, set the horses galloping. It was enough to stop all normal conversation and make the passengers hang on to their seats. They pulled into the inn at Shrewsbury at seven o'clock the following morning, several hours behind schedule.

As soon as they alighted and their bags were unloaded, they hired horses to take them to Amerleigh. They took the path over the hills, just as they had done when they had arrived in the spring. Was that only five months before? He paused when they topped the brow and could see Mandeville nestling in the hollow. There was no sign of its owner.

They continued down the hill and to the road from Scofield to Amerleigh, reminding him of the night of the Lady Gilford's ball and Charlotte's party. Had he been in love with her then? He had certainly not admitted it and, if anyone had suggested it, would have laughed. Marry the hoyden! He had gone away six years before to avoid it; little did he realise he would obey his father posthumously. *After* he had got to the bottom of her latest outrage. Suddenly he could not wait.

'You go on,' he said to Travers. 'I have a call to make.' And with that he turned his horse and cantered back up the road and into the gates of Mandeville.

Lady Ratcliffe was still abed and Charlotte was in the drawing room alone when she heard a horse coming up the drive, but she paid it no particular attention. She started up when a footman came to announce the Earl of Amerleigh and to ask if she would receive him. The words were hardly out of the man's mouth when Roland appeared in the doorway. 'Miss Cartwright, your obedient.' He handed his hat to the footman who took it away, closing the door behind him.

He was not in uniform, but wearing a frock coat and pantaloons tucked into shining Hessians, very different from the picture she had carried in her head of when she had last seen him, in soaking wet shirt and breeches and his hair plastered to his head with water and blood. She rose and curtsied. 'My lord. I had not realised you were come home.'

'I have just arrived.'

'To stay?'

'Yes, most decidedly to stay.'

'I am glad.'

'Are you?' He moved closer to her and took both her hands in his, searching her face. Her hazel eyes were bright and there were two bright spots of pink on her cheeks.

'Yes,' she said, withdrawing her hands and hiding them in the folds of her gown. It was a lemon-coloured silk, not her usual grey working garb because she meant to call on the Countess later that morning. 'Did you see Captain Hartley?'

'I did indeed. I left him going to see Dr Masterson.'

'Good. I have been talking to the Countess about the school for deaf children. When you have more pupils, it cannot continue in the schoolroom at the Hall. I have offered a farmhouse on my estate, which has recently become vacant. Now you are home you can come and see it and tell me what you think. Of course, we can do nothing until Captain Hartley comes back, but we could make a start on the alterations.' She rattled on, hardly giving herself time to pause for breath.

'Charlotte, will you stop prattling on about that school,' he said in exasperation. 'I have a bone to pick with you…'

'Oh.'

'Yes. If you imagine I am going to put my name to that document you had sent to me, you are very mistaken. I said I had dropped the lawsuit and I meant it. Why could you not let it be? Must you always have the last word?'

'I could not keep the land, not after…' She gulped and rushed on before her courage evaporated. 'Your father was right, he was cheated out of it.'

The news was enough to divert him from what he intended to say. 'How do you know?'

She went to a davenport in the corner of the room and came back with a piece of paper. 'Read that.'

He skimmed it quickly. 'So?'

'Look at the date. Do you remember the date of that ball?'

'Yes.'

'And do you know when my father acquired Browhill?'

'No.' He was puzzled.

'It was three weeks after that date.' She tapped the piece of paper he still held. 'Now, do you see?'

He did. 'Oh, Charlotte, it is you who are blind. I do not care one groat about Browhill. I do not want it. What I want is you...*you*, not the owner of mines, not the owner of mills and plantations and fine houses, not the owner of anything, except my heart. That I do care about. Now do *you* see?'

She hardly dared breathe for fear it was all a dream and he was a figment of her imagination and a puff of wind would send him back into the ether from which he had come.

He grabbed her hands again and pulled her down to sit beside him. 'Charlotte, forget about those deeds. I should like to take up our conversation where we left it off...'

'Where was that, my lord?'

'I asked you to marry me and you refused, but I had not done telling you how much I wished for it and how delightful it would be for us to become man and wife.' He paused because her lips had parted and were inviting to be kissed. It was a full minute before he could go on. 'We could do that all the time,' he said, smiling at her because her response had confirmed him in his belief that she was as warm and generous-hearted as he had always known her to be. 'And more besides. Can I not prevail upon you to change your mind?'

She wanted to say yes, truly she did, but there was still something holding her back, still the inability to let go. 'I do not know, there is so much to think about…'

'Your business, I suppose,' he said, half-expecting it. 'It will always come between us and yet I cannot see why it should. I do not want to take it from you. It is yours, part of you, part of what makes you the wonderful woman you are and I would never want to change that. I will not interfere unless you ask me to.' He laughed suddenly.

'What is so funny?'

He told her about the documents and Professor Lundy. 'So, you see, my darling, we have been fighting over nothing at all excepting a few acres of grass.'

She stared at him. The businesswoman, the employer, had not disappeared and his words woke her from her dreams. 'Does that mean the mine must be shut down? It will put good men out of work.'

'No, my love, I would not suggest that. We can always apply for the mining rights. It might be that, after all this time, they have gone by default anyway.'

'I am being a complete ninny, aren't I?' she said on a sigh. 'I wish I had never grown up thinking that nothing matters but business, that everything boils down to profit. I wish I had learned some of the feminine wiles that young ladies use to get their way.'

'I don't.'

She looked up at him in surprise. 'You don't?'

'No. It is the woman you are that I have come to love. I would not wish you to change anything about you, except to wish you would listen to me sometimes.'

'I am listening.'

'This is the last time I come chasing after you,' he said, though he was smiling as he said it. 'A man can only stand so much. Now, are you going to give me a straight answer to my question or are you not?'

'Answer to what question, my lord?' She was

shaking. She, who prided herself on having no nerves, was afraid of taking the biggest decision of her life.

'Will you marry me?'

She was silent, looking up at him. 'Are you sure?'

'I am certain. Will this convince you?' And he took her face in his hands and lowered his mouth to hers. It was not a kiss of raging passion, but of great tenderness. She felt her limbs go weak and clung to him, knowing that in his arms she could forget everything except this wondrous love. He drew back at last and studied her face. Her eyes were bright, her cheeks pink and her lips slightly parted; there was a glow about her. A strand of hair had fallen about her face and he carefully brushed it aside. 'Now, are you convinced I mean it? I love you. I want you for my wife and all I need to know is if you love me enough to put everything else aside and say yes.'

'Yes.'

'Thank the Lord for that,' he said with feeling and kissed her again.

'But we must not tell anyone, not yet.'

'Why not? I want to shout it from the rooftops.'

'Martha,' she reminded him.

'What about her? She's going to marry her Mr Elliott, isn't she?'

'Yes, but there is bound to be gossip. It is only two weeks since…'

'You are not worried about a little tattle, are you?' Roland teased her.

She laughed. 'Perhaps you are right. And who am I to worry about gossip? After all, I am a hoyden.'

'It is the hoyden I love, but no one else will dare say it after we are married. You will be a Countess.'

'That was not why I said yes.'

'I know that, I was only teasing.'

She took his hand. 'Let us go and tell my great-aunt and then we can go back to Amerleigh and see your mother together.'

Lady Ratcliffe, who was in the drawing room and knew perfectly well that the two young people were closeted in the library, was overjoyed. 'I knew it would happen,' she said, as they drank champagne to celebrate. 'It was so right. But where will you live?'

Roland and Charlotte looked at each other. 'Well?' he asked her.

'Amerleigh Hall,' she said.

He looked about him at the luxurious room. 'Are you sure you can bear to give this up for the Hall?'

'Houses are only bricks and mortar, timber and glass,' she said. 'It is wrong to become too attached to such things.'

'True,' he said, thoughtfully. 'That was why my father found himself in such dire straits; he valued his house and rank above his means to maintain either.'

'And my father valued Mandeville as a status symbol, something to prove to his detractors that he could buy anything. It is a show house, not something to be loved in the way people are loved. I have only just learned that.'

'Hurrah!' he said, making Lady Ratcliffe smile.

'But we cannot leave Mandeville empty and unused,' Charlotte said. 'Supposing we use it for our school?'

'Oh, no,' her ladyship said, horrified by the thought. 'All this lovely furniture and priceless objects in the hands of a crowd of rough school-boys. They will not last five minutes.'

Charlotte laughed. 'I was not proposing to hand it over as it is; it must be adapted. Roland, if you are willing, I can bring the best pieces to Amerleigh Hall and sell the rest. I could do with the proceeds to help with the repairs to the *Fair Charlie* and the improvements I mean to make at the mill…' She stopped suddenly. 'Oh, I forgot, they will not be mine, will they?'

'To all intents and purposes they will,' he said. 'At least until you have other things to occupy you. Then it will be up to you what you do.' He paused, smiling at the prospect of Charlotte as a mother. He had no doubt she would make an excellent parent. 'We can go into the details later and let Jacob and Mountford sort it out. Shall we go back to Amerleigh Hall now and spread the good news?'

The wedding took place two months later with everyone in the village and even further afield present. The Countess was overjoyed at the outcome that she, like Lady Ratcliffe, had always believed was right for both young people. They sat at the front, one on either side of the aisle, and behind them were ranged the rest of the congregation. On the groom's side was Geoffrey, who realised, without rancour, he was unlikely to remain Roland's heir much longer, and his wife; Captain Hartley, recently returned from London; Charles Mountford and the villagers and the estate workers. Behind Lady Ratcliffe were the mine and mill managers, Lord and Lady Brandon and Martha, whose engagement to Mr Martin Elliott had recently been celebrated with a ball at Scofield Place. He sat beside her, thoroughly pleased with himself and grateful to the Earl for his living. The Rector took his place before the altar as the bride made her entrance.

She wore a heavy brocade dress in a rich cream colour. Her hair had been partially tamed and was held in place by a circlet of flowers. She looked radiant as she walked up the aisle on Jacob Edward's arm. In the absence of male relatives she had asked him to give her away and, though it grieved him to know he had lost her, he could not have lost her to a better man.

Roland was waiting for her, dressed in a tail coat of deep blue, cream trousers, held by straps under his shoes. His waistcoat matched the cream brocade of Charlotte's dress. Everyone rose as she reached him. The service began and Miss Charlotte Cartwright became the Countess of Amerleigh. The diamond ring that sealed the union was the one Roland had brought back from the Peninsula.

Afterwards there was a reception at Amerleigh Hall to which everyone, young and old, high and low, were invited. The pieces of furniture and ornaments brought from Mandeville fitted in beautifully and the old house shone with love and attention. Mandeville was in the process of being converted into a school. 'It was worth the long wait,' Roland whispered to her as they moved among their guests. 'But now I am impatient to have you to myself.'

She laughed. 'Soon, Roland, soon. Good things are worth waiting for.'

They were to have one night at Amerleigh Hall and then travel to France and Spain for their honeymoon. He was going to take her to visit Count Caparosso, whom he had to thank for the jewels. If it had not been for those, he could not have begun on the work in Amerleigh and he would not have been in a position to marry Charlotte. For that the Count would have his eternal gratitude.

Their guests dispersed at last and they were alone. Roland took her into his arms and kissed her over and over again, and though she protested that it was too early to retire, he led her up to their bedroom where he proceeded to show her exactly how much he loved her and she, nervous but delighted, learned that material things were not important, that loving and being loved could overcome all obstacles, all doubts, all misunderstandings.

* * * * *

MARRYING THE MISTRESS

Juliet Landon

Helene Follet hasn't had close contact with Lord Burl Winterson since she left to care for his brother. Now Burl has become guardian to her son she is forced to live under his protection. He has become cynical, while Helene hides behind a calm, cool front. Neither can admit how affected they are by the memory of a long-ago night…

TO DECEIVE A DUKE

Amanda McCabe

Clio Chase left for Sicily trying to forget the mysterious Duke of Averton and the strange effect he has on her. However, when he suddenly appears and warns her of danger, her peace of mind is shattered. Under the mysterious threat they are thrown together in intimate circumstances…for how long can she resist?

KNIGHT OF GRACE

Sophia James

Grace knew that the safety of her home depended on her betrothal to Laird Lachlan Kerr. She did not expect his kindness, strength or care. Against his expectations, the cynical Laird is increasingly intrigued by Grace's quiet bravery. Used to betrayal at every turn, her faith in him is somehow oddly seductive…

⬡™ MILLS & BOON®
Pure reading pleasure™

HISTORICAL

LARGE PRINT

THE RAKE'S DEFIANT MISTRESS

Mary Brendan

Snowbound with notorious rake Sir Clayton Powell, defiant Ruth Hayden manages to resist falling into his arms. But Clayton hides the pain of past betrayal behind his charm, and even Ruth, no stranger to scandal, is shocked by the vicious gossip about him. Recklessly, she seeks to silence his critics – by announcing their engagement…

THE VISCOUNT CLAIMS HIS BRIDE

Bronwyn Scott

Viscount Valerian Inglemoore has been a secret agent on the war-torn Continent for years. Now he has returned for Philippa Stratten – the woman he was forced to leave behind. But Philippa, deeply hurt by his rejection, is unwilling to risk her heart again. Valerian realises he'll have to fight a fiercer battle to win her as his bride…

THE MAJOR AND THE COUNTRY MISS

Dorothy Elbury

Returning hero Major William Maitland finds himself tasked with the strangest mission – hunting down the lost heir to his uncle's fortune. While searching in Warwickshire for the twenty-year-old secret he meets the beautiful but secretive Georgianne Venables, who may prove to be his personal Waterloo…

MILLS & BOON®
Pure reading pleasure™

HIST0709 LP

HISTORICAL

LARGE PRINT

THE DISGRACEFUL MR RAVENHURST

Louise Allen

Theo Ravenhurst hardly believes his luck after meeting his dowdy cousin Elinor. Her family connections could be extremely useful… Theo is convinced Elinor's drab exterior disguises a passionate nature. He'll give her the adventure she's been yearning for – and discovers along the way Elinor has talents beyond his wildest imagination…

THE DUKE'S CINDERELLA BRIDE

Carole Mortimer

The Duke of Stourbridge thought Jane Smith a servant girl, so when genteel Miss Jane is wrongly turned out of her home for inappropriate behaviour after their encounter, the Duke takes her in as his ward. Jane knows she cannot fall for his devastating charm. Their marriage would be forbidden – especially if he were to discover her shameful secret…

IMPOVERISHED MISS, CONVENIENT WIFE

Michelle Styles

With his son ill, the last thing Simon Clare needs is a woman assuming command of his household – no matter how tempting her luscious lips. Phoebe Benedict knows what it is to struggle, and is drawn to the badly scarred recluse. She can tell that beneath the tough exterior lies a man desperately in need of love…

MILLS & BOON®

Pure reading pleasure™

HIST0809 LP

LORD BRAYBROOK'S PENNILESS BRIDE

Elizabeth Rolls

Miss Christiana Daventry will do anything to keep from the streets – and the insufferably attractive Lord Braybrook urgently needs a governess. Headstrong, tawny-haired Christy is unlike any woman Julian has ever met and he begins to forget how scandalous it would be to give in to this attraction for his penniless governess…

A COUNTRY MISS IN HANOVER SQUARE

Anne Herries

Country girl Susannah Hampton is confused by the attentions of the dashing Lord Pendleton. Arrogant, undeniably attractive, he is not the husband she had in mind. When he proposes marriage, Susannah accepts. This innocent country miss is determined to inflame her husband's passion – and melt the ice around his heart…

CHOSEN FOR THE MARRIAGE BED

Anne O'Brien

Elizabeth de Lacy is about to take the veil when she is told she must wed her family's sworn enemy! Lord Richard Malinder must produce an heir, and a union with the de Lacy family could serve him well – if only to keep his enemies close. Elizabeth never expected to find Richard so kind, so attractive and so devastatingly handsome…

MILLS & BOON®
Pure reading pleasure™

HIST0909 LP